# THE CRITICS THINK DAVID WILLIAMS IS A TREASURE!

"Williams's delightfully literate cozies are not to be missed!"
*The Denver Post*

"Distinctively urbane and witty"
*Publishers Weekly*

"Good enough to evoke memories of Dorothy L. Sayers"
*Kirkus Reviews*

"Delectable!"
*London Sunday Times*

"Treasure is always a great value."
*Times Literary Supplement*

"He has charm, he understands people, and his outlook on life is sophisticated."
*The New York Times*

# TREASURE
## IN ROUBLES

A Mark Treasure Mystery

# David Williams

AVON BOOKS  NEW YORK

AVON BOOKS
A division of
The Hearst Corporation
105 Madison Avenue
New York, New York 10016

First Avon Books Printing: July 1988

This one for
Edward & Elizabeth Parrack
and George Lockhart

# CHAPTER 1

Molly Treasure's gaze moved from the smoked trout on her plate and turned to wide-eyed, earnest contemplation of the wintry scene beyond the kitchen window. She took a slow deep breath through the aquiline nose: the nostrils flared: the chin lifted on the slim neck: the eyebrows arched, wrinkling the noted brow.

'It's just that I feel responsible. For their going to Russia at all. All thirteen of them,' she said in a tone redolent with concern.

'Headed for the salt mines, are they?' enquired Mark Treasure lightly, and looking about the table top. 'Is there more horseradish?'

The Executive Vice-Chairman of Grenwood, Phipps, the merchant bankers, and his celebrated actress wife were sitting opposite each other, taking a light Saturday luncheon alone at their house near the Thames in London's Cheyne Walk. Molly had a matinee to play at two-thirty. Snow, five inches of which cloaked the patio and the garden beyond, had ruled out Treasure's golf—as it had over all three preceding January weekends.

'You know, you should have gone skiing.' For the moment the ominously numbered Russian excursionists had been abandoned to their plight. Molly turned her glance inwards as she spoke, then paused as she remembered the last question. The touch of irritation showed briefly on her face as she reached for the labelled bottle

1

in the cupboard behind her. She had put plenty of horse-radish sauce on his plate when she had prepared the meal.

The table in the window of the kitchen snug was hardly big enough for serious eating: the two used it only for breakfast and snacks. This gave Molly the excuse not to let the surface become cluttered with garish branded packages, especially garish branded packages of com-modities her conscience suggested she could have made herself—or at least troubled to turn out into more seemly containers. She watched her husband apply a large dollop of the sauce to his plate.

'Good horseradish, this.' He studied the label. 'Almost as good as you make.'

They'd been eating no other kind for years: another good reason to present it in decorous disguise. Molly made an uncommitting noise, firmly re-appropriated the pot, and put it out of sight again. 'Is it too late? For you to arrange skiing?'

'In March perhaps. But I'm not going without you. You really can't get that contract altered?'

She shook her head. 'Big part. Tight budget. Filming has to start in April. It really would be too awful to break a leg or anything before. Anyway they couldn't get insur-ance cover. Not for me or any of the principals. Not at this stage. Not for skiing.' The last phrase had been pointed. She went back to dissecting her trout with a deeply solicitous look. This last, after fifteen years of marriage, her husband was equipped to judge as definitely calculating and unconnected with the condition of the fish. 'We did have New Year together, darling,' Molly added as an apparent after-thought before looking up again with an ingenuous smile. 'That was bliss. And worth it. Even for a week. Such luck.' They had spent the holiday in the West Indies. Their separate demanding careers tended to make such episodes both rare and memorable.

'And now we could press the same luck and go to Leningrad together?' Amused, he watched her expression change to one of too innocent surprise. He had suspected the Russian problem had remained pending.

'I wasn't suggesting . . .'

'Except obliquely,' he offered indulgently. 'Easter weekend, you said? That's March the twenty-seventh. I could make it, I suppose. But only just. It'd be tight.'

'Out Thursday, back Sunday. It's only three nights.'

'Four days.'

'I could go on my own.'

'With the unlucky thirteen members of the Baroque Circle?'

'I *am* president this year. And even fourteen is hardly enough to justify the effort.' Molly frowned. 'Candy Royce would have been so disappointed. If it had been cancelled. Ten was the absolute minimum. To be registered and paid up by next Thursday. That's eight weeks before we go. As it is, not everybody going is a proper member of the Circle. You'd think people who joined a Baroque Circle would be keen on a long weekend in Leningrad. In St Petersburg. Capital of old Russia.' She gave an irritated sniff, then, in response to Treasure's mildly interrogative look: 'Well it is supposed to be the most perfect eighteenth-century city. And the pictures in the Hermitage museum . . .'

'Are fabulous, but I believe the best are pre-baroque. Medieval and early Renaissance. More wine?' He held out the bottle of Chablis. She shook her head as he went on. 'In fairness you said the trip was quite pricey.'

'But well over thirty people voted for it. When we planned the winter programme last June. We expected twenty-five takers. It was to be the highlight.' She made a face. 'Unfortunately the original suggestion was mine. It's in the minutes of the meeting.'

'But you weren't going?'

'Only because I didn't think I could get away. Now I can. Now they've switched the plays in the repertory. But you'd probably hate it.' This came too dismissively, but her timing was impeccable, he noted, as always. 'I don't mean the place,' she continued. 'I mean some of the people who are going. The over-earnest ones. And I don't know all of them. And you're not the package tour type.'

'Not true,' he answered stoutly. 'And it must be a very cultured package.' He sipped at his own replenished glass while fortifying his mind with lofty insistences about his tolerant nature and plebeian origins, though neither condition would have been confirmed by objective examination. 'You said the hotel was five star?' The enquiry was meant to sound disinterested.

Molly nodded encouragingly.

'Mm,' he mused. 'Wonder if Red stars mean the same. But then, Russian cuisine has no terrors for anyone who attended an English boarding school. Charter flight from Gatwick?' added the not yet entirely committed package tourist.

'No. Scheduled airline from Heathrow.'

'Oh, that's good. British Airways?'

'Aeroflot. The only ones who go there. Very reliable.' Molly swallowed. 'Only one class though.'

'Steerage,' he pronounced flatly.

'Economy,' she corrected unnecessarily.

'It's not far.' He chose a plum from the fruit bowl. 'But your Circle's involved in everything baroque? Not just architecture?' He raised a finger to his brow as he quoted. 'Baroque. The artistic form embodying the picturesque and unconventional. Er . . . emerged from the end of the seventeenth century to counter the bleakness of the Reformation . . . and the classical rigidity of the Renaissance.' He beamed. 'Wonder how long since I memorised that? Anyway, baroque includes theatre and music, St Paul's Cathedral and the gold leaf and lurid blues in all those fruity Italian churches.'

'Which is why the Leningrad trip includes opera and a concert. Except eighteenth-century composers aren't guaranteed. There's a trip to Pushkin, as well. That's the suburb they renamed after the writer. It has two glorious royal palaces with some marvellous furniture.'

'Don't I know Candy Royce?' he enquired casually.

'Mm. She's been here for drinks. Big jolly girl. About twenty-eight. Cambridge and the Courtauld Institute. She's an assistant curator at the Simpson Collection and dreadfully underpaid. Also honorary secretary of the Circle.' Molly was pouring them both coffee. 'She's been dying to go to Leningrad for years. This way she gets there for almost nothing. The travel agency gives her a free place for organising the party.'

'I don't remember her being big. More tall and slim. Longish dark hair?'

'No, Candy has shortish mousey hair, and she's definitely not slim. You're thinking of Edwina Apse. She was here the same evening. Bit older than Candy and very glamorous. Made a great fuss of you. They both did,' Molly punctuated with a tolerant beam. 'Teaches history at a polytechnic. Except I believe she has a year off to write a book. She'll be on the trip. Nearly wasn't. Signed up last week.'

Treasure smiled blandly. 'So far it sounds an agreeable enough party. I suppose I shouldn't be the only man?'

'No, it's nearly evenly balanced. Jeremy Wander and his wife Felicity . . .'

'Sir Jeremy Wander? Baronet? Used to belong to one of my clubs. Isn't he slightly loopy? Ex regular army. Guards, I suppose?'

'No. One of those special local regiments. He told me which. I've forgotten. Jeremy's a little eccentric but quite amiable,' Molly offered carefully. 'They say he's a womaniser, but that's probably an exaggeration. He's never made a pass at me.'

'Then he's got rotten taste,' Treasure retorted loyally.

'You are sweet. He's quite young. Mid-thirties. Even younger than you, darling.' Treasure was forty-four—five years older than his wife. 'Felicity's fun in a horsey way. Anyway, they're both coming.'

'Faded aristocracy too hard-up to travel in style?'

'Not at all. They're doing up Wander Court. Opening

it to the public next year. Going to live there themselves. They're picking up ideas from wherever they can look at other eighteenth-century piles. They're both keen members of the Circle.'

'Wander Court is quite small, surely?'

'Kind of miniature Blenheim Palace. Not by Vanbrugh, of course, but good. And it's at the bottom of Easthamptonshire. On a sort of loop between Oxford and Stratford. Anyway, close enough to London, with a big tourist potential.'

Reluctantly Treasure had to concede that a travelling companion with an inherited title probably added an air— even a certain piquancy when one was travelling inside Russia. 'Any other deserving aristocrats in the group?'

'Not unless you count the Honourable Mrs Daphne Vauxley whose father was a Lord. Garrulous widow. Late sixties. Used to write a bit. Book reviews mostly. True blue. Supports corporal punishment and the old values. Not your type I'm afraid.'

'So why do I feel an immediate sympathy for her?' Treasure countered with humourous perversity.

'You should save that for Amelia Harwick, the Honourable Daphne's secretary and companion. Goes everywhere with the old girl. Suppose she can't afford to do anything else.'

'Lacks the initiative, perhaps?'

'You could be right.' Molly was disinclined to argue. 'Let's see, who does that leave? Oh, the three I've never met. The ones recruited by the travel agency.'

'To make up the numbers?'

'Mm. When it seemed we wouldn't even get ten.'

'Presumably they're deeply interested in the programme?'

'One hopes so. They're a married couple called Blinton. From Wimbledon. And a man with a German-sounding name which I've forgotten. He lives somewhere in the Midlands.'

'Rich, retired, jewellery manufacturer from Birmingham. Second generation immigrant who's potty about gold baroque trinkets,' Treasure speculated wildly. 'They made a lot of those in Birmingham once.'

'Candy's found out he's young and plays the cello professionally. In a chamber orchestra. He may have done something else first, of course.' She gave an indulgent smile over her coffee cup. 'Oh, and I've just remembered, his name's Rudolph Frenk and his home's in Coventry. And I'm afraid that's all we know about him.'

'And the married couple?'

'Were squeezed out of an overbooked group going to the Holy Land for Easter. The travel agent suggested they join us. The husband's definitely retired.'

'A pious worthy couple, no doubt.'

'So proper company for Canon Clarence Emdon.'

'You didn't say you had a cleric in the group. Splendid.' Treasure collected clergymen. 'An authority on Russian icons is he? Anglican?' This time he was enquiring not guessing.

'Episcopalian.'

'Same thing. Scottish or American?'

'American. One gathers he's lived here for ages but still behaves as if he's on a visit. Address in Belgravia. Service flat, I think. He's not old enough to be retired. Not quite. But he's not gainfully employed either. Spends a lot of time at the art auctions and says he does a good deal of research. Into paintings, I suppose. He joined the Circle last year. Terribly keen on the Russian trip. I've been meaning to have him meet you.'

'There's a Mrs Emdon?'

'Not so far as anyone knows. The canon is big and scholarly. Looks a lot like Oliver Goldsmith.'

'The playwright? Didn't he have a famous profile? Huge protruding forehead and a receding chin?'

'Also a kind of stammer. So does Canon Emdon. He's quite endearing, and very good company. Gets on well with Nigel Dirving who you do know. He's coming with us,' she ended warily.

'One of your deserving causes. I might have guessed he'd be along. Glad he can afford it.'

'Don't suppose he can really but he's terribly keen. He's agreed to share a room with Rudolph Frenk.' She paused. 'You don't mind? About Nigel.'

'Not if Rudolph Frenk doesn't. He's the one sharing the room.'

'I mean, if you came, you wouldn't let Nigel irritate you?'

'I've never said he irritates me,' he replied, trying to register injured surprise. 'It's just I sometimes find the flamboyant stagey manner rather unnecessary. In such a lamentably failed actor.'

'He's not failed entirely. He has a small part in the new film.'

'Because you fixed it with the director probably.'

She sniffed before answering. 'I may have put in a word with Bryan. People tend to overlook Nigel Dirving because of that awful divorce.'

'Which was pretty difficult to overlook in itself.' Then, smiling, he held up his hands in a surrendering gesture. 'I'm sorry, darling. I promise to be kind to Nigel in future. I don't in the least mind his going on your trip. And it's very good of you to help him the way you do.' He selected another plum and smiled at that as well. 'And that's the whole party?'

'Except for Reggie and Effie Tate. Tiny mother and tall, middle-aged son. She's getting on, but still spry and switched on. Especially when it comes to music. Australian. But she's lived in England for years—to be close to Reggie. She keeps house for him. He's an architect. Specialises in Georgian restoration. They live in Chichester.'

'Didn't you meet them three summers back?'

Molly nodded. 'During that season at Chichester Theatre. Yes. She came to I don't know how many performances. Came backstage and introduced herself. Crazy about Noel Coward plays. And that production.'

'About your performance you mean. It wasn't such a marvellous production, but there was critical acclaim for Molly Forbes and the set designs.'

'Aren't you kind to remember?' Molly almost purred. 'Well Reggie Tate used to tour me round Chichester on Saturday mornings inspecting the architectural goodies. And I used to have tea with them both. You'd enjoy them.'

'I'm sure.'

'You will come?' Her eyes had opened especially wide with an expectant expression that matched the plea.

'Of course. You know I can't resist caviare.'

'Or me?'

'Naturally.'

'Good.' Molly leaned over and kissed him.

'Don't forget to let the travel agents know I'm coming.'

She nodded, smiling. That wouldn't be necessary, of course. She'd told them several days before.

# CHAPTER 2

On the morning of Wednesday, March 26th, Sergey
Vasilefski left Leningrad's Vitebsk railway station and
crossed over to the Metro. He was a lithe figure of
medium height and fair colouring who weaved with a
gymnast's grace through the morning rush-hour crowd that
poured from the suburban line terminus. He didn't use the
Metro normally. He did so now quite openly. It was not
necessary yet to disguise his movements—or alter his
appearance.

He was wearing a short dark leather jacket. It was
commoner than his padded topcoat and he would not be
expected to check it anywhere. In Russia it's bad manners
not to leave outer clothing in the cloakrooms at restaurants, theatres, and other public places: not to do so also
makes the wearer conspicuous as well as unpopular. The
scarf he would leave later in the battered fibre suitcase he
was carrying. The light woollen gloves he could stuff in
his pockets. The cap was in the case already: he never
wore anything on his head normally.

Both the Kamenskys knew he was taking a week's
holiday. He officially rented a room in their tiny apartment in Pavlovsk, the suburb from which he regularly
commuted. They also knew that he was spending the
week in a room borrowed from a friend in central Leningrad, and that the friend was away.

Gregor Kamensky, a working man with no pretensions,
had failed to understand why Sergey was taking a vacation

10

in March when he could just as easily have had it in warmer weather. Perhaps being an international telephone operator in the Leningrad Central Exchange, like Sergey, didn't carry so many privileges, except, Kamensky had mused aloud, it almost had to carry more than you got being a road worker in Pavlovsk. Certainly he knew it didn't oblige you to take all three weeks of your vacation in the winter as Sergey was doing. It was also beyond his comprehension why a healthy athletic young fellow should always choose to holiday in the city.

The motherly, dog-doting Mrs Kamensky had understood though—that Sergey needed to take in the museums, the galleries, the opera and the other attractions that someone who worked, studied and exercised so hard never got time to see normally. He was a young man of cultured tastes, she had reminded her husband, not like some. Also, while Sergey was still waiting for that opening in Intourist it was even more necessary he should keep up his knowledge of artistic goings-on. In short, Mrs Kamensky had been absorbing what Sergey had been telling her for two months past. It was altogether enough to reassure both Kamenskys about his absence until Sunday night—and after that it didn't matter.

He came out of the Metro at Vosstaniya Place and went across to Moscow station—a grander, bigger building than Vitebsk but even more crowded. That was the reason he had chosen it. Here he planned to make the first change in his identity.

A night train from Moscow had been announced just as he entered the main concourse. There were queues for all facilities in the basement men's room but he had plenty of time. Once he had locked himself in a cubicle he pulled out the cap, changed into the black track shoes, and peeled off the beard which he dropped into the case with the scarf. He had shaved off his own beard late the night before, after the Kamenskys had gone to bed. It had taken him the best part of half an hour but he hadn't cut himself once despite his sensitive skin. It was why he had gone to such trouble over this part of the plan—not to risk ending up looking damaged or unkempt.

The false beard he had bought secondhand after a series of lunchtime negotiations with someone who worked backstage at the Maly theatre. It was a fairly old false beard but it had matched Sergey's own colouring quite faithfully.

He had left the flat before anyone was up, catching the train before the one he usually took when he was on the day shift. This was to avoid running into people who knew him by sight. Even so there had still been two travellers who recognised him, though neither had shown any surprise at his appearance. So the false beard had been worth the five roubles. He could have had the real one shaved off here in the barber's shop at the station, but not without the barber committing his face to memory. He could also have shaved it off himself after arriving in the city—except in the whole of Leningrad he wouldn't have known where he could have found a wash basin where a man could do anything so memorable as shave off an inch-long beard in total privacy. To hire a hotel room you needed a travel permit. You also needed to sleep in the room, or risk getting reported for not doing so.

'An insufficient regard for taking pains' was what his last examiners' report had said. It was why at twenty-seven he still had to face another year of compulsory classes, another year in a job that didn't begin to stretch his mental capacities—only his abilities with spoken English and German, and not even those to any marked degree. Well he was now about to show the fools that his capacity for taking pains was infinite.

He deposited the case at the Left Luggage counter, carefully pocketing the dated ticket. He killed time in the station until nine, making his few small purchases at busy kiosks where no one's custom could be remarked, and later dawdled over a glass of tea in the buffet. Then he set off briskly northwards, towards the river, along

Nevskiy Prospect, Leningrad's main shopping avenue. It was a mile and a half to his destination on the Neva Embankment. Taking the bus would have been warmer and quicker. It was snowing again, but not heavily, and he walked because to exercise was important.

To anyone not used to the sight, the length of the queue outside the State Hermitage, more than an hour before the ten-thirty opening, would have seemed daunting. But Sergey had been before at this time—often. The line of people stretched beyond the 350 metre, elegant northern façade overlooking the river, went around its eastern end and finished half way along the south front which composes one side of the immense Palace Square.

Three magnificent eighteenth-century buildings make up the State Hermitage, one of the world's finest art museums and one of Leningrad's most impressive vistas seen from any angle. Of the three buildings, the oldest is the most westerly—the baroque Winter Palace. In the centre comes Catherine the Great's slimmer Small Hermitage in the classical style. Finally there is the Large Hermitage, also classical but from a later date. The three are linked to form a continuous presentation area bigger even than those offered in London's National Gallery or the Metropolitan Museum in New York, and architecturally more refined than either.

Despite the colossal size of the State Hermitage visitors are sometimes turned away when numbers threaten to become unwieldy. This was why Sergey had arrived early even though he didn't need to be in the building until closing time—indeed, to be pedantic, till after closing time. He had come to steal a priceless painting by Raphael from gallery 229 on the first floor of the Large Hermitage, near the north-east corner. And he intended doing the job quite late.

Sergey's plan was to hide himself on the first floor near the top of the *Council* staircase—a grand, twin flight affair in the north-west corner of the Large Hermitage. From there he would emerge in the middle of the night and take the painting, using a route to and from the *northern* opening into the Raphael gallery and running eleven galleries east, then one south from his hiding place. Before the return journey he intended to actuate a false trail for immediate pursuers indicating the thief had left the building. The false route ran from the *southern* opening into the Raphael gallery through two other galleries to the *State* staircase—even grander than the other one—in the southern section of the Large Hermitage, and from there to the ground floor and a series of galleries running west to an exit in the Winter Palace.

He knew that immediate pursuit was inevitable. There was no way of stealing a small picture without setting off alarms. The success of his plan lay in the false escape route seeming believable, and the speed of his own movements seeming unbelievable.

Once admitted to the museum—at eleven o'clock—Sergey began working his way to the north-east end of the first floor of the complex. He moved from the main entrance in the Winter Palace through the length of all three buildings but by a circuitous route. Most of the way he stayed on the ground floor, eventually ascending to the one above, via the State staircase, and thereafter through the two intervening galleries to gallery 229.

It was important for Sergey to know that nothing had changed since his last visit two Saturdays before—imperative that none of the galleries, corridors or the two staircases that featured on his false and real routes had been closed for cleaning or any other reason.

Fortunately, in an art museum whose architectural features compete for attention with the pictures, there was nothing remarkable in a visitor standing as much in admiration of a doorcase by Rastrelli as a canvas by Gainsborough. Sergey was especially interested in doorways, though careful not to seem to be overdoing that interest. In every gallery, as in most open areas, aged female crones—the babushkas who are the mainstay of the Russian public building security system—keep a careful if often rheumy look-out for irregularities in the conduct of visitors. That the authorities depended too much on cheap, superannuated grannies, and not enough on advanced electronic protection, was part of the reason why Sergey had taken up the idea of robbing the place.

His fake exit route involved only two relevant sets of electronic-eye detectors. Like all those in the building they were fixed at knee height, and were not difficult to spot. On his genuine route there were three sets at different points. All were built into the pilaster supports to the openings between galleries. When switched on, they triggered an alarm if an intruder went through, breaking the cross beams. Similar devices were in use in the Great Palace at Pavlovsk where Sergey had long since become closely acquainted with one of the military guards. This was how he had come to know that once two adjacent sets of detectors were activated and an intruder's route was so indicated on a master board, it was 'standard procedure' to switch off other detectors to avoid the movements of guards being confused with those of whoever they were chasing. At both places extra alarm sensors were attached to the backs of all small important paintings—a nuisance that while it couldn't be cured Sergey had decided could be endured.

The Conestabile Madonna, the tiny Raphael picture he'd come to take, was hung quite near the opening at the south end of the Raphael gallery. This was next to a square lobby where the visitor went straight across for Tintoretto or turned right for Michelangelo—people being spoiled for choice at the State Hermitage. There were detectors in this opening and others in the one from the second gallery going south leading on to the State staircase.

There were other detectors along the fake route when it reached the ground floor, but Sergey was using another factor there to simulate his progress—indeed he was relying on it doing so since 'standard procedure' should

at that stage have led to the cancelling of detector beams.
And if it didn't his plan was badly marred.

Twice during the day Sergey gravitated to the north-
west corner of the Large Hermitage surreptitiously to pace
out the area at the top of the Council staircase. Both times
he was careful to give the impression his interest and his
pensive and protracted steps were leading from one to
another of the classical statues or the massive urns on
show there. Mentally he practised the movements of the
standing jump, the lift and body roll that had to be
completed in a two second sequence—that he *had* physically completed a thousand times in less than two
seconds, but in the gym, not here and under pressure.

Twice, too, during the day he had stood poised at the
thresholds of the three galleries out of the eleven on his
genuine route—the ones whose doorcases housed the
electronic detectors. He had breathed and walked through
the pacing of the dives that in these places would get him
clear. At the same time he had re-memorised objects and
windows he'd elected to use as markers ahead of the
alarm hazards on the return route—in case he panicked at
speed and lost count of the rooms. He didn't know how
much light there would be: very little from the inside he
hoped. But every one of the eleven galleries had windows
that looked out on the embankment. There was bound to
be reflected light from the outside.

Later he ate as well as you could eat in the overcrowded buffet back on the ground floor near the big
Rastrelli sculpture gallery and the main entrance. There
was no hot food, only open sandwiches, but the bread
was thick and filling. At five-thirty he left the buffet.
There was more than an hour before closing time but
often they stopped visitors moving eastwards through the
complex long before the whole place was due to shut. He
needed time to do the journey both ways and then to go
back once again.

Gallery 229 was thick with people when he got there.
A large conducted party of East Germans was being

lectured before the Conestabile Madonna. When the group moved on it was easy for Sergey to pretend to be one of them while dropping back to tie his shoelace at a spot quite close to the picture. Another organised group crowded in but no one's eyes were directed floorwards; no one in any case could have seen the plastic nasal spray bottle secreted in the palm of his hand. The droplets of yellowish liquid that squirted through his fingers—without touching them—settled by the wainscoting.

After leaving the gallery by the south exit he repeated the performance, applying liberal droppings of the liquid across the lobby at the side of the Tintoretto room. He did the same at the top of the State staircase, then twice in the series of galleries on the ground floor that led him back into the Small Hermitage. Three times more in the Winter Palace he bent to his shoes—once near the buffet, again in the Rastrelli gallery, then at the foot of the steps leading down to the basement.

The north-west section of the Winter Palace subregion is given over almost entirely to well staffed cloakroom counters running down both sides of an immensely wide stone-flagged corridor. The area was packed with people collecting their belongings when Sergey got there. He passed through the crowds as though he was also leaving but, ignoring the basement public exit to the embankment on the right, he stooped once more to wrestle with a shoelace beside the heavy door which led to the guard-room and a special exit.

It was six o'clock exactly when back on the ground floor he shouldered his way into the men's room. He waited till he could use the end stall. As he expected, the cover to the drainhole there was still missing. Public toilets are not subject to elaborate maintenance in the Soviet Union—even the ones in the State Hermitage. As he undid his zip, Sergey leaned forward and let the small plastic bottle drop into the open hole. It disappeared immediately as another one had done when he had experimented two Saturdays earlier. It had seemed the safest method of disposal. He couldn't have kept the bottle nor allowed it to remain anywhere in the building. He complimented himself for taking pains again.

He washed his hands extra thoroughly with the small piece of pungent floor soap he had brought with him. By this time of day there was none of the free stuff left in any case. He had shaved here earlier, not perfectly, but well enough to ensure a reasonable appearance next morning. Now he re-wrapped the soap in his spare handkerchief with the razor.

Afterwards he made his way as planned back upstairs to another of the galleries letting onto the Council staircase. He lingered there for some time pretending to study Rembrandt's Holy Family. Ruefully he considered the two hovering winged cherubims in the painting. A capacity for flight would have been useful in the next few minutes.

At six-fifteen the bells were rung to signal that all visitors should be leaving. He joined the crowd moving out to the top of the double staircase. There never was a babushka sentinel here.

In the balustraded bay between the two sets of straight white marble steps was a statue of Apollo. Opposite, across the twenty-foot-wide landing, stood a seven foot high, early nineteenth-century urn, classical in design, like a gigantic stemmed goblet. It was made of green malachite with a two foot, white marble plinth. It was under the second of three tall windows that looked out northwards on the now brightly lit embankment and the River Neva.

As he was approaching the Apollo, and making as though to descend the far staircase, Sergey let the light bulb fall unobserved from his now gloved hand that had seemed to be grasping the balustrade: then he moved back deftly.

He was in front of the otherwise deserted green urn as the bulb exploded on the ground floor with a crack like gunshot. It startled the people on the landing. Instinctively, they either craned to see down the stairwell or momentarily applied their attention that way. In one practised movement Sergey sprang up the side of the urn, rolled his head and chest over the lip and, with his arms in perfect control, brought the rest of his body down in behind.

It was all over in less than the two seconds he had allowed. The urn hadn't even trembled on its mount. His counterbalancing had been correct.

He lay still with his heart beating ready to burst. There was no way he could tell whether anyone had seen him. He could only wait to find out, curled up in the unyielding and very dusty malachite womb.

After ten minutes his confidence grew. In half an hour he was sure he was safe: the only unauthorised person left in the whole State Hermitage. He settled to a cramped vigil.

Nine hours later in the silent museum Sergey Vasilefski emerged from the urn coatless but gloved. Illumination had been reduced to maintenance lights at eight o'clock. There had been no evidence of maintenance activity before or after that, but he knew the army of State Hermitage cleaners didn't arrive until six in the morning— he had watched them as he'd jogged by in the snow twice during his last holiday. Only two security patrols had passed his hideout during the long wait—the second thirty minutes earlier. Both times when he heard the heavy footsteps turning down the Council stairs he had levered himself up to observe. Both patrols had consisted of one militiaman only, and without a dog. The guards on night duty outside the building regularly had German Shepherds with them—dogs not bitches. It was the dogs that would shortly make or break his plan—and he was thinking as much as he headed for gallery 229.

When he came to the opening that housed the first of the three sets of electronic sensors he stopped and took several deep breaths. Then he stepped back ten paces from the threshold, braced himself, lifted onto his toes, and moved forward, accelerating sharply. With extra pressure from the last stride he took off with arms outstretched on a flat dive, and straining to keep his legs straight as he went through the opening. As his hands touched the floor he coiled his body, somersaulted, and landed upright. Still and very tense he waited apprehensively for several seconds but no alarm bell sounded. He'd made it—gone over the electronic beam exactly as planned, and now he knew he could do it again. In the gym he'd been doing the same dive across stretchers set a foot higher and without touching them. But there was nothing like the real thing for building confidence. He was less tense about the other two openings—and equally successful.

He entered gallery 229 from the north, and moved past the Conestabile Madonna. He undid the top of the plastic bag and emptied the soiled, impregnated handkerchief onto the floor near the south exit, dropping the bag there as well. This was to save time later.

Next, returning to the painting, he undid his shirt, exposing the linen pouch strapped to his chest and suspended from his neck. From the pouch he extracted the putty, the glass cutter, and the retracting lino knife. Everything was now ready in his hands. He was expecting an alarm to ring from the moment he touched the picture. From then on he was to rely on speed and subterfuge.

He stood in front of the painting, swallowed and pressed the putty lump onto the centre of the glass and swiftly cut round all four edges. The glass came away in one piece. There was no alarm bell yet. He placed glass and cutter on the floor. With sweat beading on his temples he cut along the twenty centimetre sides of the nearly square canvas as close to the edges as he could get. The painting was nearly five hundred years old, but it wasn't going to disintegrate. It was modern canvas used when the work had been transferred recently from its original wooden panel. But he mustn't damage it, mustn't crop it more than by the fraction necessary to get it off its stretcher.

An alarm bell burst into life at the moment the canvas fell away from the mount. The strident clanging seemed to be under his hand; the deafening sound inside his head. Steeling himself to breathe steadily, to keep his nerve, to follow the planned sequence, he dropped the knife, rolled the canvas and put it into the pouch, pulling the top tight and doing up his shirt as he raced for the south exit. This time he broke the electric beam on purpose, streaked across the lobby to the next gallery, to the exit at its far end, broke the beam there, turned about and sprinted back through both galleries. He was leaving 229 by its northern exit just as a new squarking alarm started.

He had the same sequence of eleven small galleries to cover as on the outward journey, the same three threshold beams he mustn't activate, but this time at breakneck tempo. So count the rooms: look for the markers: pace the dives: go through, somersault, end upright and *keep moving*. He knew the course. He was fit. Forget the lights—they were coming on everywhere. He was going to win. He was faster than anyone in the building.

The first dive he nearly fumbled by ending his run-up on the wrong foot. The second was smooth as silk. After the third he felt an exhilaration he'd never expected or experienced. And by then he was nearly home.

The top of the Council stairs was now a blindingly illuminated stage. As he raced for the urn he could hear shouts for the first time, the barking of orders, the clatter of boots—but not even close yet, *and all from the floor below.*

It was another full minute before anyone hurried past his hideout, and yet another before he heard the dogs and their handlers—again on the ground floor. The men were shouting to each other about the *State* staircase.

No one used the Council stairs again for some time but there was a good deal of echoing in the distance from what had to be a group of men with dogs moving from east to west within the complex, from the Large to the Little Hermitage and beyond.

Then there was silence until Sergey heard at least two men hurriedly ascending the steps in animated conversation. They were greeted by someone who had advanced from somewhere to his right at the top.

'You think he got to the basement, Sergeant? And then out through the guard-room?' questioned the first voice Sergey picked up clearly.

'Can't doubt it, Lieutenant,' came the worried answer in a deep guttural rasp. 'Waited for his chance probably. When the guard-room was emptying. Could have been in uniform. There was a lot of confusion. But when the dogs got his scent, it led straight back there.'

'So he's got away . . .'

And from that moment Sergey believed he had done just that, even though he was still potted like an Ali Baba.

Already he was having warm thoughts about the misnamed Fleur—Mrs Kamensky's ugly mongrel bitch, the vicious and contrary animal he had pretended to care for, walking it nightly for its loving, grateful mistress.

The last time Fleur had been on heat he'd collected her urine with a sponge—the same fetid liquid he'd been laying as a false scent for sex-starved police dogs to follow.

If he hadn't been in an urn he'd have been jumping for joy. Withdrawing from the museum next day promised to be a simple task compared with what he'd achieved already. Getting out of the urn in public was potentially a far less conspicuous operation than getting in. He planned to drop down the back of the vessel when the first visitors started arriving, and then to leave with one of the conducted tour groups late in the morning. He was sure the museum would open as usual. Probably they would close the east end of the Large Hermitage 'for cleaning'. Instinctively he knew the theft wouldn't be made public.

After leaving the museum he would shave and change

his clothes at Moscow station, then head for the airport where his troubles would effectively end.

And in all but the last conclusion Sergey Vasilefski was perfectly right.

# CHAPTER 3

'They do Aeroflot at the three desks over there, sir,' said the harassed porter who had taken the baggage outside from Henry Pink, the Treasures' chauffeur. Now he was guiding them through automatic doors to the ground floor of Terminal Two at London's Heathrow airport. The admirable Pink, holding his cap, had on evident impulse shaken both Treasures solemnly by the hand before turning to close the boot of the Rolls. Not normally given to such pointed emotional manifestations, he had made it clear, more by look than comment, that his English yeoman instinct judged visits to Soviet Russia to be at the very least imprudent.

Terminal Two at Heathrow is the oldest of buildings there. It copes with airlines and passengers spurned by the three other buildings—and it does so inadequately. Departing from here is a debilitating experience at most times. At mid-morning on the Thursday before Easter it is near to purgatory.

The porter, clasping both bags, was now thrusting himself into the dense, nearly static and usually close to mutinous assemblage of people plus impedimenta that regularly clogs the space. This wide but narrow, low ceilinged area is further cramped by stairways and escalators to the less claustrophobic concourse floor above. The check-in desks line the long wall opposite the entrances, and take some time to reach.

'There's Candy Royce,' exclaimed Molly standing on

tiptoe with her mink coat pulled tightly about her. 'I can see her by one of the desks. As promised,' she ended pointedly.

'Well that's a comfort,' her husband answered, hands deep in the pockets of the lined Burberry, a garment he considered would give adequate protection against the Leningrad elements.

The Treasures had no tickets for the reason—Molly had twice explained—that for group travellers the group leader dispensed tickets at the point of departure. Treasure had accepted the fact but not the principle. He normally arrived at an airport with the token that offered a reasonable guarantee of onward progress. Their passports had been returned to them only the day before, complete with three-page Russian visas, and after spending three weeks being mulled over by the USSR authorities in London— or possibly Moscow. It happened Treasure hadn't needed his passport for any other purpose in the period, but, again on principle, he felt he might have done. Altogether he was not enamoured with the impersonality of package touring.

'Shall I leave them here, sir, or try to get 'em closer to the desk?' asked the porter who like all porters at Terminal Two was anxious not to cramp his earnings by hanging about in nearly static lines of hapless passengers. They had got as far into the building as the amorphous queues would allow. In the line they were in at least forty bodies separated them from the check-in.

'Leave them here,' said Treasure tipping the man, and electing to keep his property under his hand even though he had purposely over-insured it.

''Morning, Molly.' The sharp greeting came from behind them, but emanated from waist level. 'Exactly like the Black Hole of Calcutta,' the woman in the wheel-chair continued definitively but without seeming so decrepit as conceivably to be bearing personal witness to that disaster. She was perhaps just old enough to justify the use of the conveyance she occupied on grounds of age rather than infirmity. The lined but well tended features showed immense animation under an expensive fur hat. The strong chin was lifted high on the tightened neck to clear the topmost of the two cases that were piled across the arms of the conveyance.

'Your hip bad again, Daphne?' Molly enquired with concern, and leaning down as she spoke.

'Certainly not. They saw me using my handsome new sitting-stick and offered me this. So I took it. Cheaper than a porter,' the older woman beamed while demonstrating the perfections of the elaborate aluminium stick she was holding in one hand. Like a shooting stick, at one end it had a folding seat, but at the other, instead of a spike, there were four small rubber feet. The feet sprung out on short supports when the seat was opened—as Mrs Vauxley had contrived to demonstrate with some danger to others.

'Mark, this is Daphne Vauxley. Daphne this is my husband.'

'How d'you do. Can't shake hands.' But the woman's eyes had assessed him with confident approval. 'Great relief to have an important man of affairs with us. This is my companion, Amelia Harwick. Or it ought to be.' Mrs Vauxley glanced about petulantly.

'I'm here, Mrs Vauxley. Good morning, Molly.' Miss Harwick, who looked to be in her early-forties, was plumpish, bespectacled, and breathless. Her top coat was made of a grey, long fibred material, and her round brimmed, felt hat was also grey, but in a different shade. Altogether she seemed to affect the appearance and behaviour of a nervous nannie. 'I've got our tickets,' she offered as though in expectation of reward. She gave Treasure a bashful smile then looked away, her closed lips moving in a sort of furious chewing motion.

'Let me see,' demanded the Honourable Mrs Vauxley as if doubting the report. She took the tickets from the other's hands.

'I got them from Candy. I went up to the desk. Oh, here she is.'

' 'Morning all. 'Morning Molly. Mrs Vauxley. Hello Mr Treasure. Gosh, what a circus.' Candy Royce, Tour Leader as well as Secretary to the Baroque Circle, was a big young woman, attractive in an athletic kind of way, and dressed more for skiing than for a city vacation. She was shouldering her way to the group while proffering the hearty greetings. She was gripping a sheaf of papers and a batch of Aeroflot ticket folders. A bulging document case was jammed under one arm. 'Mountain's coming to Mohammed. Well I've got tired of standing at that desk.'

'Everybody here, Candy?' asked Molly Treasure.

'Pretty well. Hardly anyone came to the desk I've been at, of course. Not surprising. Aeroflot don't have anything of their own here. British Airways come over and cope for them. Anyway, I'm going to whip round the place looking for stragglers.' She examined two sets of tickets before handing them to Treasure with a grin. 'That's you two done. Now let's see.' She pulled out a list of names from under the tickets and started to score it with a ballpen. 'Nigel Dirving, yes.'

'He's here?' Treasure questioned with extra affability for Molly's benefit.

'First to arrive. He's gone upstairs. And he found Ma Tate and son Reggie for me. And Mr Frenk. Or somebody did. Canon Emdon and Edwina Apse helped sort people out too. They were both early. I had passports and visas for some, as well as tickets.'

'What's Mr Frenk like?' This was Molly.

'Haven't seen him myself. Nor the Tates. It's been such a crush. They're definitely here, though. All checked in. And Mr and Mrs Blinton, the other non-members. I've met them.' She looked up from her list, nodded knowingly at Molly, then went back to checking.

'Pity we've had to take on outsiders,' remarked Mrs Vauxley without dissembling, or concern for any outsiders who might be within hearing.

'The Blintons seem very nice,' Candy answered carefully.

'They were the ones who were going to the Holy Land?' This was Treasure.

'To Israel, yes,' Candy corrected. 'The tour they wanted was overbooked.'

Mrs Vauxley looked up sharply, scowled but didn't speak.

'New blood can be refreshing,' said Miss Harwick unexpectedly.

'Only if you're a cannibal,' her employer snapped. 'Push me, woman, we're losing ground.'

The queue was moving forward which involved much slow and clumsy gavotting of people and cases.

'Can we slip in here? Hate queueing. Got our tickets, Candy? Good morning Molly. How do Daphne. Miss Harwick, you're looking ravishing again.'

The male speaker with the deep fruity tone was Sir Jeremy Wander. He was wearing a long open jacket of what seemed to be practically untreated and roughly sewn sheepskin. A tweed cap sloped down his head, the front pulled well over his forehead with the peak pointing to the end of a sharp, slim nose. He was shortish, burly and very dark, with small inset eyes, and hardly any eyebrows, though what there was of them seemed to twitch incessantly. Under the sheepskin he had on a dark blazer with deeply consequential embossed gilt buttons, and narrowly cut trousers in a black and white dog tooth material. The shirt was Viyella and the tie suggested membership of a respectable school or regiment. He had continued to hold a hefty, well worn but solid leather suitcase in each hand as he spoke, bracing and unbracing his shoulders and rocking backwards and forwards on his feet either as an exercise or perhaps simply to advertise his fitness.

'It's Jeremy and Felicity. Oh good. Good. Very good. Simply wouldn't have been on without you,' volunteered the Honourable Mrs Vauxley, excessively pleased and waving an arm at Sir Jeremy, now placed in front of her in the line. It was an even more welcoming tone than she had used to acknowledge Treasure. The banker guessed that 'outsiders' like Mr Frenk and the Blintons, whatever virtues they possessed, would need to wait an eternity before being paid such extravagant addresses, and that no one lower than a baronet could queue-jump on Daphne Vauxley with impunity.

'My stick's a huge success, Jeremy,' the lady continued, waving the implement about with near abandon. 'Thanks awfully once again. Such an elegant, useful pressy. You're so kind.' She turned to Treasure. 'You know Sir Jeremy and Lady Wander, of course?' Wander's wife had now appeared beside him.

'Don't believe we've met,' replied the banker.

'Yah.' Felicity Wander made an impeccable South Kensington and District affirmative, leaving her mouth open at the end. She smiled about at everyone—including people in the other queues—squinting because she should have been wearing her glasses. She was taller than her husband, fair, with wavy hair, and slim, with a long face, a pointed chin, and a very generous mouth full of unusually large and prominent teeth. She, too, was wearing barely treated sheepskin, in her case over a loose hand-knitted sweater, a tweed skirt and red woollen stockings. 'Yah,' she repeated, this time definitely at Molly through narrowed eyes. 'Are we late? Had to fetch my ma down from Kettering before we could leave for London. Too effort making. But someone had to cope with Caroline and Roger,' she drawled on in a bored voice. 'Caroline can't be left with total strangers. Won't touch her victuals.'

'All the regular help at Wander Court's on holiday, of course,' Sir Jeremy broke in dismissively while still holding the cases. 'Firing the lot before next year. Before we open to the masses. And we're recruiting an army of part-time widows for them. From all over the county. To show people round. Pass 'em off on Americans as titled

dowagers. They like that. What?' The eyebrows twitched
in double time. 'The Yanks I mean. Plenty of widows
available. Plenty of dowagers too, it seems.'

Some Americans in an adjacent queue looked
unamused. The widow Vauxley gave a small wince, then
smiled indulgently. It seemed Sir Jeremy was allowed a
solecism or two.

'But your daughter was eating well when you left, Lady
Wander?' enquired Miss Harwick, with breathy solicitude.

'No idea. She's pony trekking with a chum in North
Wales.'

'But . . .'

'Caroline's a horse,' Sir Jeremy put in with a braying
sort of laugh. 'Felicity doesn't discriminate much.
Between people and horses, I mean. Though on the whole
she prefers the domestic habits of . . . Ah, here we go.
Everybody forward.'

In the way of Terminal Two queues the line had
temporarily fallen away in the centre through the lateral,
baggage-tending activities of some of its members, and it
had not yet re-knitted. Wander had seized the opportunity
and justified his holding on to his cases by barging a way
forward. He had Felicity in tow, but the ranks then closed
behind them like a flood tide, leaving the others more or
less where they were before.

'Molly, why don't you and Mrs Vauxley go on ahead
upstairs?' Candy Royce offered tactfully.

'Or why don't we all go home and come back
tomorrow?' suggested Treasure lightly, but to the evident
alarm of Miss Harwick.

'Don't they have to check our visas? In person? At the
desk?' Molly asked.

'No. Not this end. Mr Blinton did both theirs while his
wife was telephoning. For ages.'

'I'd rather wait. See everything through,' determined
Mrs Vauxley flatly, glancing at her companion. 'Amelia
is so easily confused.'

'Oh Mrs Vauxley, I'm not. I'm really not.'

'Anyway, in this crush we might never find you again,' Molly quickly interjected. She squeezed the arm of her mildly disaccommodated husband, thankful it hadn't been Nigel Dirving who'd usurped their place in the line.

An hour later the Treasures had checked in themselves and their baggage, gone through passport control on the upper floor, and, in response to the boarding call for Flight SU 638, were standing in the Gate 28 departure lounge. All the seats in the room had been occupied before they got there, and they hadn't moved much beyond the entrance after they and their hand luggage had been scanned, and their boarding cards checked at the desk—still by British Airways personnel.

'Must be a big plane,' said Molly brightly.

'TU-154 I expect. Not especially big. Just full. It takes a hundred and sixty passengers. I'd . . .'

'Of whom a hundred and eighty are present,' pronounced a lyrical male voice, interrupting Treasure. 'D'you suppose they allow five standing on Russian planes? Like on the buses. Hello Molly, darling. Too marvellous to see you. Hello Mark.'

'Nigel,' exclaimed Molly while the thirty-five-year-old actor, Nigel Dirving, was kissing her effusively on both cheeks. 'Did you just come through? I was sure I saw you ahead of us. Just now. At the desk over there.'

'We did,' said Treasure firmly. 'Good afternoon, Nigel.'

'Of course, I've been here hours. Popped out to the little boys' room. They let you if you say you're *in extremis*. Well heaven knows how much longer we'll wait in here.' He was a lean figure, of medium height, with sensitive, bronzed features. The short fair hair was waved at the front. His clothes were casual but nondescript for so flamboyant a wearer—though the dark blue trenchcoat draped over the shoulders lent a mildly buccaneer touch. He had been wearing a tweed hat which he had swept off

before embracing Molly. 'No seat allocations or we could
have arranged to sit together. Very tiresome,' he went on,
stroking an eyebrow with a well manicured forefinger.
'You know, you two really are fabulous looking. Like an
advertisement for . . . no, not an ad, the real thing. The
best of British. I do envy effortless superiority. Have you
seen the others?' he finished disarmingly before the
flattery could be disowned, but not before Treasure had
started to speculate on the cause of the extravagant,
nervous verbosity.

Molly beamed. 'We've seen some of them.' She rather
enjoyed elaborate compliments. 'I gather you helped
Candy Royce track down the non-members? The Blintons
and Mr Frenk.'

'Dear Candida. Such a big strong girl. I'm hoping she
has plans to ravish me on this trip. I shan't resist either.
Well not strenuously. Uh . . . the Blintons, yes. Interesting couple. Frenk no. Is he here?'

'Candy said so. But she hasn't met him yet.'

'Then Edwina and the worthy Canon Emdon must have
sorted him out. Well they were up to something together.
He's looking positively bishoplike.'

'And gr . . . rateful for the promotion. So bless you,
my du . . . dear Nigel,' came in a soft New England
accent from the large, white haired, dog-collared cleric
who had now joined them from the direction of the
checking desk. He bowed to Molly. 'This'll be Mr Mark
Treasure, no . . . no doubt. How . . . d'you do, sir?'

The canon owned the nearly caricature profile that
Molly had described—a pronounced forehead and beaked
nose above a deeply receding chin, with things in between
falling back to fit. The speech hesitancy seemed closer to
affectation than to impediment. There was an elusive scent
about him—not perfumed, more nearly chemical. Treasure
was also intrigued by the thin black cord around the neck
which disappeared under the significantly purple pullover.
Did it carry a pectoral cross, he wondered, or merely the
suggestion that it did? The cord and the purple fitted

Nigel's comment: the canon did affect an episcopal appearance.

'Guess I lost Edwina,' said the clergyman after completing introductions and greetings. 'When they announced another ha . . . alf hour delay.'

'Did they? We missed that. Accounts for the mass exodus to the washrooms. Or perhaps they're putting seats in those endless corridors,' said Molly. 'It was so much trouble to get in here, I certainly shan't go out again. I hate that metal detector arch, or whatever it's called. Makes me feel like the female figure that comes out of the toy house. You know, the one that predicts rain?'

'I always feel somehow purged or cleansed by the experience,' said Nigel.

'I wonder why?' Canon Emdon questioned absently, while pulling on the black cord to reveal that there was a monocle on the end.

'So you've been looking after what Mrs Vauxley calls the "outsiders",' said Treasure.

'Lost them too I'm afraid,' the clergyman admitted, searching the room as he spoke. 'The place is so crowded.'

'The Blintons are sitting over there, against the wall,' offered Nigel, pointing. 'He's in the astrakhan hat. She's all over leopard skin. He likes to be called Sol, and she's Gloria—*in excelsis*, you might say. He had trouble with a clasp knife, going through the metal detector. They let him keep it—for peeling apples, he said. Looked more suitable for stripping oak trees.'

There was a marked difference in age between the easily distinguishable pair. The man appeared to be in his late sixties at least, while his wife could have been in her mid-thirties. He was big, round and jolly, with fleshy cheeks and humour wrinkles discernible from ten yards. She was a short, buxom and striking blonde with nice legs and a restless manner. Her gaze met Nigel's just as he was pointing out the couple. She waved, stood up, vigorously indicated an empty seat beside her own, and motioned to the others to come over.

As the little group led by Molly was threading its way to the Blintons, the man got up quickly, said something to his wife, smiled, and stepped forward. Then, quite suddenly, he staggered, clutching his chest. For a moment he seemed to be trying to lift his head upwards, but failed in this and fell to the floor, remaining there—an ominously still heap.

# CHAPTER 4

Captain Mishka Dubenko of the Leningrad police ran up the entrance steps to the narrow, west-facing front of the State Hermitage, his long grey uniform greatcoat busily flapping open below his knees. Somebody might be watching and it was as well to look energetic; also it was snowing.

He had taken his car and driver the five hundred yards from the Central (First) Precinct police station on the east side of Palace Square, mostly to impress on people that he had a car and driver—except there was no one to see. This particular entrance was seldom used because being in the old Winter Palace Gardens it had no vehicle access. He'd forgotten this in his haste after he got the message. He'd just come back from snatching three hours' sleep— the only time he'd had off in the last twenty-four. Since he'd had to leave the car back in the square, for all anybody knew he might have come running all the way, of course—which was quite different from simply taking entrance steps in his stride, and not nearly so dignified or appropriate. People could construe that he thought like an enlisted man, not a senior officer. Dubenko stopped running.

Such considerations were important to the diminutive captain who was already forty-seven, overweight and losing hair, and whose wife still expected him to make the rank of major in the militia—the uniformed police section of the MVD in which he'd served since he was

35

eighteen. This was why his mind had strayed to promotion tactics now when it should have been occupied with practising his excuses for losing the picture: the one they said was worth ten million roubles—at least. Not that he accepted responsibility for the loss in any case.

He rattled the handles of the big double doors, and banged the panels with his leather-gloved knuckles.

There were nine hundred sub-curators of the State Hermitage working office hours, and only three platoons of policemen on guard and entrance duty covering three shifts. If ten million rouble pictures that a thief could practically put in his shirt pocket were left without being welded to the walls, then sub-curators should be made physically to watch over them—in shifts.

He rattled the doors again, although it was becoming patently clear there was no one on the other side waiting to open them. This was ridiculous.

It was five-to-seven. The museum had closed for the day. His presence inside now, with the investigator, wouldn't alert any outsider to the fact something awful had happened. His own men had been sworn to secrecy, and so had the members of the museum staff who knew about the robbery. So far as anyone else was concerned the picture had been removed for cleaning.

It had been business as usual all day at the State Hermitage with no overt signs of special police activity: there hadn't been much of it in any case. He had personally supervised the searching of the place in the early morning to no purpose. Now they were waiting for lab reports.

The dogs had made it obvious the thief had escaped through the guard-room door in the basement of the north front, just around the corner from where he was standing now. The guards had been rushing about in all directions at the time, some half dressed and others half asleep. His lieutenant had admitted as much.

This was the first time in living memory anything had been stolen from the museum, and he, Mishka Dubenko, had to be the officer in charge of the guard. He hadn't had the assignment long, and he wasn't a specialist in guarding things either. He was an expert in traffic movement and control—not that there had been much call for expertise in that area in Leningrad or anywhere else in Russia: not to date.

But they'd thought enough of his capacities to have sent him abroad to a seminar on traffic movement—to Prague only, for two days only, but it was a start. And nobody should underestimate the call for traffic movement specialists in the future, civil as well as military, not with the importance the Kremlin was attaching to greater car ownership. That's why his wife had been convinced his promotion was a certainty—and that there'd be a civilian job ready for him after army retirement. She might have been right too: up to this morning.

He hammered on the doors yet again. Special Investigator Popov had specifically directed he should come to this door. He had spent two hours with Popov earlier at the Public Prosecutor's Office where the other man worked. It was also in Palace Square. In the USSR serious domestic crime enquiry is headed by an investigator not a policeman. Investigators are part of the Public Prosecutor's staff. MVD police militia, even captains, show proper deference to investigators—and especially they don't keep them waiting, which was something else currently bothering the hapless Dubenko.

Impatiently he stayed a few more moments after the last banging, then turned and set off down the steps at the run, heading for the guards' entrance which had to be manned by someone.

'Dubenko!'

The shout from behind startled him and came as he was between steps. He faltered, half turning, slipped and fell to the ground—but he was up again in a flash, brushing himself down, staring about alertly. Only a fool would have set him off balance bellowing in that cretinous way. 'Ah, Comrade Investigator. You're there after all.' He

saluted and scurried back to the now open door, despite
the pain.

'Where else? I said this door, didn't I?'

There was no enquiry like, 'Did you hurt yourself,
Comrade Captain?' or 'Sorry to keep you waiting,
Comrade Captain,' Dubenko ruminated bitterly as he
entered the building disguising the limp, uncertain whether
his right ankle was broken or merely sprained—but sure
that walking on it now would likely incapacitate him for
life.

'Took your time getting here, Dubenko. Should have
jogged over. Good for the system.'

'Actually I came in . . .'

'The lab report makes you and your men look poor
fish,' Popov interrupted sharply. He was thin and sallow
faced, much older and taller than the captain, and being
a substantive major was superior to him in rank as well
as office. He wasn't in uniform now. He was wearing a
long black leather overcoat and a wide-brimmed black
hat. Although altogether a more important being than the
other man—in both their estimations—the special investigator should have been a chief investigator long ago and
really had nothing much to look forward to except retirement in his present rank. In consequence he was bitter,
as well as ill tempered by nature, and given to biting
sarcasm. He didn't care for Dubenko who the report
indicated was some kind of jumped up traffic cop.

'Lab report, Comrade Investigator?'

'Yes, lab report. What we'd been waiting for. And are
you proposing to shut that door or is it the militia's habit
to leave places open for art thieves every night?'

'Sorry, Comrade Investigator.' He shut the door. They
were in a narrow passage next to a stairway—a small
stairway he knew went up two floors to the attic storey,
but which he'd never used at this level. Limping badly,
he followed Popov who was already climbing. 'I don't
understand, Comrade Investigator. I haven't got the lab
report yet.'

'No, I have. Because I asked for it. Any objections?'

'No. Of course not.' The report should have come to Dubenko first but he didn't intend to protest. 'Did it throw any light . . . ?'

'Bitch's urine.'

Was this one of the investigator's especially kinky expletives—intended as some kind of twisted personal abuse? Dubenko wasn't sure, but he drew the line at being insulted like a corporal. 'I'm sorry, I don't understand . . .'

They were now on the first floor, and the investigator led on at a furious pace through to the galleries on the north side. The policeman hopped just behind.

'Seems there's nothing much you do understand, Captain,' Popov snarled. 'Read the report and you'll see your dogs were following a bitch's scent. It was on the handkerchief the handlers shoved under their animals' noses. The handkerchief you said the thief dropped by mistake. Well he didn't. It was soaked in dog's pee, and so were parts of the museum floor. Right down to the entrance to the guard-room. He dropped the plastic bag too, on purpose. Because it had the handkerchief in it.'

'You mean . . . ?'

'Well isn't it obvious? The thief put down a false scent beforehand. Ever kept a dog?' Popov glanced over his shoulder, then frowned. 'Something wrong with your leg? You some kind of cripple?' This came as an accusation.

'Certainly not. The leg, I just twisted it, that's all. It's fine now.' He tried walking normally: it was agony, but if the investigator said in his report that Dubenko was in any way handicapped the slur would stay on file for ever—a minus at promotion time. 'I had a dog once,' he lied. He hated all animals.

'Dog or bitch?'

'What?'

'Your animal. Male or female.'

'Er . . . male. Thinking of getting another. Company

for me. When I go jogging. Every morning,' he added, scaling new heights of imagination and absurdity.

'Well you should know that every normal dog will follow the scent of a bitch on heat. Even well trained police dogs. Especially if encouraged. Your thief knew it. It's how he got away.'

They had reached the landing of the vast ceremonial Jordan staircase at the north-east end of the Winter Palace. Popov pressed on along the linking galleries that led into the Small Hermitage. They had met no one so far on the journey. Dubenko had just realised this.

'The guards should be . . .' he began.

'The guards have been confined to the entrance doors. On my orders. Something I want you to see.'

They were hurrying through the white-galleried Pavilion hall, the most striking room in the building with its famous chandeliers, fountained apses, and its two-tiered rows of fluted columns. The English Peacock Clock with mechanical birds and animals was coming alive as they passed, ready to strike the hour of seven. Dubenko had always wanted to watch it perform except he had always been here at the wrong time—as now. Worse, the stirring creatures looked ready to mock him.

On emerging beyond the hall, onto the Council staircase area, Popov suddenly stopped in his tracks. Dubenko stumbled straight into his back.

'Sorry, Comrade Investigator.'

The other man sighed, straightening his hat. 'What do you see before you, Dubenko?'

'Lieutenant Glinka.' For one of his junior officers was standing some distance away at the top of the stairs. The man had quickly come to the salute when his superiors came in sight.

'What else do you see, Captain?'

'A staircase. It's the Council staircase.'

'Nothing else?'

Did he take him for a child? Of course he could see

other things. 'Statues, Comrade Investigator. Windows. Hanging lights. A green . . .'

'Urn, Dubenko. A green urn. Well done.' He raised his voice. 'Lieutenant, kindly set up the stepladder.'

Glinka hurried out of view into a side gallery, then reemerged pushing an open stepladder which moved on small rubber wheels. He placed the ladder beside the urn and locked the wheels.

'Would you care to look inside, Captain?'

'Inside the urn?'

'Looking inside anything else would be to miss the point. But please yourself. Lieutenant, give the captain your torch. You'll need a torch.'

Dubenko wasn't very good on ladders. He got to the top of this one and leaned over, shining the torch beam at the interior of the urn.

'There's nothing . . .' He realised his voice was hugely amplified through the depth of the vessel so he drew back his head before repeating almost in a whisper, 'There's nothing inside, Comrade Investigator.' And that was a smirk he'd caught on young Glinka's face for which the swine would pay dearly later.

'Nothing inside now, Captain,' retorted the investigator, clearly enjoying himself. 'Not any more there isn't. But if you'd ordered the urn, all the urns in the State Hermitage, to be inspected after three o'clock this morning, after the robbery, you'd have found a man in this one. You can come down now. In future perhaps you'll remember the capacity of an urn.'

'A full search . . .' Dubenko began after coming off the ladder, but he knew there was no purpose in protesting.

'A full search should have involved looking in all the urns,' Popov had put in rapidly. 'Do you know how many man-sized urns there are in the State Hermitage, Captain?'

'A great many . . . I should think.'

'How many, Glinka?'

The lieutenant was already standing at attention but

snapped his heels together for good measure before replying. 'We inspected thirty-eight, sir.'

'That was in the twenty minutes after closing time this evening, Captain. While you were still asleep probably. I ordered the inspection as soon as I got the lab report at my office. Because I'd put two and two together. To anyone on the spot, searching the urns should have been routine.'

And Dubenko had thought of it, too. He'd been about to include the urns when he'd got here in the middle of the night, except those bloody dogs had just gone hell for leather through the place following a scent that left no doubt the thief had got away. After that he hadn't believed getting ladders and other equipment would be worth it. 'I intended to have the . . .' he began.

'Pity you didn't go through with your good intentions, whatever they were,' Popov interrupted with bite. 'Because it followed if the thief hadn't left the building immediately after the crime, and if your men had searched the obvious places, they should also have searched the less obvious ones.'

'You'd need to be a gymnast to get into an urn. Without equipment. Without toppling it.'

'Indeed, Captain.' Popov appraised the speaker slowly from head to toe, his eyes indicating he wasn't impressed with what he saw. 'But many of us as young men, even as young as you are now, kept ourselves in enough physical trim to get in and out of an urn. One of your guards did it just now. You could do it couldn't you, Lieutenant?'

'Yes, sir.'

Dubenko had always taken Glinka for a crawler. He debated whether to say he could do it too, but decided against in case he was made to prove it: this sadist was capable of ordering him to leapfrog over rows of urns. There was not the slightest chance of promotion after this. He'd be lucky if he wasn't demoted—or sent to Afghanistan. Except he'd do anything to avoid disgrace or blame, including flattering Popov.

'Could the Comrade Investigator explain how he deduced this urn was used by the thief?' Dubenko enquired with abject deference.

'Good question, Captain. Lieutenant, fetch the evidence.'

Glinka disappeared so quickly this time he forgot to click his heels. He returned with a wooden box which he offered to Popov who shook his head, indicating he should give it to Dubenko who took it gingerly.

'You'll see—DON'T TOUCH!' the investigator screamed.

Dubenko nearly dropped the box in fright. 'I wasn't going to,' he lied.

'The stuff could be covered in fingerprints,' snapped the other without believing him. 'You'll see a chocolate wrapper, a broken packet of French chalk . . .'

'And two plastic bags tied with string and full of yellow liquid,' the captain put in to prove at least that his eyesight wasn't defective.

'He ate the chocolate. He used the chalk to improve the grip of his shoes. And what d'you think the liquid is, Captain?'

Dubenko swallowed. There could be no doubt. 'Bitch's urine?'

'Of course it isn't. It's human. It's his. He was in that bloody great vase twice. You understand? First till three this morning, then for God knows how long after he got the picture. Brought the bags so he could relieve himself and not have to sit in it after. Only thing if you're stuck in an urn.' He gave a bronchial cough. 'Lieutenant, take the evidence to the lab yourself. Tell them I want a first findings report in my office in thirty minutes. Get someone here to fingerprint the urn too, inside and out. Except the chances are the swine wore gloves. Off you go.'

As soon as Glinka was out of sight, Popov gripped the

captain's arm in so intimate a way it made him both uncomfortable and strangely apprehensive. The investigator glanced from side to side, and brought his face close to the other's before he hissed: 'Anything strike you about all this, Dubenko?' He paused, but not long enough for the captain to come up with an answer. 'The first time anyone's pinched anything from the Hermitage? Professional job? A team at work? Money no object?' Now he waited, eyes screwed up.

'Inside job? A sub-curator did it? Or a group of sub-curators?'

'No, no.'

'Uh. One of the guards?' In the spot he was in Dubenko would willingly have indicated his mother-in-law if there was a chance she'd go to Afghanistan instead of him.

'Wrong again. Remember this picture's worth millions. In the right market, of course. And which market d'you think that would be, my friend?'

So now he was a friend: it was getting more suspicious. 'Uh . . . Not Russia. I'd guess . . .'

'Absolutely.' The grip got even harder, but an explanation for the intimate advance was beginning to form in Dubenko's fevered mind as the other went on: 'Do I take it, then, we're agreed this is all a Western capitalist plot, Captain? To steal part of the people's cultural inheritance? An irreplaceable masterpiece? A picture every one of us prizes beyond measure?' Popov frowned. 'What's it called again?'

'The Conestabile Madonna by Raphael.'

'Precisely. Now on its way to Frankfurt, Cairo, London or New York no doubt. Raped. Torn from its frame by some Western thieving bastard masquerading as a tourist. I don't know why we let them in. Any of them. Do you?'

'No. Certainly not. Nor why the authorities who let them can't be made to protect the people's property. But they ought to be responsible for getting it back. When it's stolen.' Now he completely understood what Popov was driving at—not only understood it but applauded it. Hope was in sight. The pall was lifting.

Popov dropped the other's arm. His attitude was cool and remote once again. There should be no hint of conspiracy in this.

Quite simply, this investigator, who privately didn't want any part of a mess that promised to continue as a mess well into the year of his retirement, and this guard captain, who privately saw no solution that could possibly reflect anything but ill upon himself, these two had to be seen independently to have reached the same professional conclusion.

'I tell you, Comrade Captain, I shall report that in my view I should be exceeding my authority if I continued with this investigation. It clearly points to an international conspiracy, and a different authority should be alerted and involved.' Popov coughed. 'I shall commend your zeal,' he ended, trying to invest the words with conviction and nearly succeeding despite himself.

'With great humility, Comrade Investigator, I shall have to report the same. My men aren't equipped in numbers or experience to combat international crime. Better to admit it immediately, I feel. Despite your brilliant direction, which I shall record in writing. The responsibility for the crime and its quick solution should be placed on shoulders broad enough . . .'

'Yes, yes,' Popov interrupted, looking at his watch. 'I'll have my report before the Director in an hour.'

'Mine will be with my commanding officer by then, Comrade Investigator.'

Both men left the building sure that the Committee for State Security—otherwise known as the KGB, and responsible for all foreign miscreants—would be ordered to take over the investigation by morning, if not sooner.

# CHAPTER 5

'Not the most fascinating plane trip I've ever made. But I've made worse.' Mrs Effie Tate beamed up at Molly Treasure. They were standing side by side in one of two long lines of passengers waiting to have passports and visas examined in the stark immigration hall of Leningrad airport. 'It was great sitting next to you and your husband, Molly,' the spry if aged Australian added.

'Nicer if you could have sat with your son.'

'Oh he wasn't far away. Flirting with a pretty little Pakistani girl, weren't you Reggie?'

'Talking mostly to her husband on the other side,' Reggie Tate replied pointedly. 'She gave me her butter at lunch, though.'

The Tates were an incongruous pair. She was wizened, tiny and energetic with a strong antipodean accent. Her forty-five-year-old architect son was a spare, slightly effete six footer. He wore a well trimmed, reddish beard and rimless spectacles which helped to invest him with an air of quiet academicism. His very English accent was only distinguishable from that of Dirving or Wander because his tone was softer than either of theirs.

The plane had been packed for the three hour journey—mostly with immigrant families returning on holiday to Karachi where the flight was due to end. The Baroque Circle members had been scattered through the aircraft with couples travelling together in some cases obliged to separate.

46

'I hope Mr Blinton survived,' said Treasure who was standing beside Reggie. 'I still think he should have gone home after that heart attack. Or whatever it was.'

'Heart-block. His wife said it wasn't serious. Just a little fainting fit,' said Mrs Tate with all the stoicism of an early colonial. 'He's been overdosing with pills to cure his arrhythmia. Slow pulse rate. She said he's been told to get a pacemaker fitted, but he's stubborn. Don't blame him. Getting old's a rotten business.'

'But in . . . finitely more attractive than the alternative,' observed Canon Emdon heavily. He was just behind Treasure. 'The Blintons must have been first off that dreadfully crowded bus from the airplane. See, they're in fr . . . ont of the other queue. And that's . . . Nigel behind them.' The American was squinting through the monocle he had just anchored in his left eye.

The rectangular hall was fifty feet wide and three times that in length. On its far wall was a massive coloured picture of Lenin backed by the national flag. Underneath was a caption in Cyrillic letters.

Passengers had to ascend a short flight of steps after entering, then more steps some ten paces further on. Eventually they were to file singly through one of the two separate but parallel booths set into a wooden, waist-high barrier running across the width of the area. Stony-faced, uniformed immigration officers were sitting inside the booths. Another evidently official person but wearing a civilian raincoat and a trilby hat stood in the centre of the area beyond the barrier eying passengers as they passed, before they turned left into the baggage collection and customs hall.

The London flight had coincided with the arrival of one from Paris. The two lines of passengers stretched back to the entrance doors and beyond, into the open air. The Treasures and the others had just moved to the top of the second short flight of steps. It had taken them twenty minutes to get that far.

'We seem to be doomed to slow-moving queues,' said

Treasure. He was manipulating the dial of his wristwatch.
'So, with a two hour difference the time now is seven-
eleven.'

'Guess I'll leave my watch the way it is,' Mrs Tate
offered, peering closely at it—a surprisingly substantial
piece adorned with several buttons on the side. 'It's
digital,' she announced further. 'Runs away with me
whenever I fiddle with it.'

'Shall I do it for you, Mother?'

'Thanks no. I'll rely on you and Mr Treasure for the
essentials. Like getting me to meals on time. It's only for
three days.'

'I don't see anyone else from our group in the other
queue.' Molly ran her eye down the line of people to their
left as she spoke. 'Probably a few ahead of us this side.'

'Candy Royce and Ed . . . wina Apse are in front of
us,' affirmed the canon in a resigned voice. 'The last
people on that bus were the first off.'

'Thus will the first be last, and the last first. St.
Matthew, chapter twenty,' quoted Mrs Tate, her long
vowels somehow enhancing the sense of scripture. 'Never
did understand the fairness in that parable. The one about
the labourers in the vineyard.'

'The Wanders are w . . . ell in front.' The canon was
clearly not to be lured into a debate about the injustices
of Holy Writ. 'It wouldn't have pleased Sir Jeremy not
to be ahead, of course,' he concluded drily.

'We haven't seen Edwina at all yet,' said Molly. 'I
think she must have been at the very back in the plane.
Really, it was so crowded there was no incentive to leave
one's seat to look for people.'

'Oh, ab . . . solutely,' agreed the canon with feeling.
'I resisted an imperative to go the wa . . . sh room.' He
swallowed. 'A second time,' he added lamely.

'These immigration people are slower than the ones in
New York,' Treasure complained. He had stepped out of
the line towards the centre of the hall and was watching

the officials who were visible through glass windows at the sides of their booths.

'They're not that swift in London. Unless you're fortunate enough to possess a British passport,' the American cleric said with a smile. 'I recall on one occasion . . .'

The woman's scream did more than halt the canon's observation: it riveted the attention of everyone present through its sheer dramatic quality. It came from the area beyond the booths. Both uniformed officials stopped what they were doing and stood up looking agitated. The one on the left opened the door on the far side of his booth and peered out, but didn't leave his station. The plain-clothes man disappeared within the growing knot of people assembling a few feet beyond that booth. Then the woman screamed again.

'Stand back everyone. Give him air. Move back please. Is there a doctor here?' came the unmistakable, penetrating intonations of Jeremy Wander who had taken charge, accenting his status as an 11th baronet *and* an ex regular officer. He was visible as well as audible to some, like Treasure, tall enough to be observing over the barrier and to witness his actually pushing back the plainclothes official who, instead of showing anger, thereupon explicably turned on his heel and marched from the scene altogether. Close by, Lady Wander had her arm around the shoulder of Gloria Blinton who was clearly in great distress and the source of the screaming.

A tall, burly man hurried past from behind Treasure calling '*Je suis un medicin.*' When he reached the left-hand booth he attempted to press on through it, except that he was physically restrained by the uniformed official who leaped across his counter and grabbed him with both hands. Undeterred, and with much Gallic gesticulation and vehement protest, the muscular French doctor was demanding to be allowed through. His cause was soon being supported by Jeremy Wander who took up the protest from the other side.

In the face of what was threatening to become an inter-

national incident, and conscious that assistance had
diminished not increased, the perplexed officer made a
compromise. First he demanded and received the doctor's
passport, then, stepping out of his booth, he called the
other man through, closing and locking the passenger gate
beside the booth after him. In the process it became clear
that the official was a much shorter person than he had
appeared when sitting on a high chair in his domain.
Standing he was diminutive, and handicapped in his effort
to maintain the dominance he'd been displaying earlier.
His intention to take the big Frenchman's arm and to lead
his movements suffered a sort of reverse as he was yanked
along behind the doctor like a recalcitrant child resisting
the parental pace.

Treasure, who had meantime returned to the queue, had
been able to identify the patient earlier when the people
separated to allow the doctor through. 'It seems Mr
Blinton's had another turn,' he said to the others. 'He's
sitting on the floor looking dazed but recovered. As he
did after the Heathrow event. One assumes it's a repeti-
tion of the same thing.'

'But why did his wife scream like that?' asked Molly.
'In London she rather dismissed the whole thing.'

'This time it may have seemed more serious,'
commented the canon. 'In London he did rather l . . .
ook as if he'd quite ex . . . pired. Given up the ghost.
Maybe it was just un . . . nerving. For Mrs Blinton. To
have it happen again.'

'He seems to have recovered here just as quickly,'
Treasure observed.

'Well I'm glad he's all right. But he's going to be a
bit of a responsibility if he keeps dropping dead every few
hours,' said Molly ruefully.

'Don't think that'll happen.' This was Mrs Tate in her
confident tone. 'Air travel upsets people. Makes them
tense up. Even subconsciously. He'll probably be fine
from now on.'

'Or until we go back,' said her son Reggie.

'Meantime he seems to be spoiling our queue,' complained Molly.

With the left-hand booth still closed, business at the other one had been resumed, but frustrated members of the deserted line were abandoning it and crossing the floor. Their numbers included a scowling Nigel Dirving, disconsolately pulling his hat forward over his eyes.

'Looks as if we firsters are going to be lasters again,' said Mrs Tate giving the canon a purposeful look of mild admonition. 'Never did see the justice in that parable,' she completed firmly.

The attractive young Russian woman with the rich, clipped tone and charming accent, heavy on the letter 'r', was saying very fast into the microphone what sounded like: 'Ever-ryone-u in these coach is from Ba-rr-oque Cirr-cle in Lorndon only, yes? No other personus allowed, plees. Not for the whole of youru stay in USSR. Thank you.' She smiled her assurance on everyone from where she was standing next to the coach driver. She was petite, very dark, with long straight hair that spilled to the shoulders of the belted, western-style black leather top coat. She was holding a clipboard in one hand while she counted all present with a ballpen poised in the other like a conductor's baton. She waited for the Treasures who were the last aboard to take their seats near the rear of the vehicle before she spoke again. 'That's fourteen persons. It should be fifteen, I think?'—except the first number tripped out engagingly as 'for-rut-eenu'.

'Canon Emdon's gone to the gents',' boomed Candy Royce from one of the front seats and without benefit of microphone or the need for one. 'Be here in a jiff.'

'Is Mr Frenk here?' Holly called over the buzz of general conversation and looking about her. She hadn't met Frenk yet and felt as President of the Circle she should have done.

'That's me,' called the fair young man in the aged British-warm overcoat. He was sitting two rows behind the Treasures, on the very back seat with Nigel Dirving and Edwina Apse.

'Sorry. Should have introduced you,' called Edwina. She had spoken with Molly for the first time that day only moments before, as they had been coming out of the airport building.

'No chance, was there?' Molly called back and nodded behind at the three. She gave Frenk an especially warm smile, while noting his fresh, healthy countenance and feeling a stab of sympathy for what appeared to be a blotchy red birthmark over his left eyebrow. 'I didn't notice the Blintons when we got on. Should have spoken to them,' she said later to her husband who had gone back to shake hands with Frenk after dropping his hand baggage on the intervening empty row of seats, as others had done already.

'I talked to them,' he said, as he sat down. 'They're at the front. He was peeling an apple with that boy scout knife of his. He's quite recovered. Full of apologies to everyone. Looked a bit pale still, but ebullient with it.'

'Glad somebody is.' Molly glanced at the time. It was already a few minutes after eight. She had just about recovered her composure after being piqued by a particularly officious customs man. He had insisted she open her bag and had taken what seemed suspiciously like lascivious pleasure in slowly upsetting the carefully packed contents—especially the frilliest, most feminine contents. It was why she and Treasure had been last out of the customs hall—a tiny, cramped area where baggage collection, inspection and clearance had been conducted like a football scrum. 'That man obviously didn't like me. Didn't open other people's bags,' she said loudly, frowning at the memory.

'Perhaps he didn't enjoy your last movie.' Her husband smiled, squeezing her arm.

'D'you think it was my mink coat that upset him?'

'Animal protectionist, you mean?'

'I meant furs being a sign of affluence and probably decadence. But you could be right.'

'Plenty of Russian women wear furs. And he did open other cases. Candy's for one. She doesn't look especially affluent. Edwina escaped untouched.'

'Doesn't she look quite ravishing in that rather Russian ensemble?' Molly changed to a more agreeable subject. 'Like somebody romantic out of Turgenev or Tolstoy.'

Treasure had noticed as much, and was turning to do so again just as Mrs Vauxley leaned across to him from her seat on the other side of the aisle.

'I heard what Molly said. That horrible customs person opened Amelia's bag too, you know?' she vouchsafed in a shocked half whisper, the tone and glance suggesting the man's action might have been arrested only just short of his committing actual rape.

'I expect he was only doing his job,' Miss Harwick herself put in to show she hadn't been upset by the experience—and might even have enjoyed it. She was seated on the other side of her employer.

'Puh!' commented that lady. 'You're so innocent, Amelia.'

Her companion looked mildly abashed, then after a pause, some chewing of her closed lips, and a smile at Treasure she offered: 'It's a very nice coach. Quite as good as the ones at home.'

'Yes,' agreed the banker who hadn't been on a coach for years. Since the vehicle seated about fifty and there were only a quarter that number in the group he felt it boded well for their comfort on this and future journeys, making a pleasant contrast with the aeroplane. Now he watched Canon Emdon clamber aboard, and Jeremy Wander leave his seat and come down the aisle.

'Old Blinton's only just surviving if you ask me,' the baronet leaned down and confided to the Treasures, so far as his resonant voice allowed him actually to confide anything to anybody. 'Upset by that passport chap. Made a big performance of checking his visa. And his wife's.'

'Did that to all of us, didn't they?' questioned Treasure. The visas were three-part documents. Two of the sections had passport-type photographs attached. One of these sections had been taken from each visa by the immigration officers after scrutiny of the holders and a good deal of checking with thick lists of names.

'Fellow was very uncivil apparently. According to Mrs Blinton. They're sensitive because of the attitude to Jews here. They feel . . .'

Whatever they felt remained unexplained because the Russian guide blew loudly into the microphone and asked for everyone's attention. Wander went back to his seat.

'So,' said the young woman, then continued rapidly in her engaging accent: 'Now we are all here, my name is Valya Sinitseva. I am your guide from Intourist. Please call me Valya because it's easier, you see? Now we go to the five star Astoria hotel. It's situated in St Isaac's Square in the centre of the old city where is also the nineteenth-century St Isaac's cathedral, now a museum. The hotel was built in the modern style in the year nineteen-ten and is one of the finest in Leningrad. It is lucky you are staying there.' She paused for breath, or perhaps to allow her charges more deeply to savour the extent of their unproved good fortune. Meantime the coach moved off with much crashing of gears.

'Tonight there won't be time for visits to the ballet or opera. Only for dinner at the hotel, unpacking and maybe a walk afterwards if you wish. Take notice there are no unnecessary restrictions on tourist movements in the USSR.' The impact of the last statement was somewhat diminished when the speaker suddenly disappeared from sight down the stairwell of the coach—unbalanced by the driver's sharp fast turn out of the airport.

'So sorry.' Valya had climbed back clutching microphone, clipboard and this time a permanent stanchion. 'St Isaac's Square is on Mayorova Prospect, the most westerly of Leningrad's three main avenues. These avenues converge like three spokes of a wheel on the famous Admiralty building. On the other side of the Admiralty lies the River Neva Embankment. It is a few hundred metres only to the west from the State Hermitage museum where we go tomorrow. Your hotel is six hundred metres only to the south from the Admiralty which is a beautiful building in the classic style, built between eighteen hundred and six and 'twenty-three by the architect Zahkarof. Its gilded spire is seventy-two metres high and is floodlit. It is to be seen from most parts of the city like a landmark. This is why they say you can't get lost in Leningrad.

'When we reach the hotel, in about twenty minutes, please register at reception. The receptionist will give you a small card stating your room number, also the Astoria address in Russian and English. This you will exchange for your room key with the concierge at the desk on your floor. When you wish to go out of the hotel you give the key back to the floor concierge and she gives you back your card. Is that clear?' She waited a moment then continued, 'The card is very useful to you for many reasons, like if you do get lost in Leningrad.' She grinned. 'And if you can't see the Admiralty, you can show the card to someone in the street or to a taxi driver so they know where you want to go. It's much more useful than your passport which is in English only and won't be understood by Russian people who wish to help you. Incidentally, you give your passport to the receptionist at the main desk on arrival. It will be kept for a little while, or maybe longer, for entry in the city records of tourists. That's the regulation.'

Treasure chuckled. 'That's a tactful way of explaining they relieve you of your passport for a multitude of other reasons. Probably for the length of the stay.'

'Does it matter?' asked Molly.

'Not much, and I doubt you could do anything about it anyway. It stops you giving or selling it to anyone else. Or leaving the country when you're not supposed to.'

'Might bother the Blintons,' Molly observed thoughtfully.

And so it did—though the Blintons were to encounter much greater problems than that.

# CHAPTER 6

'I'm having a lovely if exhausting time. But I really could never get used to brown bath water,' announced Molly Treasure while doing something to her eyebrows in the bathroom mirror.

'Harmless if you don't drink it, I should think. Probably good for the skin. Something to do with the soil here. Neva, the name of the river, is a Finnish word meaning mud,' said her husband who was dressing in the bedroom.

It was six in the evening on their first full day in Leningrad. Following a short coach tour of the city landmarks immediately after breakfast, they had spent the rest of the day looking at paintings in the State Hermitage museum under the dual guidance of Valya Sinitseva and Candy Royce. Now they were preparing for an early dinner and the opera.

Their room was on the second floor with a view of St Isaac's Square and the cathedral. It was quite small, with a narrow antiquated bathroom, dusty grey window curtains that didn't quite close, a worn armchair, and two beds—a narrow one they used as a sofa, and a bigger one recessed in a brown-curtained alcove. A variety of other unmatching objects served mostly to inhibit free movement and looked more as if they had been dumped in the room rather than arranged for the purpose of furnishing it.

There was a huge television monochrome receiver, an

57

equally bulbous radio-gramophone—with no records—two standard lamps, and a white, family-sized refrigerator. Since there was only one wall point to power everything electrical, the Treasures had used the adapter plug they had brought with them to work two units at a time. Permanent power priority was given to the refrigerator which they had stocked with wines, and the bottle of mineral water they used for cleaning their teeth as well as drinking, in preference to what came out of the taps. The drinks they had bought at the tourists only 'beriozka' shop on the floor below.

'Valya is enormously well informed don't you think? Knows quite as much as Candy about art and architecture. I mean, apart from having very good English, she's a very cultured lady. I love those rolling ''r''s,' Molly continued from the bathroom. 'Could you pour me a glass of wine, darling?'

'Sure.' He finished straightening his tie and went over to the 'fridge. 'She has a master's degree in fine art, her husband is a senior lecturer in linguistics, and she's a good deal older than she looks under the make-up. And those sweeping false eyelashes. I'd guess she's your age.'

'Which must be a compliment to one of us.' Molly came into the room. 'Zip me up, will you?'

'She's probably a special guide reserved for ritzy art tours.'

'Pity she keeps putting in plugs about how great life is in the Soviet Union. She seems too intelligent to be doing propaganda.' She sipped the wine while critically examining the line of her dress in the long mirror on the sliding door of the wardrobe.

'Maybe she believes it.'

'That three million Russians went abroad for their holidays last year for instance? That's what she told me at lunch. So where did they go?'

'East Germany perhaps. That's abroad if you're a Russian.'

'Hm. I'm dying to ask her why the people here look

so bored and listless. Mrs Tate says it's all to do with the water. This wine is delicious.'

'You mean, so why don't they drink wine?'

'Oh, very droll.' Molly sat gingerly on the edge of the armchair. It was stained as well as worn.

He smiled and swallowed some of the cool liquid. 'It's a perfectly acceptable breakfast wine.'

'I'd still prefer coffee at that time, thank you. The half cup I got this morning really didn't switch me on for the day. And there simply wasn't any more.'

'There might have been if we hadn't had to leave. Coffee's very expensive in Russia. We should be drinking tea here. I like that dress.'

Since the advertised room service was proving to be a fiction, they had taken breakfast in the restaurant—a strategy which in most hotels ensures unlimited supplies of butter, hot toast, and coffee at least. This had not been the case at the Astoria.

Treasure had made up his mind to enjoy the cultural uplift of the trip and not to expect normal human comforts of any kind so that when he got some he could be agreeably surprised. This was why he was enjoying the wine— and his wife's band-box appearance.

'I'm looking forward to *Boris Godunov*,' he said. 'Mussorgsky's greatest work after all. And performed in his own city of St Petersburg at the Koriv Opera. Really, what more could you expect?'

'I expected Mozart's *Magic Flute*, as we were promised. Mussorgsky is hardly a baroque composer, and he goes on a lot longer than Mozart. And louder.'

'More for the money. I gather the Mozart is rescheduled for next week. Anyway, we're paying all of three roubles, that's three pounds, for the best seats in the house. Or so Valya says. At Covent Garden we pay ten times that. At least. That's the rosy face of socialism,' the banker concluded, feeling virtuously objective.

'Valya also says we'll be there till midnight. But you're

right. It should be a marvellous evening. Still feels wrong going to the opera on Good Friday, of course.'

'Except this year the Russian Orthodox Church observes Easter the week after the Western Churches.'

'And since we're here we can do the same?' She gave a contemplative sniff. 'Yes. That's all right then. But let's not bother telling the vicar. Too complicated. I wonder if Canon Emdon has a service planned for us on Sunday? Before we leave here at ten. He said there's a working cathedral just up the road.' She paused. 'I'm glad Mr Frenk is coming tonight. I saw him just now in the lift. His migraine's better, but he spent all day in bed apparently.'

'Music presumably means more to him than fine art since he makes his living at it. Sol Blinton and his wife said they'd be there.'

'Everybody's going to be, I thought?'

'Expect so. It's just that the Blintons ducked out of the afternoon session at the Hermitage. I thought he might be tiring.'

'Don't think so. Gloria Blinton told me he simply wanted to do some extra sightseeing. She's quite a character. A largely unaffected Cockney and not a bit abashed by Daphne Vauxley who's not exactly crazy about her, and makes no bones about it. There's much more to Gloria than appears.'

Treasure chuckled. 'The appearance isn't too bad either.'

'She was a dancer.'

'Bit short, I'd have thought.'

'Not ballet. Cabaret, musical comedy, and she mentioned seaside shows. A trouper in other words. That's hard work.'

'His second wife, presumably?'

'Mm. He was widowed. He's retired from the rag trade. They met in Bournemouth two years ago.' She finished the wine. 'Isn't it time to go down?'

He looked at his watch and grimaced. 'Yes, for dinner at six-fifteen.'

'It's four-fifteen in London. Pretend we're having tea.' She gathered up her things. 'Shall we go down by the stairs?'

'You don't trust the lifts?'

'It's only two floors and the stairs are so grand. Very imperial.'

'Not as grand as the ones at the Hermitage.'

'Which Felicity Wander tripped on. Nearly broke her neck.' Molly moved to the door.

'She didn't really hurt herself?'

'No, but she'd come to less harm if she wore her glasses at least some of the time. She can't get much out of looking at paintings. The way she has to screw up her eyes. How does she manage on a horse for heaven's sake?'

'Leaves it to the horse, I suppose. Jeremy seemed very uninterested in the pictures.'

'But captivated by Valya Sinitseva. Something else his wife wasn't noticing. Though in fairness, he's also charming with the older women. Especially Daphne.'

Their room was at the end of a corridor. The other Baroque Circle members had rooms close-by. As the Treasures left theirs, Edwina Apse came out of hers with Nigel Dirving.

'Confound it, we've been discovered' cried Dirving simulating surprise when he saw the others. He grasped Edwina by the waist and pulled her to him. 'Well we won't let them part us. Not ever again. Whatever the consequences.'

'Nigel don't be ridiculous,' protested Edwina pushing him from her, and obviously embarrassed by the situation or the mock histrionics, or both. She turned back to her door and locked it. 'We met out here exactly a minute ago. He came into my room to sort out my electric plugs.'

'That's her story. But I believe it. So what else can you

do in one minute? Nothing much.' The actor rolled his eyes. 'But I'm working on it.' He sloped ahead down the corridor, doing a Groucho Marx walk, disappeared through an open door, then immediately re-emerged shaking his head. 'Same problem everywhere.'

The others had now come up to the same door. 'Whose room is that?' asked Treasure.

'Wild horses wouldn't . . .'

'Oh, do dry up, Nigel,' said Edwina but in a much more indulgent voice. 'It's the Blintons'.' She knocked on the door, then stepped into the room. 'Are you there?'

'They must have gone down and left the door open.' This was Molly.

'Did the same thing this morning,' came Daphne Vauxley's voice from behind them. 'Dreadfully careless. One wonders if some people care at all about their property.'

'It could have been the maid,' offered Miss Harwick who was with her: their shared room was opposite the Treasures.

'What maid? We've just had to make our beds,' complained her employer, which the others correctly assumed meant her companion had just made them.

'They did the bathroom this morning, though. I still think they'll be coming back,' Miss Harwick excused.

'Only because you insist on thinking like a servant,' admonished Mrs Vauxley in a savagely belittling way. She stomped her stick whose metal finish glinted, but not so much as the silver lamé dress she was wearing.

There was an awkward silence broken by Treasure. 'Well, let's shut the door. We can tell the concierge. They don't lock without keys, of course.' After doing as he suggested, he motioned everybody along the corridor.

The concierge, a buxom middle-aged blonde, was sitting at her desk in an alcove across from the two lifts and the sweeping staircase. She was slightly older than the otherwise almost identical holder of the same office in the daytime. Behind her was a steaming samovar, a refrigerator, and some boxes of mineral water bottles. Keys were presented and exchanged for hotel cards.

'Room 224. It's not locked,' said Treasure not sure he would be understood.

'224?' the woman replied. Her hand darted to the appropriate space in the pigeon-holed arrangement in front of her. She held up a card. '224 key not here,' she said in a very deep contralto and shrugging. 'I tell maid. She here soon. Maid not finished yet.'

Amelia Hartwick's face reacted with a fleeting smile but she didn't utter.

'Our beds weren't made this morning. And our bath plug's disappeared,' said Mrs Vauxley unaware till now that the concierge spoke English.

'Good evening,' said that worthy who didn't speak it for some people.

'You don't understand . . .'

'We have a spare bath plug we brought. You can borrow it for tonight, Daphne,' Molly volunteered. 'I think we'd all better go down.'

'Why is it this country's permanently short of bath plugs? Perhaps Russians sit on the hole at the tap end,' said Dirving, answering his own question. 'We didn't have one in our room till this morning. Till Rudy Frenk scrounged one from somewhere.'

'It was probably ours,' Mrs Vauxley announced stiffly.

'Of course you're sharing with Mr Frenk, Nigel,' said Molly. 'Where is he?'

'Gone down already.'

'The water from the samovar must be for making tea,' Edwina half questioned as she and Treasure walked down the stairs together.

'Yes. Ready browned water too. It's free but I wouldn't touch it if I were you,' said Molly who was behind with Dirving. The other two ladies were taking the lift.

'You drank it in your half cup of coffee this morning and begged for more,' remarked her husband.

'So I did. I suppose it's all right if it's boiled.' But Molly sounded chastened.

As the visitor descends into the Astoria's long, high reception hall, the residents' lounge, the bank, the Intourist desk, and the barber's shop are to the left, with the coffee shop and night club further along around a corner. To the right is the reception desk, and beyond, past the main entrance, the cloakroom and magazine stand are two large, adjoining restaurants. The one on the right is the grander of the two with small tables, a dance band playing at night, an *à la carte* menu and a clientele in the main affluent, upper class Russian but with a sprinkling of official foreign guests. The other restaurant is much busier, has larger tables, and provides *table d'hôte* meals for package tourists.

This second restaurant was crowded at six-thirty with most of the tables occupied by groups from various nationalities. The Baroque Circle table for sixteen was near the centre of the room, set between two tables whose occupants were speaking German. All fifteen members of the British party were present: the extra place was empty because Valya Sinitseva who joined them for breakfast and lunch stopped her official duties at six.

'Wonder what they call this fish?' asked Gloria Blinton from half way down the table in her little altered from girlhood, throaty East London accent. 'Funny colour if you ask me. Tastes all right though, d'you think?'

'Looks to me like the piece of cod that passeth all understanding,' said Nigel sitting opposite. 'Sorry, Canon. Slipped out.'

'Fish slipping out. You are a card, Nigel,' said Gloria looking up and down the table for agreement. None was registered. She pulled a face at Dirving and went back to her eating.

Canon Emdon began stroking the end of his prominent nose—a characteristic gesture some of the others recognised as a preliminary to speech. 'North Sea cod probably, and better than any f . . . ish caught in the local waters,' he said. 'The brown colour would come from the cooking pans. Or the water.'

'Oh Lore!' said Gloria. 'Well, you only live once.'

'Drink plenty of the wine,' advised Wander, filling her glass. He was sitting on her left. 'Topping antidote for anything nasty.' He put down the bottle and placed a reassuring hand over hers for a moment—quite a long moment.

'*Guten Abend, Herr Doktor.*' The German who greeted Emdon had stopped behind Wander's chair. He was heavily built, and about the canon's own age. His head was completely shaven, and steel-rimmed spectacles added to his somewhat sinister appearance. Without waiting for acknowledgment he bowed, turned about and took a seat at the adjacent table. The American blinked and returned to his fish without comment.

'. . . locked it and left the key with the floor concierge. Expect a maid took it,' Sol Blinton was explaining to Molly further along the table.

'What did you get up to this afternoon, Mr Blinton?' asked Effie Tate who was across from him.

'I saw the two of you take off in a taxi. Very grand,' Candy Royce put in loudly from nearby.

'Also quite cheap, would you believe?' said Blinton, briefly gesturing towards her with one bent arm and wearing a good-natured grin on his round, cherubic face. 'The driver spoke some English. Better than my Russian, I'm telling you. He took us over the river to what's called the Petrograd side. That's the four islands to the north. Very populated. We went to the Peter-Paul fortress. It's where Peter the Great started the city in seventeen hundred and three. Everybody should see that. It's quite something. The cathedral especially. Then we toured all round in the cab.'

'The Jewish quarter's up there perhaps, Mr Blinton?' asked Mrs Vauxley in a patronising voice.

'Maybe.' He considered for a moment, then shrugged

and continued, 'My grandfather lived in this city. Died here. We were looking for his house.'

'And your father? Did he . . . ?' This was Reggie Tate.

'He died in France. In nineteen-sixteen. In action. With the City of London Fusiliers.'

'. . . I get migraines from time to time. Often after a journey of some length,' Rudy Frenk was explaining to Felicity Wander in his pedantic, accented English.

'Yah. Too crippling. A drag it kept you in today.' Felicity brought a pepper pot close up to her face to identify it before shaking it over her carrots as well as a large area of table-cloth.

'The coach will leave at seven prompt,' Candy announced, getting up from the table. 'I have to go back upstairs. Don't forget your opera tickets.'

'Not having your pudding, Candy dear?' enquired Mrs Tate solicitously. Dessert on both evenings had been slices of plain cake put on the table before the meal began.

'Reggie can have mine. He needs feeding up,' the girl joked in answer.

'No fruit at any meal so far,' complained Mrs Vauxley.

'Valya said none is grown around here, and it's difficult to transport,' said her companion.

'What rot,' countered Dirving. 'Might as well say there's no petrol because the oil wells are somewhere else.'

'We brought fruit with us,' beamed Sol Blinton. 'Apples.' His hand went to a side pocket as if he was going to produce one, but he didn't: he looked puzzled instead.

'He eats two apples a day. Throws away the best part, though. The peel,' his wife informed everybody.

Frenk made as if to speak, then thought better of it and helped himself to cake.

Treasure was sitting at the head of the table with a view of the door. Molly and Edwina were on either side of him. He had been watching Candy leave. 'Who's that chap sitting by himself d'you suppose?' he asked.

Molly turned her head. 'At the little table near the door? A music lover escaping from that dreadful band in the other room.'

'I've been watching him too,' said Edwina. 'He's not eaten anything. Just drinks and studies the people. Mostly us.'

'That's what I thought,' commented the banker. 'Did you notice the way he watched Candy just now?'

'Shows excellent taste then.' Molly smiled. 'D'you have to pay for the wine before we can go, darling?'

'Please let me pay,' said Edwina. 'This is the second time I've drunk your wine.'

'And you're welcome to do so for the duration of the stay,' Treasure replied expansively. 'There's not much choice, but it's not bad and it's remarkably cheap. I just have to remember to pay for it at each meal. They don't let you sign or put it on the bill.' He looked about him. 'Trouble is there's no proper wine waiter.'

'Or head waiter, either. No one seems to be in charge,' said Molly. 'That's why I couldn't complain about the coffee at breakfast. Ah, there's the one who served the wine. Waiter!' she called.

'My wine bill, please,' said Treasure to the man who didn't immediately understand. He tried again. 'How much for the wine?'

The waiter looked from side to side, then stooped to mutter: 'Three packs of Marlboro, OK?'

# CHAPTER 7

'Drink?' Treasure asked his wife as they left their seats for the second interval during the opera. 'This production really is tremendous.'

'Best we'll ever see,' she agreed. 'No drink this time, thanks. A glass of that nice champagne again in the next interval, perhaps. Can we go up to the perambulatory—or whatever it's called?'

'If you like. It looked fun.'

'Glad we're in the orchestra stalls. It's odd we're the only ones from the group down here.'

'Luck of the draw. What I was handed at the Intourist desk in the hotel. Seats obviously aren't allocated on a group basis. Only in pairs. Good thing in a way. Makes it less like a works' outing.'

'Daphne Vauxley's not very pleased with where she and Amelia are sitting. Second tier, I think, but I don't see them.'

Treasure raised his eyebrows but didn't comment. Mrs Vauxley was hard to please.

The elegant Kirov opera house with its bright gilded decor was built in 1860 in the classic style with rococo trimmings. It has a pitched auditorium floor, and five narrow tiers lining the horseshoe interior rising one above the next, each fronted by prettily moulded balconies. Intruding at the back, and dead centre to the stage, is the arched, blue canopied royal box occupying the width of ten seats and the height of three tiers. The stall seating

68

consists of rows of upholstered chairs in the Chippendale style.

The spectacle of the massive stage was perfect from where the Treasures were sitting, half way back in the centre. They had learned from others in their party, encountered in the first interval, that the view was not nearly so good from the three-rowed tiers, except for those in the front seats.

'I still can't get over that waiter wanting to barter cigarettes for the wine. In the best hotel in Leningrad,' said the banker as they made their way out of the auditorium. 'And after over sixty-five years of applied socialism. It's really rather sad.'

'I gather Russian cigarettes are pretty foul.'

'That is so, madam,' said the amused, well dressed man who was holding a door open for Molly, and who she found vaguely familiar. 'I'm sorry I couldn't help overhearing. I'm Russian, you understand. If your waiter asked for kind not cash, it's not exactly barter. In my country traditionally a waiter owns the food and wine he brings you from the kitchen. If you don't pay for it for any reason then he must. By extension it is thus his property to sell in kind if he wishes, so long as he doesn't ask for greater value than the cash price.'

'It'd complicate life if every waiter did it,' observed Treasure, amiably.

'Of course. And none of them should. You're right, it is rather sad. I offered the point as an explanation not a pure defence. You paid him?'

'In cash. We neither of us smoke.'

'I'm glad. Good evening. Enjoy your stay, Mr Treasure. A great honour to have you with us . . . and your famous wife.' The man bowed and melted into the crowd.

'Charming. *And* he must go to my movies,' said Molly, glowing. 'Wasn't he our lone diner at the hotel this evening?'

'I think so. I wonder . . . ?' Treasure frowned then

shrugged dismissively. 'It's this way isn't it?' He led her along the overcrowded curved corridor flanking the auditorium. It was punctuated by archways and steps to a lower, wider corridor serving the cloakrooms and the short stairs down to the box office foyer where smoking was allowed. But they took the first stairway leading upwards.

'What a divine performance,' called Nigel Dirving who they ran into on the next floor outside the royal box. 'Seen Edwina or Candy have you? Promised them a drink. But I'm dying for a smoke.' He nodded towards the open double doors to the box where its occupants, a group of high ranking army officers and their wives, were conversing over glasses of champagne. 'Never seen a British general at Covent Garden.'

'Not in uniform, perhaps,' Treasure answered. 'I know a number of musical generals.'

'Is the m . . . en's room this way, d'you know?' Canon Emdon had appeared at Treasure's side and was whispering urgently in his ear. 'Long act that one. Ah!' He hurried onwards where he could see a male queue forming.

Further along they saw Felicity Wander in the crush but she didn't see them. It seemed she was alone although she might simply have lost sight of her husband.

Gloria Blinton was definitely by herself. She greeted them at the foot of another staircase. 'Going for an ice, are you? I am. Sol's giving up. He's not musical really. And it is going on a bit. Lovely ices though. I had one in the last interval. Well you got to have something to keep you going, haven't you? See you, then.' Flushed and bubbly she elbowed her way through the wide archway that led to the icecream counter.

'Here we are, I think,' said Treasure.

The columned doorway led into the high-ceilinged, chandelier-lit reception room, which they had noticed earlier. Couples came here in the intervals to progress arm-in-arm, anticlockwise around the carpeted perimeter.

It was already fairly full, but a senior looking army officer gallantly made a place for them to slip into ahead of himself and his escort.

'Now we're here it makes me terribly self conscious for some reason,' laughed Molly taking her husband's arm. 'D'you remember doing the Military Two-step?'

'Certainly not.'

'Well it started just like this. Makes me think we should be dancing. Except there's no music. Shall we break into a skip?'

'No,' he responded promptly for fear she meant it. 'If we did we'd probably be thrown out. This is a time-honoured ritual.'

'You're guessing. That's a beautiful parquet floor in the centre. The gilt-work and mouldings in this building are gorgeous. And like everything else the place was practically rebuilt after the war. I wonder if this was the ballroom?'

'Possibly still is.'

'Is good. Good for legs. No?' the beaming officer roared from behind them.

'Good for everything, I should think,' Molly replied brightly. 'It's the voyeurs up there I don't care for. They make me feel like an exhibit.'

Around fifteen feet of wall in a corner near the doorway had been omitted. This opening, from floor to ceiling, exposed the rising marble balustrade of the staircase outside that Gloria had been descending when they met her. Above this was a balcony. Both these observation points were crammed with mostly young men regarding the people processing below—or perhaps only studying the young women involved there.

'Isn't that . . . ?'

As Treasure began to speak there was a sudden sharp commotion on the balcony. What happened was over in seconds but was no less difficult to credit for that. The watchers up there were crying out as they seemed to be thrust forward in a body, clutching each other to stop themselves falling. Then came the sound of one, piercing, agonising shout as the figure of a man at the front and centre separated from the rest, his arms reaching forward grasping at the air. For a split second he hovered like a gargoyle. Then, to a chorus of screams, he plunged head first over the balustrade, scattering the people below and crashing to the floor a few paces from where the Treasures were standing.

There were more screams and gasps while some of the horrified onlookers pressed forward to see the stricken man. Others, closer, recoiled from the sight.

It was the army officer who took charge. He conjured up, it seemed from nowhere, a handful of soldiers who at his bidding began clearing back the people. 'You, please stay,' he had said to Treasure before issuing a sharp order to the nearest soldier who immediately moved to Molly's side.

A younger officer hurried in and knelt beside the body. It was very still, splayed out, face nearly downwards, the neck twisted awkwardly. There was a clearly visible tear in the back of the light grey jacket—slightly left of centre, between the shoulderblades. One could only guess at the substance that had caused the damp patch in the material around and below the tear.

The kneeling man was presumably a doctor. He looked for pulses, then turned the body on its side and thrust his ear to the chest. The woman who had followed him in produced a small mirror from her handbag and handed it to him without being asked. He held it to the victim's mouth looking for the misting signs of breathing on the glass. Treasure was close enough to see that there were none.

The doctor looked up at the senior officer and shook his head.

By this time more soldiers had appeared, some of them wearing caps and greatcoats. They were herding the people from the room, except for a handful of designated couples. Several other senior officers—some of those

Treasure remembered seeing in the royal box—had also come in, and with them was the well dressed civilian who had held the door for Molly earlier.

After a brief conversation with the first officer, the civilian turned to the Treasures. 'My name is Grinyev. Colonel Maxim Grinyev of the Committee for State Security. We spoke earlier. In happier circumstances. The general asked you to stay because he saw you witness what occurred. He thinks if this poor fellow is a foreign tourist it would be better if . . .'

'He is. From Britain,' Treasure interrupted. 'One of our party.'

'His name is Frenk. Rudolph Frenk,' said Molly, turning away.

'I'm sorry for keeping you waiting. You're comfortable here? They've brought wine I see. Is there anything else I can get you? Anything at all?' Colonel Grinyev had entered full of solicitude.

It was thirty minutes since the tragedy. The Treasures had been left alone in this room for most of that time.

'We're sorry to be missing the third act.' Treasure, standing near Molly with a glass of wine, glanced at her as he spoke. 'But of course we understand.'

'I'm very grateful to you, sir.'

The colonel was a little under medium height, fit, thickset, and dark, and looking to be in his early forties. His normal expression seemed always to be prefacing announcements of the deferential kind, with a downwardly inclined head lending support to that superficial impression. But to the closer observer, and Treasure was one such, the darting upsearching eyes told more about the man than the gentler attributes like the soft voice and the raised hands clasping and unclasping each other in a nearly obsequious way.

Still there was more of the cultivated civilian than the intelligence officer in the outward composition of this unexpected colonel in the KGB.

The three were in the artistic director's office at the opera house. It was quite a big room but over-filled with furniture, a grand piano, sketches, stage models, musical scores, and other predictable paraphernalia. The Treasures had been conducted here by the soldier first told off to stay with them, and who had made it clear he would be remaining outside the door.

Molly was sitting at one end of a high-backed sofa most of which was piled with random swatches of brightly coloured materials.

'Mr Frenk is dead?' she said with more resignation than question in her voice.

'Quite dead, I'm afraid. There wasn't much possibility of anything else, as you saw. But, yes, it's now official. As it were.' Grinyev delivered his words quickly, but with a pause at the end of every phrase while the eyes measured reactions. 'He was stabbed from behind, and it seems his neck was broken in the fall. Either injury could have killed him. We shan't know which till the autopsy. And we don't know who did it. Not yet. It was dark and crowded on that balcony. It seems the murderer thrust in from the back. He stabbed Mr Frenk, pushing him forward like a battering ram, then disappeared. The crowd parted. They were all concerned to stop themselves going over. Nobody saw anything helpful. I'm very sorry.' The last words were directed at Molly. Now the speaker turned to her husband and gave a short, nervous smile. 'You knew him well, Mr Treasure?'

'Hardly at all, I'm afraid. Neither of us.'

'But he was a member of your art group? The Baroque Circle?'

'Only a temporary one,' offered Molly. 'He and two other people came to make up the numbers. We were short of takers from the regular membership. It was a matter of economics.'

The colonel studied his shoes, seemingly perplexed, then the glance came up sharply. 'To save money, you mean? You're on a package tour?'

'That's right,' said Molly.

'Forgive me. You are a well known actress. Mr Treasure, you are head of a London merchant bank. You would both be welcomed in this country as VIPs on a private visit. You have not been attempting to travel incognito. May I ask, do you normally take *economical* package tours?'

Treasure grinned. 'Not frequently. If you mean are we hard-up, no we're not. We came this way for cultural reasons. Also because we both happened to be free when the opportunity came up.'

'And because I'm President of the Baroque Circle and find the other members wholly compatible company,' added Molly, a touch pointedly. 'They're none of them hard-up either, not so far as I know.'

'Not even Sir Jeremy Wander, or the Honourable Mrs Vauxley, both members of the proverbially impoverished British aristocracy?'

'I'd guess quite the contrary. In both cases.' Treasure also grinned.

'Miss Royce. She comes at no cost to herself?'

The Treasures exchanged glances before the banker replied: 'Miss Royce is a distinguished academic. She's assistant curator of one of the most important art galleries in Britain. If her fare hadn't been paid by the travel agency we should probably be paying her a fat professional fee to guide us around the collections here.'

'I understand. The other two people who aren't members of your Circle?'

'Mr and Mrs Blinton,' Molly answered.

'Ah yes. He's quite elderly. She's . . . she's younger.' Grinyev spoke more slowly than before. 'So you hadn't met them before either?'

'None of us had,' said Molly.

'So far as you know. But Mr Frenk could have known Blinton or his wife?'

'Are you telling us or asking us, Colonel?' This was

Treasure. 'You seem to know a great deal about our party. Perhaps more than we do. May I ask why?'

The nervous smile came and went. 'Partly because you and your wife are in it. My office wondered why. You have explained the reason. As for the others, it's routine. I know little more than was offered on the visas.'

'You seem concerned about everyone's financial situation, Colonel. Frenk wasn't robbed was he?'

Grinyev looked up sharply. 'Not so far as I know. There were other reasons for my interest.' The speaker fell silent.

'We noticed you at dinner this evening.'

'Also routine, Mrs Treasure. My office is concerned with foreign visitors. From time to time I drop in to the principal hotels. It's a matter of conscientious application.'

'And valuable if something untoward happens. Like tonight,' said the banker moving to the piano and putting his empty glass on the tray there. 'So, what d'you want of us now?'

'Your testimony as reliable witnesses, of course. So far it seems you were the only non-Russians in the room.'

'We saw very little.'

'There was not much for anyone to see. Also, you are the only members of the Baroque Circle so far accounted for at the time of the stabbing.'

'Are you suggesting a member of the Circle could have killed Mr Frenk?' Molly asked in a genuinely shocked voice.

'It must be regarded as one possibility.'

'Until you find that the twelve members left, that's excluding ourselves and Frenk, were sitting in their seats or were at the bar at the relevant time,' said Treasure carefully.

'Which we shall begin to do in the next interval. By then I shall know from Intourist at the hotel which seats they are occupying. My officers will collect them and bring them to the room next door. There they'll be questioned. And searched.'

'Searched?' Molly questioned quickly.

'It's necessary I'm afraid.'

'And when you're satisfied there isn't a murderer amongst us, we'll be allowed to go back to the Astoria and carry on normally?'

'With one of your party dead, Mrs Treasure, it will perhaps be a little difficult . . .'

'I agree, Colonel,' Treasure interrupted. 'Obviously there's a good deal to be done about Frenk. Incidentally, someone ought to be getting in touch with his relatives if he has any.'

'And who'll be responsible for getting his body back to England?' asked Molly.

It was the two men who now exchanged looks before Grinyev replied: 'It may be some time before that will be anyone's task. In the case of a homicide there are many formalities as well as investigations, you understand? About the relatives, perhaps your travel agency can speak to them. It will probably be in order to telephone them tomorrow.'

'In order? Tomorrow?' Molly repeated uncertainly.

'It is already quite late in England. Also it's necessary to make reservations for overseas calls. The international lines are always very busy.'

'But there'll be no official reason stopping me 'phoning the news to London. When I can get a line?' This was Treasure.

Grinyev regarded his feet, then looked up. 'For the moment, yes. I'm afraid so. Until the investigation is properly under way. But tomorrow, or perhaps the next day, I'm sure it will be all right.'

'I can talk to the British Consul, of course?'

'Unfortunately there is no British Consulate in Leningrad. We shall inform your Embassy in Moscow of the situation as soon as possible.'

'You haven't done so already?'

'This is a matter of some delicacy, Mr Treasure. At the moment knowledge of it is restricted to a very few people. We shall keep it so until we have fuller details. In the interests of both our countries.'

'But a British national has been murdered, presumably . . . possibly by a Russian. It may be in the interests of your Government to keep it secret for as long as possible, but I really can't see any reason against informing the British Embassy. I'm sure they have a string of formalities to observe in such a situation too. So I expect the sooner they can get on with them the better.' Treasure had spoken with mounting assurance.

Grinyev frowned. 'The British, like the Americans, are instant communicators. In the USSR we sometimes sacrifice speed for thoroughness. In the interests of accuracy and often with the best of motives. This is not always understood. Before the presumption you make is assumed to be fact, there's an aspect of the situation which it would be better for everyone that we have clear. Before we disclose anything. Even to your Embassy. Before there's the opportunity for the news media to get the story.'

'I'm sorry. I really don't accept . . .'

'We've found the knife. The knife used to stab Mr Frenk.' The colonel had cut in without apology. 'It was dropped on the balcony. It's a clasp knife. Quite big. Made in Sheffield.'

'Quite a few are. Including many exported to Russia, I imagine.'

'This is a quite distinctive knife, Mr Treasure. A mother-of-pearl handle with silver initials. The initials are S.L.B. According to his passport, Mr Blinton's given names are Solomon Lionel.'

# CHAPTER 8

Sol Blinton was sweating. It wasn't especially warm in the cramped living room of the small apartment but his heart was beating erratically—something that always made him hot as well as apprehensive. For the hundredth time he wondered why he'd done it: why he was here.

What he'd been asked to do had seemed like a simple favour at the time—a courtesy you might say. He'd been glad to help. It was his brother-in-law who'd approached him, Jacob, his first wife's brother, the pious one—when he'd heard Sol was coming to Leningrad. Later, when Sol realised there might be complications, it seemed chicken to try to back out.

His not being well had made things worse—much worse when you took into account it had even led to somebody else begging him for help. Did he look that benign, he asked himself, that even near strangers turned to him when they were in trouble?

The heart-block at Heathrow had been genuine. Agreeing to do a phony repeat performance on arrival here had been something else again. He wouldn't have done it either if Gloria hadn't been ready—even eager—to co-operate. Maybe she wouldn't have been so keen if she'd known what else he was up to.

So now here he was face to face with a family of 'refuseniks'—which is what they called these Russian Jews who'd been stopped from emigrating to Israel. And in the condition Israel was in at the moment, Sol pondered, who needed to go to live there anyway? Except that wasn't a question he could put to these people. One day, maybe, they could argue it out for themselves in Tel Aviv or somewhere. Right now they wanted to get out of the country, and Sol was supposed to be helping them.

He nodded at Isidor Lasky, the middle-aged science teacher sitting at the dining table beside him. Olga, his wife and also a teacher, and Katrina, the pretty, sixteen-year-old daughter, were both sitting opposite. It was Katrina who spoke most English. Olga spoke some but Isidor none at all. Isidor, whose parents had been Latvian, spoke Yiddish but Sol didn't. All this had come out in the protracted exchanges when Sol had arrived—also the reason why the apartment had been empty when he'd called in the afternoon. Katrina had been at school then: her parents, who he knew had lost their jobs after applying to go to Israel, had now got work as kitchen hands in a local hotel.

Altogether communication had been slow—on top of which Isidor Lasky seemed to think Sol had joined them mostly to observe the Sabbath and the second day of Passover. There was no urgency—with Isidor it seemed everything was to do with religious observance. Now he was reading the Scripture again, aloud—in Yiddish. Two Sabbath candles flickered in their brass holders. Olga Lasky had just brought in some more matzo crackers.

It was nearly fifty years since Sol had passed a Seder evening—or even remembered a Sabbath. He wasn't against religion; he just wasn't religious. Israel for him meant sunshine holidays and not much more. But his being here at this time had acted like a profession of faith on Isidor Lasky. The Russian had shown unbelievably little interest in the money.

Sol had come on a city bus, scared most of the way about missing his stop. The bus had been packed and he'd had difficulty keeping a place to stand near a window and the door to the rear platform. Also he hadn't had a five kopek piece, the standard fare, to pass along for someone to put in the machine. Instead he had produced a twenty kopek piece so that a string of other passengers between him and the machine had made a great performance of passing back his change. He had thanked them all profusely—advertising he was a foreigner, and spoiling the whole strategy of coming un-noticed on public transport.

At least he'd known the number of the bus. He'd noted it on his first visit—also the exact location of the apartment. That afternoon Gloria had stayed in the taxi in the street below when he'd come up to check—he'd said—on what had happened to his grandfather's house. She didn't know he was helping some refuseniks. Maybe he should have told her. But he hadn't wanted her involved if anything went wrong—except she'd played up beautifully over the other business at the airport yesterday, and with hardly any notice. Definitely he should have told her. He realised that now. Well, it was nearly done. He'd handed over the fifteen hundred American dollars collected for the Laskys in London. He was only waiting for the progress report on another Jewish family that someone was supposed to be bringing. He looked at his watch. If that someone didn't come soon he'd leave without it. Katrina Lasky had said the last bus was in ten minutes.

The knock on the door was so loud Sol jumped in his seat. It was exactly the kind of knock that announced the arrival of the Gestapo in the war movies.

Lasky stopped reading: his wife looked concerned: Sol was petrified. His heart was thumping in wild patterns: the driblets of sweat were streaming down onto his already wet collar.

Katrina Lasky went to open the door at the end of the short passage. The others watched and listened to her exchange there. No one was admitted—to Sol's extreme relief—and the girl shortly returned to the table holding an envelope which she handed to the visitor. He accepted it gingerly, handkerchief in his other hand, wiping his neck and forehead.

There was no address on the missive, and it was quite

small. He knew he just had to hand it to pious Jacob when he got back to London. He stuffed it into an inside pocket.

'I have to go now,' he said, smiling at everyone and getting up from the table. The senior Laskys nodded, but then they'd done the same at almost everything he'd said.

'I take you to the bus,' Katrina offered as she helped him with his hat, coat and voluminous scarf.

'Please don't. It's cold outside. I know the way.' For the first time in his life he was uneasy about being caught in the company of another Jew—even a pretty young girl like Katrina. So maybe that was the justification for coming. He tried to shrug off the shaming thought: count your blessings Solomon Blinton. 'Goodbye then.' He smiled again. 'Next year Jerusalem.'

'Next year Jerusalem,' the others repeated the well known hope in unison, even Isidor Lasky. Sol shook hands with them. Katrina walked him to the door, then down the bare concrete stairs to the main entrance—the apartment was on the second floor. He was about to shake hands with her again, feeling awkward because he'd done it once already. Instead she did a little curtsey, put her arms about his neck, said: 'Thank you very much, sir,' and kissed him on both cheeks. That brought tears to his eyes.

There was no one else waiting at the bus-stop in the empty street, but it was sleeting and he was glad when he saw the bus coming in the distance. He was glowing still, despite the weather—pleased he'd agreed to be a courier, and grateful for his good life. It wasn't much he'd done to help others: no risk really, and now it was over—or nearly.

The well dressed man seemed to have materialised from nowhere as the bus drew up. He was youngish and authoritative, with sharp mean features and a yet sharper and meaner look. He stood close to Sol, eying him directly—blatantly summing him up. The older man's heart started to bump about again. The envelope in his pocket seemed to grow bigger and more conspicuous. He was sure from the start this man was a policeman.

There was a mere handful of passengers in the bus—three men seated apart at the front, two old women together further back. Sol glanced at the man who got on with him as they were both at the fare machine with their five kopek coins ready. Sol put his in first, then waited for a ticket to come out before remembering tickets weren't issued. The 'ticket' was the moral glow you got from having paid. Now there was a sneer on the man's face: a definitely knowing sneer. Sol blamed himself for giving away his alien status again.

He took a window seat in the centre of the vehicle across from the two women. He sensed, without seeing, that the mean-faced man had settled just behind him. One of the male passengers in front started talking to himself loudly—and drunkenly. The second was making retching noises. The third had turned about and was directing a bloodshot, vacant stare at Sol but which to the hapless, guilt-ridden tourist seemed gradually to be hardening into a look of deep contagious suspicion.

In five minutes the bus reached the Kirovskiy Bridge over the Neva without anyone getting on or off. Here the two women and one of the men prepared to get out—the man, the retching one, staggering to the door at the front near the driver. Sol was now watching the young man behind him in a window reflection. He decided to try something he'd seen done a dozen times on television—and to check if the man was following him. He stood up suddenly and made as if he was hurrying to get out. When he got to the door he frowned to show he'd made a mistake and sat down again next to it.

The experiment was inconclusive. Although the man had watched Sol with interest, he hadn't stirred, except now he was wearing a mirthless half smile. Most likely he'd seen through the ploy which Sol hadn't handled too efficiently: the automatic door had been closed by the time he'd got to it. Sol fidgeted and wiped his glasses.

On the south side of the bridge the bus turned to the right and moved along the embankment. At a stop near the State Hermitage a young couple got on. Further along, in front of the Admiralty, a group of eight other youngsters tumbled in noisily.

Sol had intended getting off at the stop where he'd got on for the outward journey. It was quite near the Kirov theatre. The group coach was to leave there for the hotel at midnight. He had told Gloria in the second interval he'd go for a stroll, then get a drink in the bar, and be waiting for her on the coach when the performance ended. There was still plenty of time for that, but if he was being followed by a policeman he had to lose him first if he could.

He marvelled at his own confidence—that he, Solomon Blinton, sixty-nine years of age, weighing 194 pounds, with fallen arches, failing sight and a heart condition was planning to shake off the Russian police. But if this man didn't know who he was yet, and wasn't aiming to find out—not with others present—then it was worth a try. Maybe he only spoke Russian and was waiting for reinforcements. So the last thing Sol should do was lead him to a coach reserved for Astoria hotel guests.

Sol planned what he'd say if he was taken in for interrogation. He wouldn't admit to any meeting for a start. He didn't have the Laskys' address on him because he'd memorised it earlier. And he wouldn't admit to passing money either. Should he get rid of the envelope while there was still time? He took it from his pocket ready to drop somewhere where it wouldn't be found. Without the envelope he could repeat the story he'd used with the taxi driver: Gloria had believed it.

Now all the new passengers were on their feet preparing to leave by the rear door at the next stop. They'd been shouting and gesticulating about another bus that had appeared right behind. They all obviously wanted to change onto it, but to their consternation it now overtook the one they were in as both buses turned left away from the river. By the time both vehicles drew up at the next stop, the anxious passengers had hustled up the aisle and were waiting at the front exit, desperate to get out and onto the bus in front.

It was then that Sol saw his opportunity—and seized it. As the driver opened the doors, Sol, from his vantage position, thrust himself in front of the others just as they poured onto the street.

A freezing wind off the river bit into his face. The pavement was slippery under him. He was dogged by fear and actually trembling—but it had been now or never. Before any of the others had passed him, he turned hard left into the narrow defile between the two vehicles. He'd seen his pursuer rise. The man had to believe he'd gone with the others to the bus in front. Please God let him believe that—Sol prayed but couldn't wait to find out. The driver of his own bus was looking down at him now disapprovingly through the cleaned arc of the snow-spattered windscreen.

Ducking his head Sol went around the front of the bus, stamping flat-footedly to keep his balance. Then he moved down the vehicle, one hand trailing its side.

There was no question of going south in the direction of the theatre, not yet. That would have taken him ahead of both buses which were still parked in line at the stop. Instead, when he reached the end of the bus, he hurried on, head down into the now driving sleet, and north towards the river.

He could hear the engines of the still stationary buses accelerating behind him as he came to the corner of the crossroads where they had turned earlier. He stopped and looked back. The two vehicles were about to pull away from the kerb—but in that instant the single figure of a man seemed to topple out from the leading bus and was left standing on the otherwise now deserted pavement.

Sol knew who the figure had to be despite the uncertain visibility. He was being followed all right: the ploy had worked—up to a point. The man had changed to the leading bus, but he'd got off it again when he'd found Sol wasn't there. Through his spattered glasses Sol could even see the man looking about him in various directions—searching for him.

Sol didn't wait to be spotted. He had joined three other people waiting at the crossroads. Breathing heavily he crossed with them eastwards, then, because there was no traffic, he crossed back, northwards again, this time against the lights towards what seemed to be an open park on the other side of the broad thoroughfare.

The light was poor on the park edge but Sol was grateful for the protection of the darkness. He headed for the dark centre, hurrying along a path between beds of unpruned rose bushes.

He didn't look around when he heard the footsteps behind him. They were loud, running steps—firm, fast, regular slaps on the wet concrete of the path some way back. Choking down something between a gasp and a sob, the frightened Sol started to run too—except he could manage nothing better than an unsteady jog. He was unsure of his balance, he was wearing too many clothes and his glasses had steamed up from his hot breath. Suddenly he was no longer thinking of escape in the darkness—only fear of the dark and what could happen to him there.

Soon the terror started to consume him. He was trembling—straining to reach light again, the street lights he could see ahead. It was then he tripped and fell on his face. Painfully he dragged himself back onto his feet, his astrakhan hat half over his eyes, the scarf coming out of his coat. The lights were closer now but the following footsteps were closer too. He looked behind. He still couldn't see the pursuer in the almost total darkness.

And now he realised they weren't street lights ahead. They were floods illuminating a statue: a huge equestrian statue. It was the man on the rearing horse—the bronze horseman of Leningrad. It was Peter the Great riding over the serpent of treason. Blindly he stumbled towards it and the succouring, megawatt pool of light surrounding it, showing off one of the city's most famous sights—visible from the embankment beyond he was sure.

'Stop!'

The voice was immediately behind him now, almost in his ear. He gulped for air. He willed his legs and lungs to carry him the last twenty yards into the light. But then his left knee buckled. He was down again and this time he knew he couldn't get up, not straight away. Helplessly, hopelessly he began crawling along the sodden path.

'Sir. Is no good running.' The voice was harsh and guttural. 'Is bad. Bad,' the admonition went on.

The mean man from the bus was bending over him. Sol cowered. The man grasped him under both armpits and began dragging him roughly to the side.

'Help! Help!' called Sol in desperation, and only conscious he was being pulled back into the darkness.

'Shh!' hissed the man. 'You bring police. Make trouble. No good.' Now he was helping Sol onto a park bench. 'This yours.' It was a statement not a question. The man was standing over him holding the envelope. 'Drop in bus. You take.' He thrust the envelope inside Sol's overcoat.

Sol thought of pulling the thing out again and throwing it away, disowning it—but what was the point? He must have dropped it in his haste and he was actually glad to have it back where it couldn't get others into trouble. 'What do you want?' he asked, still getting his breath back.

The man's stern features softened for the first time. He looked about him, then sat down beside Sol on the bench. He was less commanding than he had first seemed. 'We trade, yes? You got clothes you sell me? Jeans, T-shirts, *pulover, beg, shoozi. Niet?*' He shook his head, angry at his impatient lapse into slang Russian. 'Pullover, bag, shoes. You got? Like you sell on Petrograd side? Discs, tights . . .'

Sol relaxed as the recital of merchandise continued. It was only sad that his restored peace of mind was to be so short-lived.

# CHAPTER 9

'It's monstrous,' declared Mrs Vauxley staring around at the others gathered in the residents' lounge of the Astoria hotel.

The lounge was a thickly carpeted, irregularly shaped open area off one end of the main hall. It housed the hotel *bureau de change* behind a caged counter on one side, in use for two hours a day in the morning. Now, at half-an-hour after midnight, the Baroque Circle members, less Sol Blinton and the deceased Frenk, were in sole occupation of the rest of the place. By Astoria standards it was well if starkly furnished with several large and newish winged armchairs covered in brown moquette, some high-backed, armless upholstered chairs in the same material, and a long green velvet sofa.

The group had made a rough ring of seats around two circular, low wooden tables. They had not been told to wait here, nor to delay going to bed, but this was the first opportunity to talk about what had happened.

They had been directed from their seats at the opera at the start of the third interval, and kept in pairs under supervision, before being fingerprinted, searched and questioned one at a time. Even their short coach ride back to the hotel had been in the company of two of their plainclothes interrogators. So they had stayed together to compare notes, and later, by common, unspoken consent, as a gesture of solidarity until they knew the fate of their absent member.

Tea had been ordered and promised, but only the glasses and metal holders had so far materialised and been placed on the tables.

'Quite monstrous,' Mrs Vauxley repeated. 'It's our absolute right to telephone the British Embassy.' She was seated—almost enthroned—in one of the winged chairs. Her stick was grasped in one outstretched hand doing credible service as a sceptre. She was still wearing her tall fur hat. Canon Emdon thought the aged Catherine the Great might have looked a bit like that. He was opposite her perched on the edge of the sofa at one end.

'It's a bit di . . . fficult defining ri . . . ghts in the circumstances,' he remarked, wobbling his retreating chin, and looking at Treasure for support.

'With the hotel switchboard closed for the night, I agree,' said the banker with a shrug. He was leaning with folded arms against an ornate, dark wooden fireplace that seemed not to be used for fires. His wife was seated beside him by the hearth on one of the high-backs.

'Don't you think we should settle for getting Mr Blinton safe back for the moment?' Molly asked with feeling.

Gloria Blinton, more than a bit diminished by plight and a big chair, let out a sob and immediately had her hand patted by Nigel Dirving who was perched on one of the arms. It was noticeable he had been at her side at every permitted moment since the murder.

'What if they put Sol in prison tonight? I'll most likely never see my hubby again if they do,' Gloria uttered, tears coursing down her cheeks and making a terrible mess of her eye make-up. 'He's not well. I knew we shouldn't have come.'

Mrs Vauxley winced as much at the vulgar contraction of husband as at the prospect delineated. She was not unsympathetic as her presence witnessed, but there were limits.

'I'm sure they'll bring him back shortly. With Valya Sinitseva,' Treasure insisted but with nothing to justify the

statement except the conviction that anyone with half
Colonel Grinyev's apparent acuity would figure Sol
Blinton was no murderer.

A dishevelled but cheerful Sol had made a sudden and
brief appearance in the hall ten minutes earlier. He had
been immediately accosted by two policemen, made to
identify himself and then whisked, bewildered and weakly
protesting, straight into the manager's office. Grinyev and
several assistants were there already with the group's
Intourist guide.

'They didn't even let me speak to him,' Gloria
complained tearfully. She had been standing in the lounge
when her husband had come in at the other end of the
hall. She had been just quick enough to reach him, throw
her arms around his neck, removing his hat and
smoothing his head in a motherly way, before he was torn
away from her. She was still nursing the hat.

Earlier, when Sol hadn't turned up for the coach,
people had hoped or assumed he'd be awaiting their return
at the Astoria. When he hadn't been found at the hotel
his wife had become nearly inconsolable, though Nigel
Dirving had been doing his best.

'But at least you know now he's all right, dear,' put
in Mrs Tate from beside the canon, a statement which
almost everyone else judged to be only relatively true.

'And obviously they'll believe his knife was stolen.
Must do. As soon as they compare his fingerprints with
those on the knife.' Sir Jeremy Wander pulled himself
upright from where he had been slumped at the other end
of the sofa from the canon.

'They found fingerprints on the knife?' Gloria looked
up over her handkerchief.

'One assumes so,' put in Dirving. 'Has to be why they
took our prints. Can't think of any other reason.'

'Unless it's standard routine. In some circumstances.'
This was Treasure. Neither he nor Molly had been fingerprinted.

'Question is, who could have stolen the knife?' asked

Reggie Tate fingering his beard. He was sitting cross-legged on the floor close to his mother.

'Almost anyone,' Mrs Vauxley answered sharply. 'Those bedroom doors don't lock by themselves. If a room's left unlocked the owners have to suffer the consequences.' She was looking stonily ahead and not at Gloria, but most people understood what she was getting at.

'Our room wasn't left unlocked. Well not on purpose,' offered Gloria with unexpected spirit. 'And Sol usually has his knife with him. It was only tonight he forgot it.'

It was Dirving who broke the following awkward silence with: 'No sign of the tea, of course.'

'It's unbelievable hardly any of us had an alibi. For the time of the murder. Except Molly and Mark,' said Candy who was sitting on the floor near Molly.

'Because we were all about our separate businesses, dear,' Mrs Tate commented stoutly.

'Yah,' agreed Felicity Wander who'd said she'd been queuing for the ladies' room to no purpose during the whole interval. 'So let's hope Mr Blinton can prove he'd left the theatre before it happened.'

'I don't think he could have,' Gloria put in, and blowing her nose loudly. 'And anyway, who would he know who'd have seen him? I mean . . .'

'I could have seen him,' Dirving interrupted her which he'd been doing often, probably in an effort to help. 'I still could have seen him, come to that. I mean, he must have left by the box-office entrance. I was there. It's the only place where they allow smoking.'

'Except the washrooms,' corrected the canon.

'If only we'd had a chance to compare movements,' the actor completed ruefully.

'Don't you think it'd be unwise to invent covers for each other?' said Molly.

'And t . . . oo late,' added Canon Emdon in an unexpected and unclerical aside. 'Otherwise I shouldn't feel any co . . . nstraint. None whatsoever.' He gaped about him with an expression both benign and buoyant. He had taken against Colonel Grinyev during the questioning at the opera house.

'Quite right, Canon,' agreed Wander. 'The Russkies are noted for inventing their own versions of the truth. We're entitled to do the same, seems to me. They're always fixing up foreigners.'

'And bugging rooms,' said Treasure quietly.

Wander frowned, and shortly after his eyebrows began twitching quite violently.

'Mr Blinton may have seen some of us. Doing what we said we were doing.' This was Edwina who'd been sitting beside Frenk in the second tier at the opera. She claimed she hadn't left her seat until very late in the second interval, but no one had been able wholly to confirm her statement. Only Reggie Tate, seated close-by, had partly corroborated it. He had heard her refuse to go for a drink with Frenk, but that had been before both Tates had left the auditorium themselves—he to inspect the theatre's ceremonial entrance staircase, she to 'mosey around' as she'd put it.

'Mrs Vauxley and I weren't far from you, Edwina,' Amelia Harwick put in tentatively. She was sitting very upright on the edge of a tall chair. 'I told them I thought you were still there when we went out.'

'*You* went out,' Mrs Vauxley snapped. 'I remained in the auditorium. I'll thank you to remember that, Amelia.'

Miss Harwick seemed about to disagree, but perhaps thought better of it, and said: 'I'm sorry, Mrs Vauxley. That's right, of course. Mrs Vauxley stayed while I went to see if we could have our seats changed.'

'Because we were tired of not seeing anything,' her employer added.

'Of course. I remember now, I saw you by the box office, Amelia,' volunteered Dirving, lighting a cigarette. He gave her an ingratiating smile. 'Stupid of me not to have told . . .'

'I don't think so,' Miss Harwick had reddened as she

broke in hurriedly. 'You see I never got there. The crowd on the stairs was so thick. I'm afraid I gave up.' Her pursed lips returned to their nibbling motion after she finished speaking.

'Good try, Nigel,' said Wander giving the actor a wink.

'Yah,' agreed his wife languidly.

'Puts you back with the rest of us,' Wander added. 'Except that old crone serving in the champagne bar is bound to remember me tomorrow.'

The old crone in question had gone off duty after the second interval. She had so far not been available to confirm Wander's story. He'd insisted he'd been near the front of the line of people waiting for champagne soon after the start of the interval, and served with it around the time the stabbing took place.

'I feel so badly about not being in touch with Mr Frenk's relatives.' This was Candy.

'If he had any,' commented Mrs Vauxley.

'Where did he live?' asked Wander.

'Coventry,' Candy answered.

'Isn't that your home too, Edwina?' said Mrs Tate.

'It's where I work in term time. But it's a big place.' Edwina smiled. 'He and I did compare notes about cultural life in the city.'

'Did he mention relatives? Did he live with his parents, perhaps?' asked Molly.

'I assumed he had a bachelor flat,' Edwina replied. 'Maybe he shared with someone. Another musician perhaps.'

'I have the address and telephone number,' said Candy.

'You'd never met him before, of course, Edwina,' Wander put in, then, without waiting for a reply, he continued: 'Fancy Valya being at the opera all the time. By herself.'

'She's keen on opera. Got an odd ticket that was supposed to come to the group,' said Molly.

'She didn't know she was going when she left us this

afternoon. Told me she was spending an evening at home with her husband,' Candy offered.

'Tickets are like gold dust unless you're a tourist apparently,' said Reggie Tate. 'If you're a tourist, of course, good ones are available on the day. As they were for us. And so cheap. Don't know why the locals put up with it.'

'Not so cheap if your wages are f . . . orty roubles a week. That's average,' the canon interjected.

'It's still strange Valya didn't tell us she was going,' said Mrs Tate. 'I mean, if I hadn't run into her when I was being arrested . . .'

'You weren't arrested, Mother,' her son admonished lightly.

'Good as. We missed the fourth act, after all. Well, taken for questioning then. Anyway, if we hadn't met Valya in that corridor and spoken to her, when we were with the policeman, I don't suppose she'd have been involved at all.'

'Yah. Don't believe she was wild about being tied up with us either,' said Felicity Wander pointedly. 'Suppose you can't blame her.'

'I thought she helped a lot. During the questioning. Like having your lawyer there,' Mrs Tate observed warmly.

Mrs Vauxley gave a loud, disparaging grunt. 'Well, my lawyer doesn't work for the KGB,' she announced stiffly.

'I suppose that's f . . . air comment . . .' the canon began, but was interrupted by a shout from Gloria.

'Sol! Oh Sol!' She jumped from her chair and ran across into the hall where her husband was approaching with Colonel Grinyev.

The colonel left the Blintons to their embraces and continued into the lounge. He looked tired as well as embarrassed as he stood before the group, except many of those present had come to believe that last and characteristic impression was no more than disarming affectation. The eyes flicked quickly from face to face then dropped to examining the carpet at his feet as he spoke. His hands were clasped together before him.

'I'm sorry you have all been inconvenienced this evening. Also perhaps that you have felt it necessary to wait for the reappearance of Mr Blinton before retiring to your rooms.' He glanced up at the two Blintons as they passed him. 'As you see, Mr Blinton is quite free, although he acknowledges the crime was committed with his knife.'

'There's evidence that Mr Frenk died from the stabbing?' It was Treasure who had interposed the question.

'A verbal report to that effect, yes, Mr Treasure.' Grinyev directed one of his nervous, quick smiles at the banker. 'The preliminary post-mortem showed the blade pierced his aorta. A very accurate incision. It induced massive internal bleeding. Also, of course, some external bleeding when the blade was withdrawn. He quickly died from the wound.'

'Not from breaking his neck in the fall?'

'It's what I've been led to believe.'

Treasure nodded at the answer, while noting that Russian policemen were as careful as British ones to qualify the reliability of hearsay information—and with the same wording. 'And can you tell us whether there were fingerprints on the knife, Colonel?'

There was a longish pause before the Russian replied. 'We have not yet found any fingerprints on the knife. But our examinations are continuing.'

The last bit of dissembling earned a disconsolate murmur from the group generally, but Treasure seemed satisfied.

'There'll be a further post-mortem? In addition to this preliminary one?' This was Wander.

'Perhaps.' The tone was measurably shorter than the one used to address Treasure. 'It's also probable the British authorities will wish to carry out their own medical examination of the body.'

'Here or in London, Colonel?' asked Treasure.

'Perhaps both.' The speaker shrugged as Sol Blinton took the seat his wife had occupied earlier while she balanced herself on an arm, and not without difficulty. For some moments the Russian seemed to be wholly absorbed in watching Gloria Blinton cross and re-cross her legs, pulling the tight skirt high above her knees. 'I understand there is a British doctor at the Embassy in Moscow,' he continued with his eyes still on Gloria's legs. 'He could be sent here. It would be up to your Ambassador to decide.'

There were some muttered comments in the brief lull that followed. This was the first time active involvement with the British authorities had been volunteered by the Russian.

'You will no longer prevent us from getting in touch with our Ambassador?' This was Mrs Vauxley in a stern, reverberating voice.

Grinyev hesitated, then bowed in the speaker's direction. 'You phrase the question in that manner perhaps so that I have to say I have prevented such contact already. This is not the case. You are free to telephone your Embassy. Or anyone else you wish. Here or in Britain.'

'Except there's nobody working the switchboard here,' put in Wander.

'Nor, it seems, the one at the British Consulate attached to your Embassy in Moscow. My office has already tried to reach someone there.'

Mrs Vauxley swallowed on this disarming piece of intelligence. 'Consulates invariably keep office hours,' she rallied. 'We shall of course wish to go to the top. To the Ambassador.'

'Ah. He is, I understand, in London. For consultations.' Grinyev twitched an apologetic smile as though the Ambassador's absence was his fault. 'But tomorrow, in the morning, I am sure it will be possible to reach someone of importance at the Consulate. Or the Embassy.' He paused. 'In order not to spoil your visit further, you may wish to nominate one member of the group to handle such communication.' His gaze, and almost everyone else's, was turned on Treasure as he made the suggestion. 'Telephone arrangements will be made by the hotel.'

'And meantime we are free to go as we please? We and our rooms will not be searched again?'

Grinyev looked from Treasure to the speaker, Mrs Vauxley, and then back again before he replied. 'I very much regret it was necessary to conduct body searches. It was in your own interests, you understand? You say you think your rooms have also been searched?'

'This evening. While we were at the opera. Miss Harwick has been upstairs since our return, to fetch something. She's certain someone has rifled through our belongings. Isn't that so, Amelia?'

'I . . . I thought so,' whispered the unfortunate Miss Harwick looking absolutely terrified.

'The maids tidy the rooms when the beds are turned down.' It was Valya Sinitseva who had spoken. She had come up quietly behind Grinyev and practically unnoticed. 'Russian maids are very thorough,' she added, the last word somehow acquiring extra credibility in its deep *thow-ru* enunciation. 'Sometimes it may look like they are too thorough when they leave rooms.'

'Which is perhaps why they leave rumours as well,' the canon confided quietly to Mrs Tate, who grinned and dug him quite hard in the ribs.

The accent apart, the petite and pretty Intourist guide had made her contributions with an assurance that easily matched Mrs Vauxley's.

'Valya, what happens to tomorrow's arrangements?' asked Candy.

'The coach will take us to the State Hermitage at nine forty-five as planned. Please to be in the hall at nine-thirty.' Valya glanced at Colonel Grinyev then continued: 'I'm sorry the tea hasn't come. Now is too late, perhaps. The hotel restaurant staff have to get up very early. If you like to go to bed the concierge on your floor will provide hot water for tea from her samovar. Good night.'

Both Mrs Vauxley and Sir Jeremy Wander made as though to speak, then decided not to. Everyone got up and started towards the stairs and lifts.

Grinyev bowed to Molly as she passed then touched Treasure's arm. 'If you and I could have a last word? If it wouldn't be troubling you too much?'

# CHAPTER 10

'You've concluded Blinton is unconvincing as a murderer?'

'Much less convincing than Mrs Vauxley.' Grinyev gave Treasure one of his shy smiles. 'Your good health.' He lifted his glass in salute. The banker did the same.

The two were alone in the small and poorly furnished hotel manager's office, both seated in front of the desk. There were several beer cans on the desk, brought in earlier by one of Grinyev's assistants.

'You're right. This is better for us than spirits,' said the colonel as though the judgment was a serious one to which he had given a good deal of consideration.

Treasure nodded. 'Speaking of Mrs Vauxley, she was demanding to see the manager when we got back this evening. He wasn't here. I suppose there's no night manager?' The banker frowned at the dirty curtains and the worn carpet below them. 'He has a very . . . a . . . insignificant office.'

'He's probably a very insignificant person.'

'You don't know him?'

'There will be several managers, Mr Treasure. What you might call a committee of managers. Our grand hotels are not run the way yours are. A manager is not someone who walks through the public areas smiling at the clients and receiving their congratulations. There will be no congratulations, and where there are no congratulations in Russia it's difficult to find a manager. It's hoped such things will change soon, but it takes time.' Grinyev swallowed a large draught of beer by way of punctuation.

'And Blinton proved his innocence when you questioned him in here?'

'Quite the opposite. Blinton is foolish, stubborn and . . . guilty as hell.' The KGB man sniffed. 'But not of murder, I think. He won't explain where he was this evening. I believe he was with dissidents on the Petrograd side. He admits he was up there. Looking for his grandfather's birthplace. In the dark. In the snow.' He sniffed again, demonstrating how sorely his credulity had been taxed.

'Dissidents?'

'He's Jewish. He's probably been mixing with the awkward Jewish element. People who want to leave the country for Israel.'

'Why don't you let them?'

The Russian shrugged. 'I've no idea. We do let a good many, and good riddance. They're much more trouble than they're worth. Blinton probably took them money. People do. To bribe officials who are much worse than the Jews. Does that surprise you?'

'Only mystifies. We don't stop people leaving Britain.'

'Meaning what I said about the officials didn't surprise you. Or shock you.'

'I was surprised you said it.'

'Naturally I should deny I did. Anyway, it's a different matter from the murder. Tomorrow I may know what time Blinton took his coat from the cloakroom at the opera. According to him it must have been before the stabbing. Also the doorman may remember seeing him leave the building. Meantime I'm exercising our well known tolerance and letting him go.'

'Go where? He has no passport.'

'That's right. There are limits to tolerance, even in the USSR. It was his knife that killed Frenk. In England he might still be in custody.'

'I doubt it. Is it routine to search rooms?'

The Russian paused before answering. 'The maids tidied the rooms more carefully tonight because we're looking for something.' He scowled. '*I'm* looking for something.'

'Must have been an extra shift of special maids. The beds weren't turned down at all last night.'

'I'm surprised. This is a five star hotel.' Grinyev gave his gentle smile.

'Can you say what you've lost?'

'For your ears only, Mr Treasure, we've lost a painting. From one of the museums. It's why I was here at the hotel earlier this evening. Why I have both cases to deal with now. And why I have an army of assistants helping me.'

'A painting has been stolen, presumably a valuable one, and you think it was taken by a tourist?'

'Not by one. *For* one, probably.'

'It was stolen recently?'

Grinyev blinked slowly. 'Very recently.'

'And naturally an expensive stolen painting must be destined for export. I can see that. And you thought the theft pointed to our group?'

'Art pointed to your group, Mr Treasure, more directly than to most other foreign parties. Certainly more than any others here at the moment. So, on a hunch, I decided the theft might involve you. Not you personally, of course. Not necessarily. Then came the murder. The victim and the owner of the weapon are both members of your Baroque Circle. One is Jewish, the other may have been of Jewish origin.'

'So you figure a bunch of Zionist art thieves have infiltrated my wife's Baroque Circle, fallen out over the spoils and started doing each other in? Too convenient and decidedly far fetched I'd have thought. And anyway, I don't believe Frenk was Jewish.'

Grinyev looked momentarily sad, then his face brightened as he said: 'There was the other consideration that a great deal of money would be involved. For the painting. You could call it venture capital.'

Treasure gave a spontaneous chuckle. 'You mean the kind of capital that comes from merchant banks? Sorry to foul up your theory again, but hot pictures really don't feature in the Grenwood, Phipps current portfolio.' He opened another can of lager. 'The maids didn't find the painting tonight?'

'Not the painting.'

When it was clear the colonel, now studying his shoes, didn't intend expanding on what else the maids might have unearthed, Treasure broke the silence. 'So what's your priority?'

The other looked up sharply. 'I want the painting back.'

'That's more important than catching Frenk's murderer?'

'Of course. But the two are tied up. I'm quite sure of that.'

'There'll be international repercussions over the murder. Could be a good deal more embarrassing than losing a picture.'

'Frenk was killed with Blinton's knife. A personal feud between two British tourists. If there's no other solution we can name Blinton as the murderer. Expel him to London under guard. Then it's a British problem.' The speaker's tone was impassive.

'And you'll never admit you told me that either?'

'That's right.'

'What if Frenk was killed by a Russian?'

'Naturally I am working on that possibility too.'

'That balcony was teeming with young Russians. Mostly young men, but some girls too. I saw them myself. Have you questioned any of them?'

'Of course. All of them. And we shall do so again tomorrow. They are . . . in safe keeping.'

'I see. But nobody actually saw the crime being committed?'

'No. You said you saw the crush of people. It was also very dark at the back. The criminal saw the same and acted. With everybody looking outward. The other way. It seems he came in fast from behind and withdrew just as quickly, melting into the crowd.'

'It was an expert stab?'

Grinyev frowned. 'Or lucky.'

'And opportunist? I mean, how did he know Frenk would be where he was?'

'Unless he took him there, Mr Treasure. Persuaded him to take a look at the promenaders.'

'Which means they knew each other?'

'Most probably.'

'We should assume the murderer is a man?'

'Not at all. You think it was a woman?'

'I've no idea. But I accept it could have been.' Treasure studied the liquid in his glass. 'And the picture comes first? Getting it back, that would be quite a feather in your cap?'

Grinyev's response was firm. 'My motives are loftier than that. Surely you agree it's a terrible crime against our people and our visitors? To steal a great painting from one of the collections here? So nobody sees it again except some crooked capitalist hoarder? Understand me, how can it be shown again? Our public galleries here are exactly that, Mr Treasure. Public.'

'So are ours.'

'Of course. When I was in London I was often at the National Gallery and the others. My favourite was the National Portrait, I think.'

'You were in London? For how long?'

'First for two years, then for nearly five. I was a Commercial Attaché at the Embassy.'

'Well I never. Shall you ever come back?'

'I doubt it. *Persona non grata*. I was expelled for alleged spying. With more than a hundred others.'

'Were you a spy?'

'Certainly not. I kept my eyes open.' Grinyev made a

diffident gesture. 'No hard feelings. I'd like very much to go back. But that's not important. You disapprove of public paintings being stolen?'

Treasure hesitated. 'Are you going to tell me the name of this painting?'

'No. I'm sorry. I can tell you only that it's old and very small. Eighteen centimetres square. On canvas.'

'Did it come from one of the great private collections which you er . . . nationalised after the Revolution? The Morozov or the Shchukin collections for instance?'

'It was bought by one of the Tsars as a present for his wife. After her death it was placed in the national collection, long before the Revolution.' Grinyev was looking sternly querulous. 'You'd have reservations about the people's entitlement to any picture legally appropriated by the State in nineteen seventeen?'

'No. But I'd forgive an exiled Morozov or Shchukin for having some. Or, in certain circumstances, for trying to get a few back.'

The colonel pondered the point briefly before nodding. 'Well that doesn't arise, Mr Treasure. Your quaint capitalist moralities are not being challenged. May I take it, then, that you disapprove of the theft of this particular painting?'

'Certainly. And I'll do whatever I can to help get it back. Though frankly I don't see . . .'

'Even if it's already out of the country?' the other man interrupted.

'Mm . . . yes, I think so. And I'm taking it you'll do your level best to expose whoever killed Frenk?'

'Of course. So it's a deal, Mr Treasure?'

Treasure formally shook the other's outstretched hand. 'I assume I'm not supposed to tell anyone a picture's missing?'

'That is so. For the moment.'

'Difficult not to confide in my wife. Could be counter-productive as well. She's very discreet and I'd swear her to secrecy.'

Grinyev considered again. 'Very well. We confide in your wife on that basis.' He stood up. 'This office and the telephone here will be available for your use from nine in the morning. That's seven o'clock London time.'

'I could use the 'phone in our room.'

'This one will be better.' The short nervous smile was clearly intended to excuse further explanation of the point. 'The telephonist will get any number you want. Remember it's Saturday. Easter Saturday. Nobody in England will be working. Don't expect much from the British Embassy in Moscow except shock about the murder and feeble excuses for not doing anything. Here's the number. Half the staff there will have flown home on leave. Like the Ambassador. The rest will be working a holiday roster. Won't be anyone there of much importance, and no one to spare to come to Leningrad.'

'Not even over the murder of a British subject?'

'Unlikely. They'd send someone over the *arrest* of a British subject. It's why I haven't arrested Blinton.'

Treasure chuckled. 'You don't have a high opinion of diplomats.'

'They get in the way of investigations.'

'What d'you expect me to find out that's going to help over the picture?'

'You have employees in London who will go to work fast on Frenk. His background. His friends. His contacts. Why he came on this trip. They'll do this for you, even on a holiday. It'll be quicker than official channels. Speed is important.'

'The British police . . .'

'Are very professional, but they'll wash their hands of this. What else should they do? It's not their business. We are not in Interpol even.' Grinyev had been pacing the carpet between the desk and the door. Now he stopped, arms folded, head down. 'Frenk will be the key. I'm positive.'

'And assuming my army of conscientious employees in London unearth anything useful about Frenk, who lived

in Coventry incidentally.' Treasure made a pained face.
'Assuming they do . . .'

'I have a list of questions here, Mr Treasure.' Grinyev
went to the desk and picked up a sheet of paper. He
handed it to the banker.

'Hm.' Treasure scanned the list. 'Seems straightfor-
ward provided we can find people who knew him well
enough. These other trips in the Eastern Bloc you ask
about. Do we know he ever made any?'

'There's nothing in his passport to say so. But he may
have had some contact in East Germany.' Grinyev took
a deep breath, then exhaled it noisily. 'Mr Frenk was a
curious man. He was a cellist in a chamber orchestra, but
his physique suggests he might have been a professional
athlete. This is what the pathologist said.'

'Playing the cello is hard work. Maybe he had a fitness
bug too.'

'It's possible. His clothes also are strange. Everything
he was wearing tonight was new. But the clothes in his
room, the ones people say he wore yesterday, for the
journey, they were well cared for and good quality, but
old. Some were threadbare, like the overcoat from
Harrods. Also a jacket from Gieves, and a pair of
Church's shoes. Those are all expensive I think?'

Treasure nodded and said: 'So, although he probably
didn't have a large income, he went in for good clothes.
Things that endure. Very wise. I try to do the same. Good
British tailoring takes some beating. Lasts for ever.' He
was self-consciously aware that the well cut, dark-blue
suit he had on looked anything but worn—and definitely
beyond the means of a provincial cellist. It seemed from
the direction of his gaze that Grinyev was coming to the
same conclusion. 'So what about the new stuff Frenk was
wearing today?'

'They were all one brand. St Michael. That's the trade
mark of . . .'

'Marks & Spencer the chain store. Also shows sense.
Mass produced but good value. My wife . . .'

'Even though it doesn't match the other philosophy you expounded, Mr Treasure? That best quality lasts longest?'

'Suppose not. Not quite. Maybe his circumstances had changed.' He shrugged. 'You say all the things he wore to travel in were good quality British?'

'No. The trousers were bought in the USA, also the shirt. Both from Saks Fifth Avenue, but a long time ago. The tie was from Paris, silk, very wide, very old fashioned.'

'What about his underwear? I'd guess Marks & Spencer on both days.'

'Today yes. And new. What he had discarded in the room were undershorts from Simpson of Piccadilly. Again quite worn.'

Treasure's eyebrows lifted. 'Those could belong to Nigel Dirving, of course. They were sharing a room.'

'Dirving confirms the undershorts were Frenk's. Also an undervest, soiled but fairly new.'

'New you say?'

'Unlike everything else he wore yesterday. It's special also because it came from a store in Leipzig, East Germany.'

# CHAPTER 11

'I thought you must have gone on the town with Colonel Grinyev.' Molly Treasure looked up from her book as her husband came into their room.

'And I thought you'd be asleep by now.' It was nearly one-thirty.

'Missing the latest news from the Politbureau? Not on your life.' She laid the book open on the bedclothes and took off her glasses. 'So tell me all. D'you think the room's bugged?'

'Very probably. Also the manager's office. But I doubt the recordings go any further than the colonel. I'd guess he keeps them for his own protection.' He took off his jacket.

'So shall we go in the bathroom? Run the water?'

'Not unless you want to bath.'

She snorted. 'I meant so we won't be heard.'

'Ah, depends what you have in mind. The obscenity laws here are pretty stringent.' He sat on the bed and kissed her.

'Very droll, and you smell of beer.'

'Russian lager. Quite palatable and very light. Blinton's still under suspicion of murdering Frenk. He could be tried and sentenced here, or just bundled home, depending on what suits the authorities.'

'A scapegoat in case they find a Russian did it?'

'Full marks for a broadly correct conclusion.'

'I'm not just a pretty face.'

'Because you have a lovely young body as well.'

'I didn't mean that.' Absently her hand went to cover the V of her neckline.

'Did the room look as if it'd been searched?' He glanced about as he spoke, then started to remove his shoes.

'I thought so. But probably because Daphne Vauxley insisted hers had been.'

'Well she was right. They're looking for a small painting someone pinched the night before we arrived. Probably from the Hermitage.'

'Which picture?'

'I don't know, but very valuable. Could be a Leonardo or a Raphael, I suppose. Or perhaps a Giorgione. Anyway, you're not to tell anyone about the theft. It's top secret. I'm allowed to tell you because I've said you're utterly discreet.'

'There must be another reason,' she offered flatly.

'There is. Grinyev is quite convinced Frenk and the theft are related, which could mean he knows something we don't. The picture wasn't in Frenk's room, and it wasn't on him when he died.'

'It's that small?'

'Mmm, just over five inches square. No frame or stretcher.'

'Does Grinyev think Frenk had it, and gave it to someone else in the group?'

'That he may have done. I said you know the other Circle members better than I do.'

'And are you both expecting me to shop the one who's got the picture?'

Treasure got up and went to the chest of drawers. He began turning out his pockets. 'I suppose that's a possibility.'

'Not remotely,' Molly replied with firmness, smoothing her neck. 'They're all friends of mine.'

'Frenk wasn't. Nor are the Blintons.' He went on undressing. 'Actually, Grinyev's much more concerned to get back the picture than he is about nailing whoever took it.'

'Anyway, you said it went before we got here.'

'But one of the group could still be taking it to London.'

'By prior arrangement? Imagine the Baroque Circle being a front for international picture thieves!' She frowned. 'Didn't the Communists appropriate most of the pictures in the first place? After the Revolution?'

'They er . . . nationalised a lot, yes. Mostly modern stuff. Former property of rich industrialists. People who abandoned all and fled the country in nineteen-seventeen. This picture was come by honestly though, as you might say. Otherwise it could have fitted a sort of re-requisition attempt by anyone convinced he had a putative claim. I told Grinyev that. And that I wouldn't have found such an action wholly indefensible.'

Molly's mouth opened in surprise. 'You didn't? I'd have thought that would have written you off entirely as a fellow traveller.'

'Not at all. He understood my reasoning.'

'But didn't agree with it?'

'Didn't need to.' Treasure went into the bathroom.

'So you and I are obviously in the clear. Teacher's pets,' said Molly two minutes later when her husband reappeared. 'I mean we weren't even fingerprinted. Or searched. Wasn't Daphne livid about being done over like that?'

'Don't blame her either. I gather the search was a fairly perfunctory affair though. And it didn't seem to bother the others. Nobody cares to be fingerprinted, of course, because of the sinister and enduring overtones.'

'Well honestly, I can't believe anyone in our party's a crook.' She shook her head. 'And that definitely includes sweet Mr Blinton.'

'Who Grinyev says is involved helping the refuseniks.'

'That'd be quite different. And I can't believe anyone with his kind of heart condition is involved in anything strenuously illegal. Anyway, Colonel Grinyev's pretty ingenuous if he thinks we're going to inform on fellow countrymen.'

Treasure made a querulous face as he hung up his suit in the wardrobe. 'He's a very laid-back member of the KGB. And a pretty irreverent one. I don't think he was being indiscreet just to impress me.'

'To win your confidence?'

He sniffed. 'It's possible.'

'He's an Anglophile. Marvellous English. He must have lived in England or America?'

'Both, but mostly London. For years. Some kind of diplomat. Kicked out for spying. Seems to me that most of them are, after a bit. Anyway, he'd like to go back to England.'

'What, defect?'

'Shouldn't think so. I'd say he's committed to the new order. Harder work. Competition. Greater efficiency. The stamping out of corruption. That sort of thing. All based on a higher standard of public morality than they've had here for decades. The kind Grinyev believes still applies in Britain.'

'You didn't disillusion him?'

'Why should I? Our moral standards are a lot higher than theirs.' He paused, brow still knitted. 'Broadly, anyway. It's why I said I'd turn in anyone I knew was downright guilty of stealing that picture. Or of committing a murder.' He got into bed beside her.

'So he conned you into that, darling. Played on your sense of national pride. Your feet are freezing. And this bed's much too small. Cosy though.' She rearranged the pillows and the duvet. 'Well I'd turn in a murderer perhaps, but not an art thief. Not in Russia. Not till we got home.'

'And I'd like to see them get the picture back, and certainly if that nailed the murderer as well. Anyway, being what you call a fellow traveller has bought me

special privileges in the morning.' He told her about the
nine o'clock arrangements.

'So who will you 'phone first? The Embassy?'

'Yes. To get the official part under way.'

'Then the estimable Miss Gaunt?'

'I thought so.' Miss Gaunt was Treasure's secretary.
'But there's a limit to what she can do for us in Coventry
since she lives in Islington. Anyway, she's a devout Holy
Roman and I'm not intending to interfere with her Easter
arrangements. Not more than absolutely necessary. No,
I've decided to throw our problem at Peregrine Gore.'

'Good for Peregrine.' They were speaking of a
Grenwood, Phipps's executive who Molly knew well. 'I
used to think he wasn't terribly switched on. Before he
got engaged to Vanessa Arkworthy that is.' Molly delivered the point as though it completely made up for Gore's
former lack-lustre reputation. 'Vanessa's making a new
man of him. Her mother thinks so too. Don't know about
her father.'

'Peregrine's come on a lot. And he aims to please. And
I happen to know he's spending the weekend in Chipping
Campden, with the Arkworthys. Wish we were too,'
Treasure ended with feeling. Harold Arkworthy, born a
Yorkshireman, was a prosperous Midlands manufacturer
and a client of the bank's. The Arkworthys were close
friends of the Treasures who stayed with them often in
their Cotswold manor house.

'Oh darling, I'm sorry. This is all my fault.' Molly
moved closer. 'Is Chipping Campden near Coventry, I
forget?'

'Less than thirty miles, I'd say. He can be there in half-
an-hour in the morning probably. Peregrine will help in
a good cause. Even on a holiday weekend,' Treasure
asserted with justification. Gore had got his job in the first
place because he was a nephew of Lord Grenwood, the
bank's Chairman. He had kept it largely because of recent
commendations from other superiors, including Treasure.

'Vanessa shouldn't mind either. We introduced them after all, remember?'

'I'd say it depends what their plans are.' Molly sounded less confident. 'What about the police? Can't they get what you want?'

'Possibly, but I'd rather use one of our own people. Grinyev expects it. Also he could be right about official channels being too slow.'

'But what is it you want Peregrine to do?'

He paused before replying. 'Difficult to explain. I want him to follow up on some questions. To get us a better picture of Frenk. Better than we've got so far. That fellow was an enigma, and he's become more so.' He told her about the pathologist's comments and Frenk's clothes. 'Anyway, we can leave it to the Embassy or the Foreign Office to brief the police. And I'll have Miss Gaunt ring the travel agents as soon as they're open.'

'Well I think it's very noble of you to take charge, darling,' Molly said. 'Candy was dreading having to explain everything to Mr Frenk's relatives.'

'If he has any. I doubt the travel agents will know. That's a job for the police in any case.' He looked about the room. 'Why's the 'fridge so quiet?'—earlier it had been juddering ceaselessly.

'I think I must have disconnected it when I switched over from the television to the bed lights. Didn't mean to. The TV wasn't compulsive viewing. Let's leave the 'fridge till the morning. It kept me awake last night.' She yawned.

But Treasure wasn't quite ready for sleep. 'Did you know before we came that Edwina Apse and Rudy Frenk came from the same area?'

'Around Coventry? I knew, but it hadn't registered. Not as significant. They'd never met. Oh come, you don't think . . . ?'

'That they'd known each other all the time? That they were the front, as you put it?'

'Coventry's a big place.'

'Sure, but the academic and arts community can't be that huge. She's a lecturer in modern history, doing a book on baroque influences. That must include music as well as art. She's very keen about the music part of this trip. Told me so. He was a professional, classical instrumentalist. Doesn't that mean they almost had to have been at the same concerts? To have mixed in the same cultural groups?' He pouted, then shook his head. 'Perhaps not.'

'Edwina said not,' but now there was a tinge of doubt in the tone. 'They were together a lot on the first night. And they were sitting next to each other at the opera, of course.'

'That needn't have been by design. Just the way the tickets were dished out. Or maybe they simply took to each other. If they'd been plotting anything sinister they're more likely to have gone out of their way not to be seen together. Come to think of it, it's surprising Frenk wasn't seen more with Nigel. They shared a room after all. Wasn't that by arrangement?'

'By agreement. At the time of booking. Sharing a double room was much cheaper than paying extra for a single.' She turned her head on the pillow to study his face. 'I hate to say it, but I don't believe Nigel has the acuity for sophisticated thieving.'

'I'm inclined to agree, but this bit of thieving may not be that sophisticated. Not if it's gone wrong in some way that's led to murder.' He paused, staring at the ceiling. 'Canon Emdon sat with Frenk on the coach going to the opera. Edwina was with Nigel then.'

'And the canon was with Frenk before dinner. Remember we saw them when we came down?'

'And we saw him at the start of the interval. I suppose he was in the men's room the whole time, as he said? He got there early enough. Of course, it's the only place you're allowed to smoke, apart from the ticket office foyer. Does he smoke?'

'No.'

'Hm. Funny chap. He can be very uncelestial at times.'

'You don't think he was doing anything uncelestial in the men's room?' She didn't wait for an answer before going on: 'As a matter of fact, now that I'm seeing him at close quarters, I don't find him celestial at all. Pictures are obviously his ruling interest. It's almost an obsession.'

'And he spends a good deal of his time at auctions in London?'

'Yes. But he's got to be a non-starter as a murderer and a thief. Or a murderer at least,' she insisted sleepily. 'Of course, he's American. I suppose one would sell an important stolen picture in America?'

'Not nowadays. Not necessarily. They can afford to come by them honestly. They say Greece and Egypt are the big centres.'

'Oh dear.' Molly came momentarily wide awake. 'Clarence Emdon was in Cairo last month.'

'He told you that?'

'Not directly. Reggie Tate ran into him there.'

'So Reggie was there too?'

'With good reason. He was there professionally. Darling, could you put the light out? I'm terribly tired.'

He reached over and worked the switch. 'What was Reggie doing in Cairo?'

'They're doing up an old embassy building. He's in charge.' She sighed. ''Night.'

'Good night.' He turned to embrace her.

It was just then that the refrigerator burst into throbbing life, which would certainly have disturbed Molly— even if her husband hadn't.

'Talk about electric responses,' she murmured much later.

Once more Canon Emdon opened the door to his room a fraction and waited. This time there was no sound of voices or movement outside so he edged the door open more, and slowly stuck his head out. The last time he had done this he had only just missed being seen by Mark

Treasure who had been on his way to his own room further along. Now the corridor was empty.

It was not that the canon had failed to provide himself with an excuse for nocturnal sallies. He had complained to the floor concierge after dinner that his lavatory was defective again—and still nothing had been done about it. This gave him the reason for heading in the opposite direction to the concierge's desk, to the communal lavatory at the very end of the corridor. Since the concierge's seat was set well back into her alcove he figured she wouldn't see him in any case—which suited his purpose of not wanting to draw attention to himself unnecessarily.

Silently, and remarkably swiftly, the dressing-gowned cleric reached the appointed door and very gently turned the handle. Once inside he noiselessly shot the bolt, then again with the kind of agility no one else in the Baroque Circle would have judged typical of him, he stepped up onto the down-turned seat, grasping the pipe from the overhead cistern, first for leverage and then to steady his balance. Squinting through his monocle he observed with satisfaction that the cotton strand was still in place. He had gummed its ends on either side of the cistern's two parts, near the back. Next, very gingerly, he lifted the cistern cover.

The flat package was where he had left it, securely taped to the cover. Its contents being irreplaceable it might have seemed profligate in the extreme to be risking them in this way. But Canon Emdon was used to taking calculated risks. His room had definitely been searched this evening whereas this cubicle had evidently not been disturbed for weeks by even cleaning staff, let alone the police. There was no toilet paper, and the pan was in a disgusting condition. People would only use the place as a last resort: every room on the floor had its own 'private facilities'.

Without hesitation he replaced the cistern cover and refixed the cotton with rubber gum from the tube in his pocket. Earlier he had considered shifting hiding places but later dismissed the idea.

He returned to his room as quietly as he had left it, turning the heavy key in the lock with care. He leaned against the door when he was inside, breathing deeply but well pleased with himself.

As it happened the floor concierge had watched Canon Emdon's expedition through the nearly undetectable mirror angled against the ceiling opposite her booth. At first she had been only mildly intrigued by the apparent stealth of his movements, and not at all once she had determined where he was going. The mirror gave her a view of the whole corridor. She made a note of the time. He was one of the guests whose movements she had orders to log. She remembered twice reporting the defective lavatory in his room. She had been reporting that lavatory on and off for weeks.

# CHAPTER 12

The black Volga saloon had covered the short journey from the hotel at speed. The driver was a sallow-faced youth with bad breath, wearing a black peaked cap, and a Party badge in his lapel. He had ignored the two traffic lights set against him, hurtled down Dzerzhinskovo Street with headlights blazing before screeching to a halt outside number six, a late eighteenth-century, classical building close to the corner with Admiralty Place.

To locals this is perhaps the best known anonymous house in Leningrad—the place where, in December 1917, Feliks Dzerzhinsky set up the very first office of the Soviet secret police.

None of the three people squashed in the back of the car was impressed with the driver's dangerous display of arrogance. Even so, two of them, men in dark coats and snap-brimmed trilbies, knew that the extent by which government drivers overlorded other road users was in direct ratio to the importance of the people they were carrying. Of course the woman they were escorting knew this too, and while it was something that increased their self-esteem, it added considerably to her disquiet.

As the car stopped the man sitting nearest the kerb was already half way out. He marched across the pavement and pressed the bell. The door was opened almost immediately, but not before the woman had been unceremoniously pushed from the vehicle by the other man and was standing ready to be admitted. She was hurried through the opening into the dark panelled hall.

The man at the desk made a downward sign with his thumb and muttered a number. One of the escorting KGB men who had kept a rough hold on the woman's arm now thrust her towards a basement staircase, while the other busied himself signing a form at the desk. Neither of the men had uttered a word during the journey.

She gave a little cry as her foot slipped on the metal edging on one of the steps. The man prevented her from falling with a grip that hurt her shoulder, and a muttered oath about her carelessness: the orders were to deliver her scared but undamaged.

The bleak room she was put in was large, stone floored, and low ceilinged, with two cast-iron radiators but very little furniture. There was a small wooden table holding a lamp and a telephone, with an upholstered desk chair behind. Arranged ten feet in front of the table was a stark deal chair on which her escort had motioned the woman to sit before he left.

There were two ceiling lights but they were not switched on—only the desk lamp was lit. This was why Colonel Grinyev surprised her when he stepped out of the shadows at the back of the room: she had thought she was alone when the door had slammed.

'They got you here safely, Comrade Sinitseva?' Now he walked quickly to the desk. 'No, don't get up. Would you like to take off your coat? Your nice leather coat?'

'No thank you, I'm cold.' The last words were hardly audible. She swallowed, trying to dispel the fear. He had been considerate earlier.

'I'm sorry?'

'I said I'm cold, Comrade Colonel,' she repeated but still with a falter in her voice.

'I see. I find it quite warm in here. You're not frightened, are you? Nothing to be frightened about.' The look seemed genuinely solicitous. 'We're only here because they were getting very testy at the Astoria. Did you notice? Keeping people up with our being there, and so on. No, I thought it better to continue our little chat in private. And this place being so near. It's not where I have my office. But they never close here.' He sat in the chair and leaned forward with his forearms on the table, his gaze fixed on his clenched hands.

'It's . . . it's very late, Comrade Colonel. If we could continue tomorrow, I . . .'

'Because you have a long drive home across the city. In your nice little Zhiguli. To your nice little three-roomed apartment on Marshala Zhukova Prospect.'

'It's my husband's car, Comrade. I borrow it only if I'm going to be late.' She drew in her breath, then added: 'Our apartment has two rooms.'

'Ah, that's right, of course. No children. So no problems about baby sitters. But you wouldn't have had tonight in any case because your husband isn't with you. He's at home I expect?' He looked up briefly.

She nodded. 'It's a busy time for him. At the Institute . . .'

'Where he lectures. And he doesn't care for opera, perhaps? Strange. Most Lithuanians like opera. Very cultured people.'

'He's only half Lithuanian. Only his mother . . .' She faltered, confused, then blurted on nervously: 'He likes opera, but not as much as me. And . . . and there was only one spare ticket tonight.'

'So he made the sacrifice. And lent you his car so you wouldn't be bothered by the drunks on the Metro.' Grinyev gave a sharp cough. 'Excuse me, Comrade Sinitseva. Or, I tell you what, why don't I call you Valya? Hm? Is that what your husband calls you?' He looked up again, taking in her nod of assent.

She could almost feel as well as watch his gaze. Instead of returning to a study of his hands it ran down her figure, lingering on her legs.

'When you go abroad you can go together of course,'

he continued. 'You've both been abroad a lot. To Warsaw, Leipzig, Belgrade, London, Paris?'

'Not together to London or Paris. To the other places, yes. I've been to London. For two weeks. For Intourist. My husband was in Paris and New York for conferences. At the universities. The Sorbonne and Columbia. He's a linguist. An assistant professor.' She knew she was rushing her words—saying too much. She recrossed her legs, pulling the bottom of her coat across her knees and wishing she was wearing a longer, looser skirt—and boots, not the court shoes she had on: she'd left her boots in the car.

Grinyev watched the movements. 'And you haven't yet been able to go with him. Not to the West. Not together. Couldn't get away at the same time. Is that it?'

Since he knew so much about her of course she knew he had the answer to the question already. 'We don't have double clearance . . . Not yet,' she finished feebly.

He looked puzzled, then his expression relaxed into an understanding smile. 'So you've applied . . . ?'

'Often, Comrade Colonel,' she'd interrupted on impulse, and meaning to say they'd been told that the next time . . . But he must know it. So all she'd done was stupidly underline how many times they'd been turned down already.

'Often? The Foreign Ministry being over-cautious, would you say? I mean because of the Lithuanian connection? Sorry, half-connection. The Ministry can be very stupid. Because someone's half Lithuanian doesn't prove he's plotting revolution. Or illegal secession from the USSR. Not unless there's some kind of proof.' He shrugged. 'After all there are two-and-a-half million Lithuanians. They're not all potential traitors.'

'My husband is a Party member.'

'There you are. Exactly. Total proof of his loyalty. His suitability to hold a teaching post. How would he have got the job otherwise? So how could anyone think he belongs to a subversive organisation?'

'I'm sure our double visa hasn't been held up because anyone thought he was unreliable, Comrade Colonel.' For the first time there was a note of confidence coming back to her voice.

'Isn't that what I'm saying to you, Valya? He's been abroad often, after all. Without you, of course.' He gave a dismissive grunt. 'It wasn't as if it was he who threw the acid at the Rembrandt. In the State Hermitage. The man who said he belonged to the Lithuanian Liberation Movement. You remember that?'

'Yes, Comrade Colonel. The painting was Rembrandt's *Danae*. A masterpiece. The action was an outrage. My husband and I were shocked. The man must have been mad.'

'Ah, I'd forgotten you'd know all about such things. I know the work slightly myself. Nude princess reclining on a couch and gesturing invitingly to Zeus who's disguised as a shower of gold. Not very convincingly disguised, but those mythological subjects are often a bit bizarre.' Grinyev was studying the woman before him as he continued: 'Yes, Princess Danae. Small, rounded, voluptuous figure. Beautiful.' He paused. 'It was a foolish thing to harm her. Pointless too. More sensible to have stolen her. Sold her for millions of dollars to help the Lithuanian Liberation Movement. Don't you think so, Valya?'

'Only for such evil people, Comrade Colonel. Except it would be difficult to steal such a big painting, perhaps.'

'But not a smaller one, you think?' he came back swiftly. 'The principle is the same, though. Open vandalism leads to martyrdom and imprisonment. Steal a picture on the quiet and you can make a fortune. A much more mature way to help a cause. In this case an evil cause, as you imply. But perhaps the revolting Lithuanians are growing up. Have you heard of any pictures being stolen recently?'

'No, Comrade.'

'Just so. And you and your husband have applied to

join a cruise ship this summer? To go round the Baltic and also to Britain and Holland?'

She knew that question would come. 'For a working vacation. We hope to be accepted on board as lecturers.'

'But no permission yet. I wonder what's holding it up? Perhaps one of you'll be allowed to go? A bigger sacrifice for the other than the one your husband made tonight. Or you could go one at a time? Not a bit the same, of course. Not the same opportunity . . . to get away . . . together.' He was watching her very intently as suddenly he demanded: 'Valya, where is your husband tonight?'

She started. 'He's at home, at least . . .'

'He's not at home, Valya. So where is he?'

'I don't know. Perhaps he's gone to see his mother. She lives close.' Her fingernails dug into her palms as she steeled herself to stay calm.

'He's visiting his mother at one-thirty in the morning? And where were you at four-thirty this afternoon?'

'At four-thirty?'

'Precisely. Quickly, where were you?'

'I was . . .' She drew in her breath in a sort of backward sob. 'I was at the Astoria. At the Intourist desk. Arranging the opera tickets for the group.'

'You're lying to me, Valya. Why? At four-thirty you were on the third floor of the hotel. Who were you with?'

'I'd forgotten. After I'd arranged the tickets I went up to deliver . . .'

'WHO WERE YOU WITH?' He roared the words, slamming the table with his fist.

'The people called Tate. A mother and son.'

'Who have separate rooms. You were in his room not hers. What were you doing there?'

'I've told you, Comrade Colonel, I went to give them their opera tickets. They'd come back from the Hermitage ahead of the others.' She was leaning forward in the chair, conscious she was gabbling her words again. 'Mrs Tate was tired. They'd seen me in the lobby and asked about the tickets. I promised to take them up. I wasn't sure who was in which room. I'd meant to go to hers.'

'You're in the habit of going to the rooms of male tourists?'

'Never, Comrade Colonel.' She felt the blush rising in her face.

'Never? Last November the deputy director of a Washington museum called . . .'

'That was different, Comrade Colonel,' she broke in with the protest. 'That time I was ordered.'

'And two years before that? A British Member of Parliament staying at the Moskva hotel? That was on orders too?'

'Yes. That too. Nothing happened. I mean I was told to be especially nice to them. To make lasting contacts. Cultural contacts. Over drinks. That's all.'

'Drinks in their rooms. How much do you earn, Valya?'

'A hundred and eighty roubles a month, Comrade Colonel.'

'And your husband?' he demanded quickly.

'Two hundred and twenty roubles a month.'

'And you have a car, and a country dacha.'

'It's a very small dacha, Comrade Colonel.' She was desperately searching for a handkerchief in her bag.

'But it has to be paid for. Like the elegant clothes you wear. Does your husband know about your being especially nice to visitors? In their rooms?'

'Yes. He knows. Also that it's harmless. That in such cases it's always my duty.'

'Your trade?' he put in roughly. 'And he doesn't mind because he has his own . . . arrangements? Like tonight. Another woman, perhaps? Or a man? Ah, would that explain why you have no children? That your husband prefers . . . ?' He raised his eyebrows but didn't complete the sentence. 'And you were going back to the Astoria, after the opera tonight? To join Mr Tate in his lonely room?'

'That's not true, Comrade Colonel.'

'I see. After all, you were there in the afternoon.'

'Only for a few minutes. And my husband is normal. He's not unfaithful, and neither am I.' Now the tears she'd been holding back had begun coursing down her cheeks.

'So what did Mr Tate give you when you were with him so briefly? In exchange for these opera tickets, and whatever else you provided? Clothes was it? He's a smart dresser, your Mr Reginald Tate. He'd have plenty of saleable clothes.'

'He gave me nothing. Nothing except six roubles for the tickets.'

'So he gave you money? You didn't tell me. Pounds in exchange for roubles?'

'Nothing, sir. Nothing except six roubles.' She sobbed, shaking her head. 'And I gave him nothing except the tickets.'

'Not even a painting? Just a small painting?'

'What painting? I know nothing about a painting.'

'Which room are the Blintons in?' He stabbed out the words.

'Number . . . I don't know. They're all on that floor.'

'I'm told the Blintons are always leaving their door unlocked. It was open when you passed at four-thirty and again when you left twelve minutes later. When you were just delivering those tickets to Mr Tate. Or did you spend some of the time in the Blintons' room? I understand they weren't back till later. Did you see Mr Blinton's knife on the dressing table? Did you pick it up? Did you take it?'

'I don't know what you're talking about.' She buried her head in her hands and was sobbing uncontrollably.

'Or did your friend Tate take the knife and give it to you at the opera? Where you'd arranged to meet? At the ceremonial staircase? In the interval? And do you have a pair of cotton gloves in your bag right now? ANSWER ME!' he roared.

Slowly she dropped her trembling hands. One of her

long false eyelashes had come away on her palm. She stared at it without it seeming to register. Her cheeks were blotched with mascara and her eyes were red with the weeping. She took a deep breath, still staring downwards, one hand clasping her black evening bag.

'Comrade Colonel, I'm a loyal Party member,' she uttered in a just audible and broken whisper. 'I love my country. My work. My husband. I have done nothing dishonest . . .' She gasped. He had come round the table and was standing over her.

He snatched the bag from her, snapping it open. He thrust his fingers into it, then, impatiently, tipped it over, emptying the contents onto the table. The gloves fell out last.

# CHAPTER 13

At eight-fifty on Saturday morning Peregrine Gore parked his open Scimitar two-seater outside number fourteen, Picton Avenue, a quiet, tree-lined main road tributary on the south west side of Coventry.

The drive from Chipping Campden had taken him thirty-nine minutes. Mark Treasure had called him at the Arkworthys' just after seven-thirty. Peregrine had been doing press-ups when the 'phone rang. The call had changed his plans for the morning. Mr Arkworthy had offered him a round of golf at Stratford-on-Avon, although he hadn't seemed to mind when it was called off. Peregrine wasn't sure Mr Arkworthy entirely enjoyed playing golf with him—not since the last time Peregrine put a ball through the club house window. It was the sort of thing that could have happened to anybody, of course, except that it had happened to Peregrine twice—at his future father-in-law's golf club.

Vanessa Arkworthy, Peregrine's fiancée, had still been sleeping when he left. They'd been to dinner with friends in Oxford the night before and had been late getting back. He might still have woken her and taken her to Coventry if Mr Treasure hadn't suggested there might be an element of danger involved.

Peregrine was as over-protective towards women as he was over-ingenuous about them in almost every other connection. When he had been a serving officer in the Brigade of Guards his gallantry towards women had become legendary. Sadly, that was all Peregrine had been commended for in his entire term as a Guards officer—not that it had been a long term.

Peregrine Gore was a twenty-five-year-old lantern-jawed, flaxen-haired, healthy heavyweight. Reasonably intelligent and by nature agreeable, courageous and alert, he had the physique and disposition for manly activities and the outdoor life—altogether, one would have guessed, promising army officer material. But unhappily he had lacked that indefinable something which leads to the smooth co-ordination of the impulse, consideration and decision-making process. His tendency to take prompt, masterful action proved so often to lead him from dangerous situations into impossible ones that he came to be regarded by his superiors as a liability when placed in charge of men—particularly under battle conditions, or even simulated battle conditions. In such circumstances Peregrine's fearlessness only exacerbated the effects of his wilfulness and was the reason why ultimately his short service commission had ended as one of the shortest on record.

His discharge had been honourable—early termination attributed to the late discovery of colour blindness. This tactfully covered the conviction by his colonel that Peregrine was uncommonly accident prone.

The young man was better protected than most against protracted periods of unemployment thanks to well placed relatives in positions of authority in business, commerce, the Church, and many branches of the armed services. One of these was usually able to open the door to a new career. Although he had failed in the army and industry—there had been a short and predictably disastrous period as a management trainee with an explosives company—merchant banking had then beckoned. Not only were the entry requirements much less onerous than they were for the Guards, but also Peregrine's half-uncle was Chairman of Grenwood, Phipps, as well as its largest shareholder. And through a series of happy judgments and coincidences, banking was so far proving the most promising piece in what could loosely be referred to as the growing mosaic of Peregrine's career pattern.

Above all, and as Treasure had observed the night before, Peregrine aimed to please by working as far beyond the line of duty as it was possible to stretch it. This was why the line was stretching now to the outskirts of Coventry in the middle of a holiday weekend.

The house on the corner of Picton Avenue and Picton Close was one of a semi-detached pair of dwellings put up between the wars. It was white rendered with Tudor-style embellishments, and a pointed front gable above bays with casement windows. There was a low, manicured privet hedge growing beyond an even lower pavement wall, and behind this a patch of lawn skirted on one side by a concrete drive leading to the front door and a wooden garage at the side. Edging the grass in front of the house and along the next-door boundary was a border of evergreen shrubs. On the grass there were two coloured plastic gnomes and a large spotted plastic mushroom. Peregrine had ample time to observe these features while waiting to see if the bell would be answered.

The house was evidently divided into two flats. There was a pair of illuminated bell pushes with name cards at the side: the top card offered FRENK, the lower one LLOYD.

Peregrine had pressed the top bell without expecting any response, but because he thought it the right thing to do. After a minute he registered a slight movement in the net curtains behind the downstairs bay window, and following a further decent interval he pressed the second bell. The front door was opened almost immediately to the accompaniment of shrill canine yapping.

'Yes? Quiet Tai Fung. Good boy.' The slim woman with the affected accent was a tight-skinned, brassy platinum blonde wearing a lot of make-up, a yellow quilted housecoat with big pockets, and fluffy high-heeled open slippers that featured her coloured toenails. Her manner was determined, her voice rasping, her age about forty, and her cough unnerving as she exhaled smoke. She held her cigarette holder high and in the Russian manner—like a teacup, between taloned forefinger and thumb. The fat brown and white Pekinese leaning on her ankles stopped barking as ordered and made nose clearing noises instead.

'Oh, good morning.' The caller raised his cap. 'Sorry to disturb you. I'm here to see Mr Frenk,' he lied affably, under orders. He knew Frenk was dead and trusted this wasn't Mrs Frenk.

'Upstairs flat, dear. But he's away. I heard you ring.' She squinted at him through a fresh wreath of smoke, but it was a carefully appraising and partly tutored gaze that had already taken the new-looking sports car into account. The dog now seemed to be choking on something but the woman took no notice.

'Would you know when he'll be back Miss . . . er . . . ?'

'Mrs Lloyd, dear. I'm a widow. She patted the side of her tightly dressed hair. 'My husband was killed quite recently. He was very young. Now I've only got Tai Fung to protect me, haven't I then, sweetie? Such a little angel.' She bent down and wiggled her head several times at the dog which rolled on its back in response, giving a wet snort. 'I think Mr Frenk'll be back tomorrow or Monday. He didn't say for sure. You a friend of his?'

'Sort of. But I'm here on business. I need to make some arrangements with him. Is he abroad, d'you know?'

'I really couldn't say, dear.'

'He doesn't have any relatives living here?'

'No. Nor any living anywhere else that I know of. I could take a message.'

'You don't know where I could reach him?'

She hesitated. 'I'm not sure, dear. Is it about a booking?'

'That's right. Could be important to him.'

'Band or orchestra?'

'I'm sorry?'

'Dance band or chamber? He does both, you know?' She glanced up, down and across the street. 'Look, it's cold standing out here. Why don't you come in for a minute?'

She closed the front door behind him. The cramped hallway accommodated only the stairs to the upper floor and the open door to Mrs Lloyd's flat through which he followed her into a small lobby. To the right he could see into a bedroom with chintzy curtains and a dressing table with a draped front in the bay window.

'Don't know what the neighbours will say. Me entertaining a handsome young man at this hour of the day,' said Mrs Lloyd coquettishly and noting the direction in which he was looking. She leaned her shoulders back on the door to shut it—twice, because Tai Fung got jammed in it the first time. 'You'll have to forgive the mess.' She touched his arm, directing him into a meticulously tidy living room with every hard surface shining and all the cushions plumped like risen soufflés. There were French windows at the end and an archway to a kitchen area on the left. Over the tiled mantelpiece was a large framed coloured photograph of Mrs Lloyd, when younger, in a low-cut sequined bolero-skirted dress doing the Cha-Cha-Cha, or something of the sort, in the arms of a Brylcreamed Lothario in white tails: Mrs Lloyd had been leaning back into camera. 'Please sit down, Mr . . . ?' she invited, sitting herself with the light behind her.

'Sorry. I should have introduced myself. I'm Peregrine Gore.'

'I see. I'm a pro myself. You've probably guessed.' She crossed her legs. The housecoat parted above the slim knees.

Peregrine coughed nervously. 'How interesting,' he answered uncertainly. He sank into a deeply yielding sofa opposite: it was all gold-threaded silk damask with carefully combed fringes. Gingerly he put his cap and

muffler down beside him, hoping they wouldn't make the
place look too untidy.

'I was Doreen Daynar, the dancer.' The uppermost leg
leaped up violently from the knee as if being tested for
reflexes: its owner paused for a reaction to one or both
disclosures.

'Of course,' Peregrine provided, making relief sound
like recognition.

'So I know what it is to miss a booking, dear. Expect
you 'phoned and didn't get an answer. Mr Frenk's got an
agent, of course. Very unreliable, though. Aren't they all?
Especially at weekends. Birmingham are you?'

'And London.' The Peke had started licking the
visitor's skin between the top of his sock and his trouser
leg. Peregrine put his hand down to stop it and had a
finger nipped before the animal retreated backwards
yapping loudly.

'That's just his little game, the sweet. You've made a
hit there,' said Mrs Lloyd indulgently. 'We don't usually
go for the men visitors, do we Tai Fung? Only the good-
looking ones,' she added archly, keeping her neck
extended and her chin up. 'So you're London as well? Me
too in the old days. I don't accept many engagements
now. Exhibition turns now and again perhaps. And some
judging. But there isn't the call. Not for professional
ballroom any more. Not for the quality stuff. And I can't
do the other. Then there's my little business in the city.
Health and sauna clinic,' she paused. 'And therapeutic
massage. Unisex it is. Very nice clientele. Lot of
businessmen like yourself. Closed this weekend.' She
nodded knowingly. 'So you'll be more the instrumental
side I expect?'

'Backing mostly,' he replied promptly, ad libbing.

'String backing for vocal artistes?'

'Actually, financial backing.' The bank did occasion-
ally put money into theatrical ventures. Mr Treasure had
instructed him to keep as close to the truth as he could.

'Fancy.' Mrs Lloyd seemed visibly impressed. 'Would

you care for a coffee, dear? It won't take a minute. No? Later perhaps. Will you be involved with Rudy, Mr Frenk I mean, when he moves to London?' she asked guardedly.

'Indirectly. We're pretty big,' Peregrine volunteered expansively, interested in the information and warming to his role. 'When is Rudy likely to move, do you know?'

'End of next month. He gave me three months notice, of course. As agreed. The flat's furnished. I converted the house after my husband died, five years ago.'

'Would that be your husband? In the picture?'

Mrs Lloyd gave a bronchial trill. 'No, that's my partner. Arnold was a soldier, a corporal, in the infantry. King William's Eastwick Yeomanry. God rest him.'

He assumed she meant Arnold not King William. 'Did he die in Northern Ireland?'

'No. Potter's Bar. In London. In a car accident. Nothing heroic. Like a cigarette?' She pulled a packet from the pocket of the housecoat.

'No thanks. Allow me.' He heaved himself out of the sofa, went across to her, and picked up the table lighter near the telephone on the table beside her.

Mrs Lloyd held his hand with hers as she lit the cigarette from the flame he proffered. 'Thank you, dear.' She looked up into his eyes while pressing a leg against his—so hard he mistook it for part of the chair. 'My Arnold had nice manners too. Stop it Tai Fung. Mr Gore's a friend.' The animal had interrupted its mistress's determined advances by trying to nibble Peregrine's trousers. It retreated once again, issuing malevolent hisses as Peregrine went back to his seat.

'Have you re-let the flat?' he enquired earnestly.

'Nothing definite. You wouldn't be interested, I suppose?' There was more hope than solid expectation in the question.

'For a colleague, perhaps.'

'Would you like to see it? Wouldn't take a minute.'

'I'd like to. Before I go perhaps? You mentioned an address. Where I might be able to reach Rudy?'

'Oh yes.' She pulled an address book from under the telephone. 'It's a friend's cottage. In the country. The other side of Evesham. A male friend, you understand? Not your type. Not Rudy's either you wouldn't have thought.' Mrs Lloyd's features stiffened for a moment as though she might have been recalling a bitter memory. 'Takes all sorts, of course. They often spend weekends there together. No 'phone, I'm afraid.'

'The friend's another musician?'

'No, a telephonist. In the Birmingham Main Exchange.'

'And you think Rudy may be at the cottage?'

'Couldn't say, dear. He might be. We could . . . we could try. He only said he'd be away the whole weekend. If he has musical engagements he usually tells me.' She came over and sat close to Peregrine, placing the address book on his leg with her hand under it. 'Nice to have the house to myself, in a way. Lucky I was here. For you, I mean. I'd no plans, as it happens. There's the address if you want to copy it. I've never been there, but Rudy says it's less than an hour from here by car. Quicker in a car like yours I expect. Pretty drive too, I should think,' she finished wistfully.

Peregrine finished copying the address. 'Do you think we could go upstairs now?' he asked. He felt her body give a little start.

'But my . . . Oh, to see the other flat? Yes. I'll get the key.'

The disappointment in the voice hadn't communicated itself to Peregrine.

Their progress to the upper floor involved a contrived performance by Mrs Lloyd, in the lead, showing a generous amount of thigh as well as plenty of nicely developed calf. She had purposefully bunched the skirts of the housecoat to one side at the bottom of the narrow stairs. 'Own front door, you see?' she said, turning at the top to give a frontal view of the same anatomical features and which were quite her best.

'Very nice,' said Peregrine, but thinking it a fairly ordinary door.

The furniture inside the flat was what had probably been excess to requirements in the Lloyd place after Arnold's demise: the rooms had a threadbare appearance but they were as tidy as those downstairs. The bedroom was nearly as feminine as Mrs Lloyd's own and had a lingering but distinctive smell of joss sticks about it. The double bed was shrouded in a pink taffeta cover with frilled edges, and decorated with small cushions.

'Plenty of hanging space,' said Mrs Lloyd, rolling back a built-in wardrobe door to reveal amongst other things a short, bright scarlet silk dressing gown and some other items that demonstrated Frenk's taste in leisure clothes veered toward the exotic. 'I go over the place once a week when Rudy's away.' She swept her hands sensuously over the bed cover. Then she straightened herself, adjusting the edges of her housecoat—a prim gesture but with the result they parted to show a bit more of what lay beneath. 'That's by arrangement, you understand. Not included in the rent. Like some other things,' she added, treating Peregrine to a long, unblinking stare. She stepped towards him, but just at the point when he'd turned about to move to the room at the front. He'd been interested in the several framed photographs in the bedroom.

'This is the lounge,' Mrs Lloyd explained, following him in. 'The opposite of the way the rooms are downstairs. Better for me because he does his practising in here. But not after eleven at night. Well, you can't have a man playing one of those things on top of you, not when you're in bed, can you? Oh, what am I saying?' she finished archly with a cavernous cough and pointing to the cello in the corner.

'It's a good big room,' said Peregrine affecting to look about him, but darting looks at the numerous photographs on the fireplace, the bookcase beside it, and the walls above both.

'Rudy takes a good photo,' remarked Mrs Lloyd, picking up a portrait, an action which served definitely to identify her tenant for Peregrine. Frenk appeared in nearly all the pictures, usually with others—in most cases other men, but there was one of him with an older woman. 'That's him with his mum. She's dead now,' Mrs Lloyd volunteered.

But Peregrine had become more interested in the dark young man who was depicted often with Frenk, and also in one professionally posed group photograph that didn't include Frenk. The group showed eight young men all wearing fur hats and heavy coats carrying airline bags and standing in snow beside a motor coach. It was a large framed print embossed with the distinctive Aeroflot insignia—like the bags in the picture. Peregrine picked it up. 'Rudy didn't go to Russia?'

'Not on that trip,' Mrs Lloyd replied guardedly. 'Oh Lord, he's left that window catch off.'

While Mrs Lloyd went to fix the window, Peregrine—in the line of duty—pocketed the small snapshot of Rudy Frenk that was at the front of some folded papers stuffed behind the clock. He'd been sure Mrs Lloyd hadn't seen what he'd done. Only the Pekinese had been watching directly and now stood in front of him fixing him with a watery, accusing stare and wobbling its rear.

'Nice Typhoo. Good dog,' Peregrine bent down to pat the tiny brute.

Tai Fung rolled on its back and sneezed.

'Twisting both of us round your little finger, Mr Gore? Or can I call you Peregrine? Always supposing that's your real name. Anyway, dear, before we go any further, and before I start screaming rape, which I may have to to get any action, why don't you tell me why you're really here? And you'd better take your things off so I can go through them and find out what else you've taken. That's besides the photo you just palmed. Oh, and I haven't got a licence for this, dear, so let's hope it doesn't have to go off.'

In her right hand Mrs Lloyd was holding a small automatic pistol of indeterminate vintage. She was pointing it at Peregrine's chest which at close range was a very large target even for a very small gun.

# CHAPTER 14

'You were right about the Embassy. Hardly anybody there.' Treasure was sitting at the Astoria manager's desk. Grinyev, who had just entered, was standing in front of it. The banker drained his coffee cup. 'It's been a useful morning, though.' He looked at the time: it was just after eleven.

'And the exchange connected you to all the numbers you wanted? Here and in London?'

'With remarkable speed. Can't imagine why people complain about the service.' Treasure grinned.

'I arranged a certain priority. And other things,' Grinyev replied somewhat woodenly.

'Like the coffee. Will you have some? There's plenty in the pot. My wife will be insanely jealous. We never get enough here at breakfast.'

Grinyev refused the coffee, but sat down. 'Who did you speak to at the Embassy?'

'Eventually an Assistant Counsellor. A woman. Sounded intelligent. Seemed to be coping single handed. She rang me back a moment ago. It was early, of course.'

'Someone from our Foreign Ministry has also spoken to her. Everything appropriate is being arranged.'

'So she said. Our Foreign Office will handle the search for Frenk's relatives through the Home Office. That actually means the police in Coventry I should think. They'll be sending someone to his address there for a start, but I shouldn't think they'll be ahead of the chap

I've sent. My secretary's contacting the travel agency which isn't open yet. Oh, and the Embassy is already in touch with your people about a post-mortem with a British doctor present. I mean, if our Government want that before the body's flown home.'

'They'll decide that after the weekend. Meantime the body is being properly protected.' The colonel nodded as though he knew that part already.

'Seems it's the standard international option in cases like this one. Understandable.'

'Not peculiar to British nationals who meet their deaths in the USSR,' Grinyev pronounced solemnly.

'Cause of death is pretty obvious, of course. It's the name of the murderer Frenk's people will want to know.'

'Which we all want to know, Mr Treasure.' The colonel gave his nervous half-smile. 'You've been shut in here for a long time. Would you care for a walk around the square? It's quite warm and fine today.'

'Good idea.' Treasure pushed back the chair and got up. 'It'll also enable the hotel manager to re-possess his office.'

Grinyev shook his head. 'This room is yours for as long as you need it. I shall tell the telephonist to hold any calls until we return. You are expecting some soon?'

'Possibly from my secretary. The more important one, from one of my executives, we've booked at noon Leningrad time or six this evening, depending on how soon he's gathered the information I've asked for. That should mostly cover the questions you . . .'

Grinyev had put a finger to his lips and picked up the telephone. He issued some instructions in Russian, then afterwards he asked: 'Your wife and the others have gone to the museum?'

'There didn't seem any point in not doing so. Candy Royce volunteered to stay but I told her not to. You know, it really is quite difficult to decide on the right thing to do. In the circumstances. My wife, and Miss Royce for that matter, they both feel it's probably disrespectful to go on enjoying a holiday, when one of our number's been murdered.'

The two men had emerged from the hotel lobby and into the street before Grinyev replied. He moved quite quickly with short steps, directing Treasure across the road and then between some parked tourist coaches until they were on the road-bound island with the cathedral in the centre. 'But it's the British tradition to carry on, I think. Like they were playing cricket in Kent before manning the little boats for Dunkirk. In nineteen-forty.'

The banker scratched his nose. 'I suppose so. It's just that one wonders what Frenk's people may be expecting us to do. Or not to do. D'you follow? Probably not. You possibly think I'm barmy.'

'If it eases your conscience, I could lock you all up on suspicion.'

'No, please don't do that. You've made me feel much better already. And you're right. It's like a spring day in England. And that's a very powerful building. The golden dome's magnificent in the sunlight. Must be about the same height as St Paul's in London.' He stopped to consider the cathedral structure. 'We were admiring the four porticos yesterday. There's a great deal to be said for using the Greek cross principle in church design. Makes for a wonderfully balanced effect.'

'We'll walk round the outside if you choose. The place suffered a lot in the nine-hundred-day siege, but it's been well restored. Inside it's more beautiful.'

'A beautiful museum with an enduring air of sanctity. We were there for a bit yesterday too.'

'Is it then so different from London? For the people who rubber-neck around St Paul's it's a museum, surely? Aren't they also non-believers like here?'

'I shouldn't be drawn on that, but I will. Formal worship goes on all the time at St Paul's while a good deal of informal worship seemed to be going on in there yesterday. Judging by the expressions of many visitors. I think most were Russian.'

'Elderly peasants over-awed.'

'Well *I* said a silent prayer.'

'For the conversion of Russia? I hope you did it standing up not kneeling. It's an offence to obstruct other citizens when you practise religion.' The colonel smiled, then his expression changed as he continued: 'So the executive you mentioned. The one who's telephoning at noon. He's trained in fact-finding?'

'Yes. Not as a criminal investigator, but to dig for information certainly. It's his normal job to ferret out critical knowledge of private companies who come to us for loan capital. He's very good at it, too.' Treasure went on as though he were justifying something to himself. 'Curious chap. He's never been much use at anything else.'

'But you picked him for this morning?'

'Couldn't think of anyone better at short notice. He was well placed geographically too. He's totally trustworthy and a big chap who can look after himself. Of course he won't have all that much time before the official teams get to work.'

'But he knows about the missing painting. They don't.'

'You're still sure the two events are connected?'

The colonel shrugged. 'I still have the hunch.'

'And that tourists are involved? Incidentally, we had a new guide allocated to us this morning. Met her at breakfast. A younger girl. I hope nothing's happened to Valya Sinitseva.'

Grinyev hesitated. 'Ah, she's indisposed. But only temporarily. She'll be back probably for lunch. I expect she's tired.'

'We were all up pretty late.'

The colonel solemnly regarded the sculpture high up in the pediment of the eastern portico of the cathedral. It depicted an episode in the life of the obscure St Isaac and involved a great many semi-recumbent people. 'Mrs Sinitseva and I were up even later. I had to question her,' he commented almost absently.

'Third-degree stuff?'

'What do you mean?'

'Were you hard on her?'

'Quite hard.' Grinyev gave a pained expression. 'It was necessary. To get at the truth. In her own interests.' This seemed to be his standard justification for unpleasantness. 'It's not an aspect of investigative work I enjoy. Questioning women. Harshly.'

'You could delegate it?'

'Taking the easy way out? It's also difficult to explain to one's subordinates the extent . . . the limit to the firmness required.'

'Sounds as if Valya's in trouble. Or was. You haven't arrested her? Temporarily?'

Grinyev scowled. 'Soviet citizens who indulge too evidently in *blat* are open to suspicion of more serious misdemeanour.'

'What's *blat*?'

'I'm sorry. It means unfairly to use the influences at your disposal to get what you need. Valya Sinitseva belongs to Intourist. Her husband is well placed in the academic world. They can apply a great deal of influence for their own ends.'

'Through what in England we'd call the old boy network? Or is it something more sinister? I mean how does *blat* work?'

'It works so that by doing favours you get favours repaid by others. Thanks to your position. So you may have better clothes. Get a car without waiting. A little dacha for the weekends. Theatre tickets when you want. Superior vacation arrangements. Foods out of season. Such things can be organised through reciprocal favouring.'

Treasure pouted. 'So *blat* makes for easier living but doesn't need to involve corruption or bribery? I can see Valya and her husband might be in positions to give and receive favours . . .'

'The dividing line is very slim, Mr Treasure,' the

colonel had interrupted quite hotly. 'Over-indulgence in comfortable living by people of limited income but good position. It invites investigation. Also it invites the proposition they may be getting greedy. And greed leads from *blat* to straight corruption.'

'And that's what you feel may have happened with Valya and her husband?'

'I didn't say so.' The other folded his arms in front of him as he walked. 'One must always be vigilant. Of oneself as well as others, of course. For instance, the manager of a refrigerator factory may be especially grateful that the professor gives extra tuition to his son.'

'So he provides the professor with a cheap refrigerator?'

'Also ahead of the queue. Precisely, Mr Treasure. But what if the professor later asks for several refrigerators? One as a favour for the dress shop manager who is providing his wife with first choice of fashionable clothes. One for the mechanic who is mending his car on Sunday morning with parts removed from the factory stores. Another for the civil servant who can hurry the allocation of building materials for the extension to the professor's dacha.' Grinyev shrugged. 'Then it can mean the professor is forced to give away not only tuition, but also high marks in the examination to the factory manager's son. And the sons of others who can provide reciprocal favours. It has happened. And worse.'

'Valya's husband is an assistant professor.'

'I used a professor only to illustrate.'

'And presumably Valya can offer quite as many favours as her husband? Through her job?'

'Through Intourist. Many commercial favours. And more. Because of her sex. She is quite attractive. Haven't you noticed?' The colonel scowled, indicating he had certainly noticed. 'It seems her husband also is attractive. To women.'

'You mean they have affairs?'

'From time to time. He is having one at the moment

with a dull woman in the Foreign Ministry. Possibly with his wife's knowledge.'

'The woman's lack of attraction suggesting she is providing er . . . *blat* to compensate?'

Grinyev smiled. 'Also possible. In addition it's suggested Valya's been giving sexual favours to influential men tourists, perhaps for hard currency or for helping her with a project. She especially asked to be allocated to your Baroque Circle group this week. If the Sinitsevas have been involved in the theft of the painting, and the stabbing of Frenk, one can see a sinister thread of logic in what they've both been doing.'

'You mentioned help over a project.'

'They're . . . pulling strings to be posted to a cruise ship this summer. As lecturers. Together. It's a cruise ship that calls at Western ports.'

'You think they could be planning to er . . . leave Russia?'

'The people involved in the theft would have large sums of money waiting for them abroad. So large it would be impossible to bring to Russia or to use here without raising heavy suspicion.'

'They both speak fluent English and both could presumably find satisfactory work abroad.' Treasure sniffed. 'But you have no evidence against them except circumstantial stuff? Valya asking to look after our group, which you can only surmise is tied in with the theft.'

'And Valya being at the opera last night when Frenk was murdered.'

'Understandable since there was a spare ticket left over for the group.'

'Except there wasn't, Mr Treasure. An extra ticket was obtained through *blat*. Also Valya Sinitseva doesn't much care for opera. Not as much as her husband, although she claims the opposite. She most likely got the ticket for him, but he couldn't go because he was meeting his lady friend. So Mrs Sinitseva goes herself. I am now close to believing she did so out of pique. It was important to find out whether there was a different reason. Why she didn't sell the ticket to someone else. Why it might have been necessary for her or her husband to have been there in person. I had to delve for this. The process was distasteful. You would like to sit to admire the view?' Abruptly the speaker had changed the subject, while pointing at an empty park bench.

They were now abreast of the northern end of the cathedral in a part of the precinct that was nearly empty of people.

'So you haven't arrested her?' Treasure sat.

'As you say, because there is no firm evidence.' The KGB man gave the banker a sidelong glance before he also sat and continued. 'And while it is possible to hold people on suspicion in this country, as it is in yours, sometimes it's better to allow them rope.'

Treasure frowned. 'Why are you telling me all this, Colonel?'

'Because I trust you, and because we have our agreement. Has Mrs Sinitseva made advances of any kind to you?'

'Good lord no. Not that there's been much opportunity for sexual dalliance. I don't believe we've ever been alone together. D'you think she's been at it with the other chaps?'

Grinyev was studying his shoes. 'In your case I wouldn't have expected sexual advances, Mr Treasure. She wouldn't have been so stupid. Has she once mentioned money to you? How money is handled in Britain perhaps? How it is transferred between countries? You're a banker.'

'No, money hasn't cropped up at all. But what do you mean "in my case"? Are you trying to give me an inferiority complex?'

'It was meant as a compliment to your intelligence. She has certainly made an opportunity to be alone with the bachelor Mr Tate. And according to his passport, Mr Tate is in Cairo quite frequently. Stolen pictures are often disposed of there.'

'Hm. He has an excellent reason for being in Cairo. And I don't think there's any future in Tate as a criminal. In any context. And I don't believe he's crazy about women either. Nigel Dirving's the lady's man. Also Jeremy Wander when his wife's not looking. Neither fits as a thief or a murderer.' He invented the last comment to protect the two men, and without stopping to consider whether he wholly believed it.

'Why does Miss Amelia Harwick visit men's rooms in the early morning?' Grinyev enquired quietly.

'Because she's lost I should think. Whose room?'

'Frenk's.'

'You mean Dirving's? They shared. When was this? After Frenk's death?'

Grinyev paused. 'At seven o'clock this morning.'

'She was probably on her way to the bath. She shares a room with her employer, Mrs Vauxley, who apparently occupies their bathroom for hours on end and doesn't let Miss Harwick in. My wife got that from Candy Royce. There's a communal bathroom down the corridor. And a loo next door. Miss Harwick uses that. That'd be the reason for her being in the corridor.'

'Her excuse for being there. She went into Mr Dirving's room and stayed half an hour. She did not go to the communal bathroom.'

'Well bully for Amelia.'

'I'm sorry?'

'Nothing. It's just . . . Well, never mind.'

'In consequence Mr Dirving's room was searched again later this morning. Also Miss Harwick's.'

'That won't please Mrs Vauxley.'

'There's no reason she should know. They found nothing.' The colonel sighed. 'Canon Emdon also uses the communal facilities.'

'His lavatory doesn't work.'

'So he told one of my officers after breakfast. He was very frightened.'

'I'm not surprised. Being interviewed by one of your officers could be a very frightening experience for someone who leads a sheltered sort of life. Why was he questioned?'

'Routine. He's in the corridor too often. We asked why.'

'I should have thought that was obvious. He's getting on. But you didn't question Miss Harwick. Is the subject of lavatory visits too delicate for your officers to discuss with ladies?'

'I am interested to know how much pressure has to be applied to the frightened Canon Emdon before he demands to see his consul.'

Treasure traced a finger across his forehead. 'There's an American Consul in Leningrad? I didn't know that.'

'Canon Emdon does. But he has no inclination to call on his services. Strange.' Grinyev's gaze had strayed to the sculpture enclosed in the northern pediment. It was a scene of Christ's Resurrection by Lemaire. 'Just as well, perhaps. I'm afraid the American Consul's away. For Easter.'

# CHAPTER 15

'I've had to complain about my ba . . . throom again,'
Canon Emdon said loudly as he and Treasure handed their
room keys to the floor concierge in exchange for their
hotel cards.

It was after lunch and the party was due to assemble
in the main lobby of the hotel ready to board the coach
for Pushkin. The canon's pointed remark had been
intended more for the blonde concierge than for the
banker. It also explained why the cleric had come
hurrying back along the corridor from a region beyond his
own room—chin sunk into neck like a threatened tortoise,
his expression alternating between dismay and mystifica-
tion. He was well wrapped up, despite the mildness of
the day, and carrying the small black handbag he
sometimes took with him on excursions.

The concierge seemed unmoved and too preoccupied
with other things to deal with the canon's indirect repeti-
tion of his standard grumble. In any case she had understood from the housekeeper that the bathroom had been
repaired.

'No news from London?' called Mrs Tate who was
waiting for the lift with her son.

'Afraid not,' answered Treasure who had been interested to observe the concierge painstakingly making
pencilled entries beside the names on the list under her
hand—the least sophisticated but patently quite efficient
section of Colonel Grinyev's intelligence system in full

operation. No doubt the canon's daytime visitations to the 'communal facilities' were as carefully logged as the night-time ones.

'This lift takes ages. The coach leaves in five minutes. Let's take the stairs,' volunteered Mrs Tate leading the others across the large circular landing to where Molly was already waiting for her husband.

'They won't go without us, Mother,' offered Reggie Tate.

'And there's no cha . . . nce the trip to Pushkin will be cancelled?' the canon questioned with genuine apprehension in his tone as he glanced from face to face for enlightenment. 'I mean on account of Mr Frenk?'

'None at all, Canon. Not according to Valya at lunch,' Molly answered.

'It was nice to have her back. I didn't care for that other girl this morning,' commented Mrs Tate, reaching up to pull a long pin out of her hat. 'Younger, but not nearly so well informed. Not as pretty either.' She jabbed the pin back again with frightening aplomb.

'Valya didn't eat much,' said her son. 'Hardly worth the effort of joining us. And I understand the free breakfast and lunch are a valued part of the perks for Intourist guides.'

'Then they can't be difficult to please,' muttered the canon whose stomach had been upset since the first day.

Treasure missed the comment because he had his attention fixed on Reggie Tate. He was trying to decide whether a close personal encounter with an Intourist guide would rate as a valued perk for this particular visitor: on the whole he still thought not. The question remained whether Valya had visited Tate's room just to deliver opera tickets.

'I don't believe Valya looks at all well. It's why she had the morning off,' came the slight voice of Miss Harwick from behind the descending group. She had been sent back from the lobby to get her employer's spare glasses and was on her way down again.

'She was up very late,' said Treasure, allowing her to overtake him on the wide stairs. 'Later than us, though she may not have been up so early.' He was viewing Amelia Harwick in a new light since the revelations about her early morning visit to Dirving's room. Almost as though she were reading his thoughts—or perhaps more into his comment than was intended—Miss Harwick coloured, lowering her gaze as soon as it met his.

'We'll be back in time for Peregrine's six o'clock call?' asked Molly quietly as she and Treasure came together in the lobby.

'Mm. Provided he remembers to make one.' The reply was clipped and acerbic. 'Pity he didn't call at noon, just to say how he was doing. A call was booked.'

'Perhaps he wasn't near a telephone.'

'He's in the English Midlands not outer Mongolia. Miss Gaunt managed to get through even though we didn't have a line booked for her.' He had been called to the telephone to speak to his secretary only minutes before this, at the end of lunch.

'But she had nothing to report.'

'Nothing substantial. Except it's good to know she got through to Geoffrey and most of the others, even though everyone seems to be out of town.' He frowned.

'Like us, darling.' Molly squeezed his arm affectionately.

The Geoffrey referred to was a Member of Parliament, a Minister at the Home Office, and a trusted friend of Treasure's. The others Miss Gaunt had been told to reach were also people of influence. The banker was satisfied that the situation of the Baroque Circle members would not now be overlooked or go unexplained in London if there was a sudden clamp down on information—or on them. And this despite the distractions of a holiday weekend that seemed, from his point of view, to have prompted far too many people to abandon their basic responsibilities—despite his wife's implication that he was being unreasonable for thinking so.

'And you're coming to Pushkin?' Molly pressed as they joined the assembling group near the reception desk. He had been undecided to this point.

'Yes. I don't see why not. The Embassy in Moscow won't be calling back today. There's no point really in my hanging about on the off chance of a call from anyone.' He fell silent as they halted beside the others.

'. . . to Pushkin which is a small town of imperial palaces, renamed in nineteen thirty-seven after the Russian writer who lived there,' Valya Sinitseva was in the middle of announcing to those already around her. 'Take notice, it is twenty-five kilometres from Leningrad and we should be there in forty minutes. We shall have time only to visit the famous Catherine Palace built in the baroque style by Catherine the Great but named after an earlier Catherine, wife of Peter the Great. It is usual also to visit the Great Palace at Pavlovsk which is two kilometres further than Pushkin, but on a four day visit to Leningrad not everything is possible. Next time you come we go to Pavlovsk perhaps.' She gave an unconvincing smile—politely returned only by Miss Harwick—before she continued. 'Take notice also that your tickets for the concert tonight at the Philharmonia Hall have been reserved. They should be picked up and paid for at the Intourist desk here in the lobby when we return from Pushkin. Now please to board our coach which is waiting across the street outside.'

Although her face was drawn—something make-up and effort didn't disguise—Valya was noticeably turned out in an elegant fur jacket over a tight red sweater, a well cut black tweed skirt and matching leather boots. Treasure considered the effect to be a tribute to natural defiance and *blat* resource.

'In case you didn't hear earlier, Valya says we'll be able to walk in the palace gardens,' called Candy Royce to the group at large as they moved towards the street door. 'It'll be later in the afternoon though. Colder. Everyone got proper coats?'

They all seemed satisfied with what they were wearing,

but Mrs Tate stopped suddenly and exclaimed: 'Oh Reggie, in the rush I forgot my camera.'

And immediately afterwards Mrs Vauxley, who had been talking with Jeremy Wander, announced: 'I must have left it in my room. Well I can't do without it. Especially if we're going to tramp through gardens. Clever of you to notice, Jeremy. Please go back and get my stick for me, Amelia.'

'But Mrs Vauxley, you did say you'd do without it this afternoon. I did ask.'

'Don't be tiresome, Amelia. I'm an old woman and have to be indulged.' She nodded pointedly at Wander, affirming the bond between gentry.

'Have we got time, Valya? To get things from upstairs?' This was Reggie Tate.

'If you're certain to be quick, Mr Tate.' It was the first time either had spoken to the other—or even acknowledged the other's presence—that Treasure had recorded that day. And the distancing had seemed to be mutual.

'Let me. I'll go for both of you. I need a different coat. Give me your room cards for the keys,' offered Wander—and curiously since he was already wearing his untreated sheepskin, the warmest garment he had with him.

'Would you, Jeremy? Thanks a lot. My camera's on the dressing table.' Mrs Tate handed over her card.

'And my precious stick is in the wardrobe,' said Mrs Vauxley doing the same thing with the ingratiating smile she reserved for Wander and Treasure, but mostly for Wander. 'It's very good of you to go to the trouble. Amelia could easily have done it.'

'Jeremy's been a boy scout at heart for yonks,' his wife subscribed with a grin that bared a lot of teeth. 'Darling, bring me my long scarf as well, will you?'

'The yellow one?'

'Yah. With the Fred's label.'

Gloria Blinton gave Dirving a puzzled look as they went through the door. 'Is Fred's a shop?'

'It's what the rich call Fortnum and Mason's, love.'

'Oh, I see,' she responded, although she didn't see at all. 'And you reckon they'll let us all go home Monday?' she went on as they waited to cross the street. As usual, the coach was parked with others on the far side. Dirving was between her and Edwina Apse. He spent a good deal of time with both and, as Treasure who was now behind them was noticing, surprisingly little with Miss Harwick who was ahead, approaching the vehicle with Sol Blinton.

'I'm sure we'll be free to leave.' Dirving looked over his shoulder. 'Ask Mark, he's the expert . . .'

'Oh, my God, Sol's being arrested again,' Gloria blurted the interruption, her hand leaping to her mouth. She dashed across the street, ignoring the traffic—only to reach the coach as her husband was being courteously helped up the steps by the tall young army officer she had earlier seen tapping him on the shoulder. The soldier—it was Lieutenant Glinka from the State Hermitage militia— also took her arm as she pulled up her short, over-tight skirt before starting a confused ascent into the coach behind Sol. But Glinka was paying little real attention to the women—even to Gloria's knees. He was closely studying all the men though, while Valya stood opposite watching him apprehensively.

'What did he say to you? What did he want?' Gloria hissed to her husband as she sat down beside him.

Sol shrugged. 'How should I know what he's wanting? He didn't say a thing. Don't suppose he speaks English.'

'He was looking at you hard enough.'

'So he's looking at all the men. See?' He nodded in Glinka's direction through the window. 'So maybe he's doing some kind of identity check. Perhaps he's after a deserter.'

'Could it be anything to do with that black marketeer of yours?'

'He wasn't in the army. Too undernourished.'

'Don't tease, Sol. It could be serious.' She was keeping her eyes on what was going on outside. 'You're right, he's only looking at the men.' She lowered her voice even more. 'I wish you'd get rid of that letter.'

'That's safe enough. Praise God I didn't have it on me when they searched me.'

'Because it was in your hat. I had your hat.' She shivered every time she thought of it.

'But I didn't mean you should have it. Like I said. Act of God.' At the time he'd forgotten where he'd put the letter until it was too late.

Most of the party were now in the coach. Only Valya was outside with Lieutenant Glinka.

'What d'you suppose he's after?' asked Edwina as Dirving came to sit next to her.

'Well not just Sol, obviously,' he remarked loudly, glancing around and nodding encouragingly at the Blintons. 'Probably waiting for us all to get on. Then he'll have us driven to the Lubyanka prison.'

'That's in Moscow,' called Mrs Tate from across the gangway.

'Plenty of time for a group interrogation on the way,' Dirving joked back.

'Careful, Valya could hear,' Miss Harwick cautioned from a forward seat.

'Too bad. This is police harassment,' countered Mrs Vauxley beside her, disagreeing with her companion's comment probably on principle since she had never before shown antipathy to Valya. 'Ah, here's Jeremy.'

They could all see Wander advancing across the road still dressed in his sheepskin coat but with a yellow scarf draped around his neck, stick in one hand, camera in the other. As he went to get into the coach Lieutenant Glinka suddenly barred his way. Valya stepped forward and translated something the soldier said. Then the three were joined by a thickset civilian who some of the others had noticed hovering in the background. The man seemed to have a frightening effect on Valya who instinctively took a step back on his approach.

There was an apprehensive silence inside the coach,

with those at the front trying to pick up what was being said beyond the door. All could see Wander expostulating and getting very red in the face.

After some moments Felicity Wander half rose from her seat in front of the Treasures, but the banker was into the aisle ahead of her and making for the door. Then the drama ended as abruptly as it had begun.

'What a load of nonsense,' Wander declared in a voice that was nervously loud and assertive as he stepped inside the coach. 'They wanted to know if I could have been in Leningrad late last Wednesday afternoon. I mean, how could I have been?'

'Yah. So why should they have thought so, Jeremy?' asked his wife.

'Heaven knows.'

'The lieutenant believes he saw one member of the Baroque Circle at the State Hermitage on Wednesday. He was in charge of the guard there that day.' This was Valya who was standing in the aisle behind Wander as he distributed the things he had brought—the stick for Mrs Vauxley, the camera for Mrs Tate and the scarf which he handed to his wife. 'His superior wishes to know if he recognises anyone else.'

'Well in that case his superior ought to have the man's head examined. Or his own,' commented Dirving. 'I spent last Wednesday afternoon making a recording in a BBC TV studio in Shepherds Bush. As millions of viewers will shortly be able to attest. Well a few hundred thousand anyway. Programme doesn't have a top rating,' he finished modestly.

'None of us could have been in the Hermitage on Wednesday. So who is the officer supposed to have seen there, Valya?' Reggie Tate enquired.

'He's not saying. Perhaps he is mistaken.'

'He could have seen you, perhaps, Valya,' joked Candy Royce.

'I was there, yes, with another group,' she answered

after some hesitation. 'The authorities know that. I think it's the men they are looking for.'

There was silence for a moment while everyone searched for a significance and only the Treasures found one.

'Someone looking for you upstairs, Canon,' Wander called to Clarence Emdon who was sitting by himself half way along. 'German by the name of Dr Klaus Brendt. Chap with a beard. Spoke to you at dinner on Thursday night I think.'

'I know who you mean.'

'Well his party's leaving this afternoon. Wanted to say goodbye. Said if there's anything he can do for you, you only have to let him know.'

'Thanks.' The American was for some reason embarrassed by the message and clearly not anxious to pursue the topic of Dr Brendt.

'Comes from Dresden, he said. Art dealer I gathered.'

'Do they have art dealers in East Germany?' questioned Mrs Tate.

'If Dr Brendt is one, then they must have, Mother,' her son replied with unusual briskness.

# CHAPTER 16

' "The garden façade of the palace is three hundred metres long, punctuated by white pilasters and columns. The gold mouldings and the blue wall renderings are once again as the architect Rastrelli intended. Also the elegant gilded domes of the church at the south end." ' Molly Treasure looked up from her reading of the guide book. 'Isn't it gorgeous?'

'A baroque extravaganza,' Treasure agreed, smiling. They had completed their tour of the inside of the Catherine Palace and were standing in the centre of the upper terrace overlooking the long formal gardens and the start of the park which spread out beyond. 'Busy, and just possibly short of great architecture, but immensely pleasing as a composition. Amazing restoration after what happened to it in the war. The rooms were very good. I don't believe I know anything in the style quite so elegant or refined.' He sniffed appreciatively. 'Your Circle is getting its money's worth in Pushkin.'

'Guess we can go as we please in the gardens,' said Mrs Tate who had just appeared beside them. The tour of the interior had been a strictly conducted one. 'Valya's staying inside with the people who wanted to look at the picture gallery again. Don't blame them. But there's so much to see here.'

'Remember the coach leaves at five,' Molly cautioned.

'Which gives us a half hour to view the geometric paths, the marble statues, the fish canals, the Great Pond, and all those pavilions. I'll never make it, but I'm going to try. Wish Reggie would hurry. He's gone to the men's room.' The Australian matron beamed at the others. 'Say, you doing the outdoor Cook's tour as well, Canon?'

Clarence Emdon had been purposefully making for the steps down to the next terrace. He paused briefly on hearing the question addressed, raised his hat, nodding and smiling sheepishly. Then he moved onwards without speaking, though he did utter a benedictory kind of noise.

'Well there's one who'll be able to tell 'em back home he took in everything,' said Mrs Tate. 'Ah, here's my talented son. See you all later. Don't miss the Marble Bridge. It'll remind you of home.' She took Reggie's arm and they hurried off in the canon's wake.

'Cripes it was hot in there, wasn't it?' This was Gloria Blinton who had arrived arm in arm with her husband. 'I learned a lot though. Let's see.' She closed her eyes to think better. 'Most of the rooms are by the Scottish classical architect Charles Cameron. He had to do the inside all over after Rastrelli the Italian had finished. That was because Catherine the Great went off a lot of the baroque stuff after all. Can you imagine? Around a hundred and fifty rooms and they had to do it again? And a Scotsman gets the job. Right here in seventeen seventy-nine.' She gave a satisfied sigh. 'My mother was half Scottish.'

'Did you see what happened to the detectives, Mr Treasure?' enquired Sol as both couples moved down the steps. A car with two easily identified plainclothes detectives had trailed the coach all the way to Pushkin. The two men had followed the party on the inside tour at a discreet distance. Now they were not in evidence.

'I was wondering where they'd gone. Thought I saw one of them waiting down there when we came out, but I could have been wrong. It's very crowded.' The banker nodded towards a lower terrace. There were a great many people who had come out of the building heading in the same direction as themselves. 'Either they've been called off or they've given up the unequal struggle. It'd be a bit difficult for the two of them to cover fourteen of us, once we split up out here.'

'I thought perhaps they'd be concentrating on special people,' said Sol, whose definition of special in this context included himself but involved no kind of compliment.

'But for your part you're keeping out of trouble?' Treasure enquired lightly but with a similar thought in mind.

Gloria Blinton heard the question, frowned and was about to speak when Sol put in with forced bonhomie: 'You bet. On my best behaviour till we get home. Then I can start living it up again.' The older man's eyes twinkled as his wife bore him off in the direction of a small blue pavilion set in the centre of a grass bordered etoile.

'Don't really want to go down there. The less formal part of the park's to the right,' said Molly, again consulting her guide book. 'And some of the best pavilions are there too. Around the lake.'

'The Great Pond,' Treasure corrected absently. 'This place must be pleasant in the summer.' There was still a good deal of snow in untrampled areas.

'And to think these beautiful buildings were half flattened in the war.' Molly stopped to look back at the impressive white, blue and gold façade.

'Like most of Leningrad. During the nine-hundred-day siege everyone keeps telling us about. You know, it's a paradox these people have spent millions on restoring the cream of Church and Tsarist architecture, after it was virtually obliterated by a capitalist enemy. The cathedrals and palaces are monuments to a religion and a regime they claim to detest. And now they've spruced them all up again, good as new.'

'You think the money would have been better spent on housing or something?'

'No. Although those ghastly high-rise flats we passed

on the way weren't wearing very well.' He pouted at the wide stretch of water they were skirting along its south bank. 'It's the irritating inconsistency. What they've done here is so civilised, a quality they lack in so many other ways.'

'Isn't Colonel Grinyev too civilised to be in the KGB?'

Treasure frowned. 'Yes. Although perhaps he personifies what I'm getting at. The soul of courtesy and common sense so far as we're concerned, while I suspect he's making life hell for a lot of others. Like Valya. Ah, this must be the Little Admiralty pavilion. Gothic and red-brick. Reminds one of Keble College, Oxford.'

'Used as a restaurant in the summer,' said Molly consulting the guide book.

'Hm. I don't think Keble's ever thought of that,' he mused.

'D'you suppose Colonel Grinyev ordered the harassment when we got on the coach?'

'That was Mrs Vauxley's description. I didn't feel harassed. Wander looked a bit uneasy. Must have been instigated by Grinyev, of course. I couldn't think of the reason at the time.'

'But you have now?'

'I should think it was to test the young officer's acuity. As to human recognition, if not time.'

'He said he'd seen one of us. One of the men. At the State Hermitage. But on Wednesday? Impossible.'

'Yes. But he must have been asked to identify a corpse.' The banker paused, brow knitted. 'Or maybe he'd been shown a photograph of the corpse.'

'Of Mr Frenk? But he could never have seen him alive.'

'Not on Wednesday, certainly. But he may have been in charge of the guard at other times. Frenk may have been there before.'

'On a previous visit? He didn't say he'd been to Russia before.'

'But perhaps he had and didn't want us to know. The

officer may have remembered him for a wrong reason. More likely than the other kind.'

'So why did he want to look at us if it was Mr Frenk he thought he saw?'

'Because on this other memorable visit, whenever it was, Frenk may have been accompanied by someone else.'

'All very hypothetical,' said Molly dismissively. 'And since he'd got the date wrong anyway.'

'This is part of the stolen painting investigation, not the one about who killed Frenk. Grinyev's obsessed with getting the picture back and he's leaving no pebble unturned. If that officer volunteered he'd seen Frenk before, Grinyev would want the point followed up on the off chance. And even if the chap was wrong on the date. Anyway, it gave us two facts we didn't have before.'

'That the painting was stolen from the State Hermitage? And it was pinched on Wednesday?'

'Well done. You know, I don't believe our party was supposed to be told where that officer came from.'

'But only you and I know about a stolen picture. So there wouldn't have been anything incriminating about the others admitting being in the Hermitage on Wednesday. Supposing any of them had been here then.'

Treasure nodded. 'Grinyev told me last night the painting had gone very recently. It happening so close to the murder of a Western art tourist at least suggests the possibility of a link.' He pointed ahead of them. 'Look, the famous Marble Bridge.'

Molly opened the guide book again. 'Copy of the stone Palladian Bridge at Wilton House. Faithful copy too. It's why Mrs Tate said it'd remind us of home. Except we don't live at Wilton,' she added wistfully. 'Wonder where she and Reggie are?'

'Well forward I expect, but there's the canon.' His eyes narrowed. 'What's he doing?'

The covered bridge, with its Ionic columns and green copper roof, was a hundred yards ahead. Canon Emdon was emerging from it and moving rapidly. When he saw the Treasures he increased his pace even more, and without making any sign of recognition he swerved left onto a tributary pathway. At the same moment three men also came off the bridge—one of them clearly in the custody of the much bigger figures on either side of him who were holding his arms.

Now someone came running from behind the Treasures—a heavily built man with a scarred cheek and wearing a black overcoat and trilby: he was one of the detectives who had followed them from Leningrad and through the palace. Treasure looked about for the man's partner, but it was the canon who saw him first—coming towards him on the pathway he'd chosen.

Canon Emdon turned around, and then froze at the sight of the three men bearing down on him. He made to go left towards the Treasures but recognised the other advancing policeman. Half turning again, he pulled a guide book from the handbag he was carrying, opened the book at random, fixed his monocle in his eye and stared earnestly at a miniature stone pyramid near the water in front of him. Almost immediately he was surrounded by the other five participants in the unfolding drama.

'Hello, Canon,' called Treasure briskly and enlarging the group still further. He elbowed through to the canon's side. 'Interesting monument. Three of Catherine the Great's dogs are buried under it.'

'One was called Sir Tom Anderson,' Molly observed valiantly at the top of her voice from behind her husband. 'Long name for a dog.'

'Ah, Tr . . . easure. I thought I saw . . .'

'Please to move away.' It was the scar-faced detective who spoke to the Treasures. He then said something sharply to the other Russians in their own language. The small man being held in the middle of the trio had his face partially obscured, but he seemed to be quite old. His body was stooped, and wisps of grey hair protruded from around the battered Homburg.

'Come along then, Canon,' said Treasure taking Emdon's arm confidently. 'Seems we're not wanted.'

'He stays. You go. You and lady, please.'

'Do you want to stay, Canon?'

'No,' the cleric almost whimpered.

'So I think you must be making a mistake,' Treasure advised the policeman politely. 'This is Canon Emdon, a distinguished American. My name is Treasure.'

Scar-face was unimpressed. 'These two make an exchange.' He pointed at the small man and then to the canon. 'On the bridge. We watch.'

The knot of people was now expanding rapidly, but when scar-face's partner gruffly ordered newcomers to disperse they did so promptly—all except for the Tates, now exposed on the fringe.

'This man is trading with foreigners. It is an offence.' Scar-face was pointing to the small man whose eyes showed bewilderment over the top of his muffler. 'Both are under arrest. You please now go.'

'No, we're staying with Canon Emdon,' Treasure insisted. 'My name is Treasure and I've been working all morning with Colonel Grinyev. I wish to telephone him immediately.'

The statement was not received with quite the degree of reverence the speaker had expected. It wasn't even evident that the name Grinyev meant anything at all to scar-face who looked more puzzled than impressed. Even so, he didn't repeat his insistence that the Treasures leave.

'I received nothing,' said the canon, but more to Treasure than the policeman.

'He gave this one a package. These officers witness,' scar-face stated bluntly, indicating the small man's escorts. 'Is most likely foreign currency. Is a bad offence.'

'You in trouble, Canon?' This was Effie Tate who by moving forward with Reggie, deep into disputant territory, had put a better nominal balance on things.

'Who are you?' demanded scar-face.

'We're with the Baroque Circle which you must know perfectly well. You just trailed the lot of us through the palace,' replied Mrs Tate affably. 'Now we're supporting Canon Emdon.'

The policeman gave her a disapproving look, then said something in Russian to the small man who replied haltingly, then slowly began turning out the pockets of his blue raincoat. First came a folded newspaper. Scarface's partner snatched it, examined the front page closely, then shook his head. Everything else produced was treated in a similar way. These comprised two letters, a coloured postcard of the Catherine Palace, and the blade of a car windscreen wiper. The last item brought a challenge from the second policeman, answered satisfactorily it seemed, in mime, by the small man's production of an ignition key.

The next sequence happened quickly. Following a roughly couched order, the small man slowly began to remove his outer clothing—first his scarf, then his raincoat and finally his hat. The grey hairs were attached to the hat: the owner was about thirty with a crewcut. While most of those present were registering this, he made as if to hand the garments to scar-face then, swiftly whipping about, thrust the hat and scarf in the face of the first escort and the coat over the head of the second, shoving both men hard backwards into the water before sprinting away from them along the tributary path.

Scar-face's astonished partner was still holding the newspaper and the wiper and continued doing so. In contrast, his companion's reaction was prompt and decisive. He moved after the fugitive for only as long as it took to produce a stubby handgun from beneath his coat. Then he dropped on one knee, taking aim with both hands, as the crowd scattered in the wake of the target and out of the line of fire. One shot rang out. The small man was forty yards distant. He buckled at the knees, then fell on his face.

'Oh God,' the canon beseeched, the monocle falling from his eye.

'Winged him, by the look of it,' said Mrs Tate in a matter-of-fact tone.

Treasure and Reggie Tate caught up with scar-face as he knelt down beside the wounded man. He began tearing open the jacket. Its owner lay moaning on the ground, blood oozing through his fingers. His hands were fastened over a rent at the top of one trouser leg on the outside.

'Flesh wound,' said scar-face coldly, by way of information not apology, and perhaps to advertise his skill as a marksman. He also said something to the victim as he came upon a flat package in an inside pocket, and roughly hauled it out.

The detective pulled off the black plastic wrapping of the package, tearing away the layer of tissue paper beneath. What he revealed was a small dark oil painting. The work was about five inches square.

# CHAPTER 17

At the time the coach transporting the Baroque Circle members arrived in Pushkin, Peregrine Gore had already been locked inside the windowless bathroom of Frenk's flat in Coventry for several hours.

He was entirely naked. Mrs Lloyd had even insisted he surrender his watch, so he could only estimate how long he had been there and roughly how much longer the incarceration would continue, unless he could extricate himself. She had said she was expecting a 'phone call at two and that after that she would know what to do about him.

That a strapping, healthy, athletic male—and a trained soldier (well, broadly)—could be rendered so totally helpless by a passed-over blonde dancer armed only with a .22 automatic should have challenged normal understanding. It didn't challenge Peregrine's, though, just as it wouldn't have taxed the credulity of those who knew him well.

Peregrine abominated hand-guns, trying never to be involved with them unless it was absolutely unavoidable—all as a result of one of those army accidents to which he had been so prone. On top of this, his chivalrous attitude towards the female sex was positively Arthurian. Thus, the present impasse had not come about through a lack of courage on his part—only a conjunction of two principles rigorously observed.

Even so, it is probable Peregrine would have tackled a

167

male holding a pistol on him. What had deterred him was having to take on a *woman* armed not only with a pistol but also with one of positively French Resistance vintage. He'd had plenty of time to look it over and come to the conclusion that it was the kind of weapon which often blew up in people's hands. So what had weighed heavy with him was the chance—and with his luck—even the probability of this gun doing Mrs Lloyd a serious mischief if she fired it. Quite simply it wasn't in Peregrine's nature to expose any woman to the risk of injury.

However, his imprisonment had at least allowed him time to reason why things had turned out the way they had.

From the start he simply hadn't been ready for Mrs Lloyd's preparedness. It was as if she'd been expecting him—or someone like him. And when she'd decided he wasn't all he'd been pretending to be she'd had a programme ready to implement—to hold him pending advice. She'd been a step ahead of him the whole time, except for the brief period when she'd relaxed her defences—when she'd stopped suspecting his motives, and begun making plans for dalliance in the Scimitar. That was when she'd given him the cottage address in the hope he'd drive to Evesham and take her with him. He was sure she wasn't meant to have parted with that address— that his knowing it was the reason she couldn't let him go, as well as the reason why it was imperative he escape in time to reach Evesham by two.

She had kept her distance while he had been undressing in the living room—making him empty his pockets onto a table and place his clothes in a neat pile. He had not been particularly aware of the way she had assessed his revealed physique but she had given him a good and un-erotic reason why she wanted him stripped.

'I may have to keep you here for quite a bit, dear,' she had explained as she'd motioned him into the bathroom, keeping the same safe distance she had done since producing the gun. 'Don't try breaking down the door.

It's a good solid one. So's the lock. The airduct behind that fan's too small to get your head in even, and it goes out through the kitchen. Don't try flooding the place or I'll switch the water off at the stopcock. And don't try shouting, or banging on the walls. Nobody'll hear you. The next door people are away for the weekend.' She had looked him up and down slowly, with the gun pointing at an area of his anatomy he felt was even more acutely vulnerable than his chest. 'Pity you didn't turn out the innocent I thought you were. As it is, you can stay in the raw in case you give trouble. If you do I'll scream blue murder and swear you're trying to rape me. It'll be your word against mine. And with your clothes off I know whose word'll get taken.'

It was then she had announced she was expecting the call.

'Is it Rudy who's ringing?' he'd asked.

'Never mind who's ringing, dear. I can tell you you'll make life easier for yourself if you'll say why you're here. And who sent you.'

'But I've told you. Nobody sent me. I brought myself. To enquire about a painting Rudy's interested in. An old painting.'

'And I've said I don't believe you. Rudy isn't into pictures. So I still want the real reason.'

'Mrs Lloyd, I've given it to you. And I can't see why you won't tell me where Rudy is. If I can talk to him I can explain. There'd be nothing underhand in that.'

'Taking his photo was though. Sneaky that was. For someone who's supposed to know him. So, you going to answer my question?'

She had waited for a response. He had made none. Treasure had told him not to say Frenk was dead. In any case he didn't know what effect that piece of intelligence would have on Mrs Lloyd and hadn't been minded to find out at the time.

'Well, please yourself,' she'd ended. 'If you're thirsty there's plenty of water in the taps. I'm not bringing you food, but you don't look as if you'll starve for a few hours.'

Ever since she had locked the door and left he had been able to listen to her movements. Despite the solidity of the building the sound insulation was poor. She seemed remarkably busy, vacuum cleaning and shifting furniture a good deal of the time below and in Frenk's flat. Latterly she had been clattering about in her kitchen.

Peregrine had small hope of Mrs Lloyd going out. With his car parked outside, the possible need for her later to claim he had been detaining her against her will was enough to keep her in. It was just that dog owners usually walked their pets at ritual intervals, and even though Tai Fung didn't look like a keen exerciser, there was still a chance in that area: from time to time Peregrine had listened hopefully to the animal's complaining yaps. There had been no purpose in trying anything so noisy as breaking down a wall or door while Mrs Lloyd was in. It wasn't until later he'd found a more promising escape method—and quieter too.

Peregrine's prison comprised half the space occupied by the original bathroom. The other half—the part with a window—had been made into a kitchen. Mrs Lloyd had explained that when she had been showing him around.

The room was an oblong measuring about seven feet by four, painted blue, with a white panelled bath against one long wall and a matching washbasin in the centre of the other with an empty, mirror-fronted medicine cabinet sticking out above it. The WC was on the narrow wall opposite the door. There was a strip light on the ceiling, and cork tiles on the floor. The only movables were a plastic nail brush, a roll of toilet tissue, a hand towel and a bath mat. Frenk had taken all his toilet accessories with him. The small extruder fan was set in the kitchen partition wall which was made of breeze block, not board as Peregrine had hoped before he'd scraped away some of the plaster. That wall might still have been the most promising place for a forced exit, but again a noisy one.

Peregrine was determined not to attempt anything that would precipitate Mrs Lloyd having him taken into custody accused of sexual assault. The consequences of such a happening could be too awful to contemplate. Vanessa, his fiancée, was broad minded and trusting; her father sometimes proved to be less so: the effects of being charged with something unsavoury anyway tended to linger, even if innocence was later proved. Peregrine had been framed by an unscrupulous woman once before—a general's mistress who had not been above using gullible, chivalrous Subaltern Gore to save her reputation after she'd been found in a compromising situation during a brigade ball. That episode had done him lasting damage and so, he felt, could Mrs Lloyd: being accident prone over a long period at least offered object lessons in caution.

The young banker had also worked out that anyone accused of a serious crime on the eve of Easter Day would risk spending two days in cells before a magistrates' court was convened. That could conceivably meet Mrs Lloyd's purpose better than having him locked in Frenk's bathroom, but the prospect hardly suited Peregrine.

It was why he had done two hours' exhausting work on the access hole to the roofloft. Now at least he knew it *was* an access hole.

Searching the room earlier, he had noticed an oblong patch in the ceiling plaster, next to the kitchen wall, immediately above the washbasin. It was roughly thirty inches long and half as wide. The proportions fitted with the masking of what could have been the recess below a loft access cover—something made over with plasterboard during the partitioning. Probably a new loft access had been cut somewhere else.

By standing with one foot on the basin and the other on the bath, Peregrine had just been able to reach the edges of the patch with the hard corner of the nail brush. He had worked around the outline, applying as much pressure as he could with his upstretched, aching arms until the patch had separated from the rest of the ceiling on three sides. There was no edge at the partition wall which confirmed that the patch was probably square, with its other half on the kitchen side of the ceiling.

Bending the patch downwards, Peregrine could see the shallow, square empty space behind it, boxed around in wood. Six inches above that was what he had expected—an easily identifiable loft access cover. Before attempting what he next had in mind he needed to be sure the cover would open. There had been a pause in operations at this point before he thought of unclipping the metal arm and attached ballcock from the inside of the low level WC cistern. With this he was able gradually to push the cover aside into the roof space: he used the same rough implement to saw off the bathroom side of the ceiling patch.

The work so far had been fairly noiseless—after he'd stopped the cistern from overflowing by jamming down the ballcock joint with the nail brush. Sitting on the side of the bath he listened for Mrs Lloyd's movements. For minutes there was no sound at all, then, praise be, came the familiar staccato notes of a familiar signature tune. She had turned on the TV for the BBC one o'clock news with the sound level very high. There wouldn't be a better opportunity for covering noise.

After stuffing the bath rug and hand towel inside the porcelain washbasin, Peregrine set himself up, balancing with both feet on the edge of the bath and opposite the basin. Next, treading as lightly as he could, in a continuous movement he stepped onto the basin with his left foot, sprung the right foot up onto the narrow top of the cabinet, brought the left alongside it as, with arms outstretched, he thrust upwards with both feet.

Before the cabinet came off the wall, which he had guessed it would, there had been enough upward purchase for his fingers to have reached and grasped the edge of the loft access. Still using the momentum of the initial thrust, his arms pulled his head and shoulders through the gap. The wooden cabinet fell into the basin but the noise was muffled by the bath rug and towel: the mirror hadn't smashed. The back of his head had hit the frame of the hole which had also grazed his shoulders, but his trunk was sprawled inside the loft with legs dangling outside before the pain registered—along with the relief.

There was no time to listen for a reaction from downstairs. Kneeling on a roof joist, he tore at the kitchen side of the ceiling patch. It came away easily. He lowered himself through the hole onto a solid working top, then to the kitchen floor. Soundlessly he moved to the corridor and made for the front room. His possessions were still where he'd been made to leave them. It was as he reached for his shirt he heard, then saw, the police car draw up outside. The two men, one in uniform, were approaching the front door as he was pulling on his trousers. Either they had come because Mrs Lloyd had sent for them or, more likely, they were the first manifestation of official authority following up on Frenk's death. Mr Treasure had estimated Peregrine would be several hours ahead of police enquiries, and the timing seemed right. Also the two men had looked too relaxed to be apprehending a sex maniac.

Whatever the reason for the police visit Peregrine figured he didn't want to be involved in it. He grabbed the rest of his things. At the same time as Tai Fung began his yapping progress from the kitchen to the front door, no doubt at his mistress's heels, Peregrine was creeping along the passage to Frenk's bedroom.

There was a downpipe on the outside wall at the back of the house, quite close to the bedroom window. Peregrine swung out onto it gingerly, hoping it would take his weight—it was cast iron and it did. He figured he was safe escaping at the back of the house while the others were talking at the front. As he reached the ground the voices stopped and he heard the door slam. Mrs Lloyd must have asked the policemen in: it was too soon for her to have sent them away.

He vaulted the low hedge at the side of the house. It wasn't high enough to hide him—nor was the wall beyond, which he fell over. He moved along the pavement of the side street on all fours towards the front of the house. Two little girls playing tag around the corner lamp post stopped to point at him and giggled. He made a funny face at them. They made funny faces back and got onto their haunches, hopping about and screaming with delight. Peregrine had always found it easy to amuse children. Perhaps he could use these as cover—not that he really needed it. Mrs Lloyd and her visitors must be in the living room at the back by now.

When he was opposite the front door he stood up, and hurried forward, waving a farewell to the girls who were turning into a gateway further along the street. He even smiled at Mrs Lloyd's plastic gnomes while reaching in his pocket for his ignition key. He was feeling a certain elation at the success of his escape plan while he blinked into the sun which was shining directly into his eyes.

The police car was parked immediately behind the Scimitar. There was another uniformed constable at the wheel.

'Excuse me, sir,' the officer called, getting out. 'Could I have a word?'

# CHAPTER 18

'But Clarence Emdon's painting wasn't the one you were looking for. It wasn't even valuable. Or that old,' observed Treasure.

'It has great superstitious value to the people of Brutsky,' replied Colonel Grinyev in a tone indicating he had no intention of having the matter dismissed that lightly.

The two men were walking briskly along the wide Neva Embankment. They were just across the road from the statue of the Bronze Horseman—scene of a dramatic encounter involving the other elderly male member of the Baroque Circle, but an episode which fortunately neither had heard about.

When the coach had returned from Pushkin the colonel had been waiting to see Treasure. It had been the Russian's idea to walk up to the river. It was 5.45. The weather was cold but dry.

'Incidentally, where is Brutsky?' Treasure enquired.

'East of here. On the way to Volkhov. It's a small place.'

'And the portrait was of some kind of local saint?'

'Not a saint,' said Grinyev gruffly. 'Not canonised or anything like that. He was Dymitry Pavlych, the village priest. A century and more ago.'

'Miracle worker and champion of the people. Canon Emdon said he supported the peasants against a wicked landlord. Bit of a revolutionary. Before his time, perhaps?

Anyway, that's why they revered him. Wanted the likeness back.'

'Your Canon Emdon is a fool. He'd say anything.' The colonel frowned. 'There were no miracles. The picture is a peasant daub. I've just seen it. It used to be set into the stone cross on the priest's grave. Nothing special, even if it's the original, which I doubt. In later times photographs were used on graves for the same purpose.'

'But this picture was taken out of Russia. To America. By immigrants from Brutsky. After the Revolution. And now it's been sent back as an act of faith. From an Orthodox congregation in Chicago. It's a touching story really. The canon volunteered to bring the picture.'

'By stealth. It wasn't necessary. And none of his business. He's not even a member of the Orthodox Church.'

'Ah, Christians try to pull together these days. You mean he could have declared the picture at customs? Then posted it on to the devout of Brutsky where they're trying to get their church going again?'

'Something like that,' Grinyev replied less certainly than before. 'If they lease the old building, and find money to pay a priest, probably they will get their church. There's freedom to worship in the USSR. There are four working Christian churches right here in Leningrad.'

'Serving a population of four million?'

'Very few people are religious. Also there are other places of worship for other religions. The Orthodox churches are not always full. In Moscow there are fifty of them.' Grinyev frowned. 'It was underhand to bring the picture that way. Also to involve the man from Brutsky.'

'But he involved himself. It was he who arranged to meet Canon Emdon on the bridge at Pushkin. I don't know how. Nor why the chap couldn't have come to Leningrad.'

The other man loosened the scarf he was wearing in a delaying gesture. 'His internal passport didn't allow him

to come here. Unless he got special permission. Which
he could have done. Easily. For any innocent reason.'
The Russian ended emphatically.

'But his passport was good for Pushkin?'

'Yes. And many other places.'

'They wanted the portrait now because next week is
grave-cleaning time. When they wash the stones. Paint
the railings. Cut the grass. Before the Orthodox Easter
Sunday. I'm told it's an old custom being revived all over
the country.' It was Valya who had told him that the day
before, but he didn't intend to say so. 'And on the actual
day of remembrance—that's next Saturday—I gather
relatives come to the graves bringing flowers, and painted
eggs, and . . .'

'Bottles of vodka. It's just an excuse for drunken
parties.'

'And that's the worst harm it can do?' Treasure paused,
also in his steps, drawing the other to stand with him at
the embankment balustrade looking across the river. 'You
know, the views in this city could be compared with any
in the world,' he remarked carefully and pointedly.

'The floodlit building over there is the Academy of
Sciences.' Grinyev removed his gloves and began to
smooth the stone under his hands, watching the movement
of his fingers. There was silence for a moment. 'But you
meant the other kind of views. The spoken kind. Our
judgments.'

'I meant those as well.'

The colonel looked up. 'Canon Emdon will be returned
to the hotel later. He will not be allowed out tonight nor
in the morning until it's time to take the coach to the
airport. He has caused a great deal of trouble. He is very
lucky we are so tolerant of mischief makers. And bloody
fools. It's not surprising he hasn't been in touch with the
American Consul here. He is well known as an agitator. In the German Democratic Republic. We've been
checking. He's had contact here with an East German

who only pretends to have legitimate business in the USSR.'

'Chap called Brendt? From Dresden? He's an art dealer.'

'Also suspected of criminal activities.'

'Not another religious agitator? Didn't look like one.'

'A trader in icons. The kind forbidden for export. He's been watched since he's been here.'

'But he's now left. I don't believe Emdon knows him at all well, and he certainly wasn't cultivating him. Quite the opposite. I'm sure it was coincidence they were here together. At the same hotel. I know Brendt was enquiring for Emdon as we were leaving for Pushkin today, probably . . .'

'We knew it also,' the other interrupted.

Treasure shook his head. 'So that's why your blood-hounds followed Emdon around Pushkin.'

'That was fortunately the case,' Grinyev replied sternly. Then after a pause continued, 'So this time we excuse him. But he mustn't come back.'

Treasure hesitated. 'Thank you, Colonel. I'm very grateful.'

'And I am disappointed.'

'Because you thought you'd found the stolen painting?'

'Exactly. So would you have been.'

The last comment seemed to re-establish the easy, earlier relationship.

'What happens to the Blessed Dymitry?'

'He's confiscated.' Grinyev managed a wry grin. 'As an art lover what would you expect? It's a terrible piece of painting.'

'Will he ever get to Brutsky?'

'That's an internal matter. Not for me to say.'

'Not even if we found your important picture? Or caught Frenk's murderer? Or even both?'

The colonel turned sharply to study the speaker's face. 'You have some new information?'

'Not yet, but that may be a good thing. We've been

wondering during the afternoon why my . . . my assistant in England didn't call earlier when he could have done. My wife thinks he may have had good reason. That he was onto something he couldn't interrupt. It's just her intuition at work. But she could be right.'

'He has a call booked for six, I think?'

Treasure nodded. 'Which means I ought to be getting back to the hotel.' He moved away from the river wall. 'D'you want to listen to the call?'

'That's not possible. I have someone to see now. But I shall be back quite soon.'

'I'll bring you up to date then.' It was only an exchange of niceties: Treasure was quite sure the calls from the hotel manager's office were being recorded.

'Shall I drop you at the hotel?' Grinyev indicated the black saloon drawn up at the kerb nearby. It had been following them at a discreet distance since they had left the Astoria. Now the driver got out. There was already a passenger in the back.

'Thank you. Just one more thing.' The pavement was wide and they were still out of hearing distance of the car. 'You mentioned the airport coach in the morning. You're not intending to hold anyone from our party here?'

'No. Not at the moment. You should be free to leave.' The Russian shrugged. 'Of course, the body of Frenk will remain. That is already agreed with your embassy in Moscow.' He had been studying his feet. Now he looked up into Treasure's face. 'That birthmark on Frenk's brow. It was fake. A long-lasting dye. It looked so real the pathologist didn't give it priority. Frenk's idea of an adornment you think?'

Treasure looked surprised. 'Bit unusual, I'd have thought. But people do curious things to their appearances these days. So perhaps it was some kind of decoration. Hm, I imagine it might have been illegal to have it on his passport picture.'

'In your country and mine. Did I tell you he had especially good teeth?' the other man rejoined unexpectedly. 'No fillings. No extractions. Pity. You can learn a lot from dental work.'

It was half an hour later when an angry Treasure left the Blintons' room and stalking further down the corridor knocked at Nigel Dirving's door.

'Come in. Take a pew,' the actor invited. 'I'm bathed and changed already. Killing time before dinner. Like a Scotch? I've got plenty. Duty-free. You look peeved.' He was even more ebullient than usual—and more verbose. 'Expect you know they're releasing old Emdon. He'll be on parole apparently. Confined to the Astoria till we leave, Candy says. Fate worse than death. No, what am I saying? He's probably lucky in the circumstances. Did you have a hand in fixing it?'

'Not really.' Treasure accepted the proffered drink and sat in the only armchair. The room was similar to the one he had just left, but not as tidy. He had half expected to find Miss Harwick here, but was glad Dirving was on his own. There was a woman's silk headscarf on top of the television receiver: he couldn't place the owner, except it was too expensive to be Miss Harwick's. 'I've just talked to one of my people on the 'phone.'

'In London?' Dirving picked up his own drink and settled on the edge of the bed.

'Actually Evesham.'

'Where they grow all the fruit? Charming old town.'

'Frenk shared a cottage near there. Did you ever visit it?'

Dirving looked puzzled. 'Of course I didn't. I never knew the chap. Not before we met here. That is, at Heathrow.'

'During the flight from London you persuaded Sol Blinton to stage one of his heart-block attacks on arrival here. On a signal from you. When he and his wife had cleared immigration and were waiting for you to do the same.'

'But that's preposterous. Why should I . . . ?'

'That's exactly what I need to know,' Treasure interrupted stiffly. 'Why did you? As to its being preposterous, both the Blintons admit it. I can get them in to say so if necessary. If you want to waste the time?'

'I still don't see what business . . . Oh, very well. I did ask them. And to keep it to themselves,' he added in a hurt tone. 'I was worried about something in my passport. I wanted them to create a little diversion. To stop the inspector dwelling on the fact I'd been to Israel twice recently.'

'Which is the nonsense you fed the Blintons, and which Sol accepted, for natural reasons. But he was a late recruit for what appears to have been a vital job. So who did you have lined up for it earlier? Someone not so convincing?'

The other man remained tight lipped.

Treasure decided not to press the last point. 'Well, I'm sorry, I don't accept your explanation. The Russian authorities had our passports for examination weeks before we came. If your visits to Israel bothered them—and heaven knows why they should have—they'd have done something about it earlier.'

'But you can't tell with these people. They might have assumed I'd been cooking up something for those refusenik people.'

Treasure shook his head impatiently. 'You had Sol time his attack for the moment your passport was handed back to you. The first passport.'

'I don't understand.'

'Neither did I till just now. Your passport was cleared, but you didn't go through the barrier. I was watching and it puzzled me at the time. I thought I must have been mistaken. That you hadn't been cleared before all that fuss over Sol. Before the passport man got involved with the French doctor, and closed the booth. Anyone else might have reached the same conclusion. People don't normally fail to go through an immigration barrier once they've been cleared. It's not logical. But what you did was bend down and fiddle with your hand baggage. Then, at the height of the fuss, you dropped back into the queue. That's when you switched across to the other line. The one Molly and I were in. It was also when you put a hat on. At a curious angle.'

'I'd no idea you'd followed my movements so meticulously. Pity you hadn't asked for an explanation earlier. I could have . . .'

'I was interested when your actions didn't fit with the expected,' Treasure interrupted, sure of his ground. 'Was the hat to cover the phony birthmark? Something you'd prepared? As some kind of transfer perhaps? Using stage make-up? Something you put on when you were messing about with your hand baggage?'

The colour had suddenly drained from Dirving's face. He made as though to speak, but no words came. He got up to refill his glass, turning his back on Treasure who was watching his movements alertly.

'The person we knew as Frenk was more thorough,' the banker continued. 'He used a long-lasting dye for the mark. But then he needed to wear the thing the whole time. You had to get rid of it after you went through immigration the second time, with the other inspector—and customs clearance too, of course. You must have had to do that twice. But it was much easier than immigration. Such a crush of people humping baggage about, with five or six inspection tables. Not at all organised. I wasn't watching but it was probably easy to clear two bags and get two customs declarations stamped. With your hat on of course, and the birthmark under it still, ready for showing if required. To go with Frenk's identity. That mark was a brilliant invention on somebody's part.'

'God's, I imagine,' said Dirving with an attempt at coolness. He had turned about to face Treasure but continued to stand with his back to the refrigerator. 'Poor Frenk had a natural red birthmark above his left eye. I assume that's what you're going on about.'

'Wasn't natural, I'm afraid. But that's of no consequence. You and Frenk's impersonator looked a bit alike, of course.'

'What d'you mean, impersonator?'

'I think you know well enough. Look, this is a hell of a lot more serious for you than you seem to imagine. And I'd advise you to stop being so obtuse. In your own interests.' The other man lapsed into stolid silence as Treasure went on: 'You're a bit taller and older than our Frenk. But height doesn't signify on a passport photo, and that short haircut you've had makes you look younger. But, in any case, the birthmark provided instant identification. It would fix anyone's attention who needed to recognise you from a picture. Clever. Like the whole plan. So was the execution. I'll give you that. You went through immigration and customs here as two people.'

'And I'm supposed to have done the same at Heathrow?' Dirving suddenly responded, but more enquiring than challenging.

'Undoubtedly you did. Much easier than at this end.' Brow knitted, Treasure studied his drink which he had hardly touched. 'You began by pretending to find Frenk for Candy, and checked him in with his passport, visa and luggage at a different desk from the one she was at. Nobody else saw Frenk, of course. But then nobody else knew him. Or could have seen him, since he wasn't there. Later you actually volunteered to Molly and me that you'd come into the departure lounge twice. Naturally you omitted to say as two people. When we left to get on the plane you gave two boarding passes to the checkers so they had the right apparent number of passengers. I didn't think it could be done, but now I see it can. And how.' Treasure looked up. The other man said nothing. 'The person passing as Frenk was waiting for you here at the airport. Met you as soon as you'd cleared customs for both of you. He took over the bag you'd brought for him and, presto, he was one of us. He was already dressed in second-hand clothes bought here on the black market. Very thorough. They were all British or American made.

That's except for a bit of underwear carelessly acquired in the wrong Germany.'

Dirving had demonstrably paled. 'You can't prove any of this,' he faltered. 'I shall naturally deny . . .'

'Your fingerprints on Frenk's visa?'

'But I made sure . . .' the other stopped in mid-sentence.

'Did you now? Well, the visa's clean enough as it happens, but what about his customs declaration? It's covered in prints. None of them his.' It was the only lie Treasure employed—based on a lucky guess because it eliminated the remains of Dirving's crumbling denials.

The actor sank limply onto the bed again, head between his hands. 'My God. I knew it,' he uttered. 'I just wasn't thinking properly at that point. It was the strain.' He looked up sharply. 'And Grinyev's onto that? He's told you?'

This time it was Treasure who remained silent, staring at the other man.

'All right, it's true. What you've said,' Dirving admitted. 'So what'll they do to me, Mark? You've got to help me. You will, won't you? It was all innocent. And I didn't kill Frenk. It's what you're thinking, isn't it? That I killed him?' The words came in a rush now; the speaker was beside himself with fear.

'Colonel Grinyev is shortly going to know that Frenk isn't dead. The real Frenk, that is. He was seen at the cottage this afternoon, where he was supposed to be lying low for the weekend. So who was the murdered man, Nigel?'

'I don't know.' The sentence came in a despairing whisper.

'You mean you went to all that risk to establish his existence as one of our party. You shared this room with him. And still you don't know who he was?'

'I swear I don't.'

'Why did you get involved in the first place?'

'For money of course. I was broke. They were going

to bankrupt me. But if I co-operated I was in the clear. It didn't seem such a difficult job. Not for a competent actor.' The words flowed easily now. He'd straightened a little as he spoke. 'I carried it off, too. If only the cretin hadn't got himself murdered.'

'How much were you paid?'

'A hundred thousand. Half in advance. It was more than I owed.'

'Who set it up?'

'A woman in Coventry. She'd been lending me money. When I'd been desperate. She took over some of my other debts. Then all of them.'

'A Mrs Lloyd. Blonde. Widow.'

'You know her, Mark? But how . . . ?'

'I know of her. And enough to know she doesn't have that kind of money. So she's an intermediary.'

'I expect so. I don't know.' Dirving's head went between his hands again.

'You've no idea who she works for?'

'None. I only met her once. The rest was done by 'phone and letter. Mark, what'll happen to me?'

'You still swear you weren't involved in the murder?'

'On my life I wasn't. Can't you see I had no reason? Quite the opposite. That death has probably cost me fifty thousand pounds.'

'Then there's a chance nothing will happen to you, if you behave sensibly.'

'But my fingerprints on the customs form?'

'With any luck won't come to light until we're home.' Treasure wasn't prepared to admit to his long-shot guess—but there was every chance he was right. 'What nationality was the dead man?' he demanded after watching the look of partial relief developing on Dirving's face.

'Russian I suppose. I don't know for sure. He wasn't at all communicative.'

'And what else did you have to do for him?'

'Nothing. My job was over once I'd introduced him

. . . that is, once I'd handed over the suitcase and the passport.'

'And introduced him, you said. To whom?'

Dirving hesitated, then swallowed. 'It was an instruction I got. A typed instruction.'

'From Mrs Lloyd?'

'Via her. In a sealed envelope she sent on to me. There were others like that. I don't believe she knew what was in them.'

'And the introduction?'

'As soon as Frenk arrived. As soon as I'd given him the suitcase, I was to introduce him to . . . to Mrs Vauxley.'

# CHAPTER 19

'Did you tell Colonel Grinyev everything?' asked Molly Treasure smiling brightly as she stopped and glanced about her. Onlookers might have deduced she and her husband were exchanging comments on the design of the room—which is exactly what it was intended they should deduce.

'I told him some of the bare truth. That the real Frenk is still in England,' Treasure answered while actually admiring the rows of massive chandeliers that lit the main space.

The couple were standing apart from other people, near the orchestra podium, at the narrower south end of the oblong, unraked, classical auditorium of the Shostakovich Philharmonia Hall.

In any event the hall is impressive and deserved remark. Internally it is constructed along the lines of a Greek temple, with a sentinel, tight unbroken row of white Corinthian columns spreading out from the north end and advancing up the east and west sides to mark the limits of the central space, and shutting off the balconied side aisles. The columns rise to support a handsome architrave, frieze and cornice under a rounded ceiling with inset windows.

The Philharmonia's great height is somehow unexpected because it lies beyond a grand if dauntingly high, straight entrance staircase only relieved in the ascent by a half-landing with cloakrooms at either side. The stairs culminate in the very centre of the hall's north end where arriving concert-goers find themselves emerging in narrow files between the dwarfing columns and onto the central aisle.

The rows of gilt, red plush chairs were slowly filling with people. The Treasures' seats were on the aisle, ten rows from the front.

Molly had come early with the group by coach. Treasure had just arrived by taxi after seeing Grinyev who had turned up at the hotel, at the end of dinner, for the promised report on the telephone call from England. Before this there had been only the briefest opportunity for private conversation between the banker and his wife since he had spoken with Peregrine Gore.

There were still several minutes before the concert was timed to begin: the orchestra—the visiting Leipzig Symphony—had not yet appeared.

Molly took her husband's arm. 'You didn't tell him Frenk's imposter was here all the time?' They began strolling in the area at the side of the podium.

'Certainly not. I don't think he'd have believed me anyway. Not yet. It's such a knock to their security.'

'And ours. So we have to hope he doesn't work it out for himself.'

'Not while we're still in the country. If he knew one of our group had come in as two people he'd certainly keep us here till he found out which one.'

'Nigel would own up, of course.'

'Hm. Since I know it was him I suppose he'd have to.'

'You don't give him much credit.'

'He'd done nothing that deserves any. He's made the whole lot of us accomplices in his wretched conspiracy.'

'But you said he couldn't have killed Frenk. Or whoever it was.'

'I know he couldn't have. And fortunately for him, Grinyev knows it too. Incongruously, he's the only one of the group who couldn't have done it. Apart from you and me. Your precious Nigel has an alibi for the whole interval, though he doesn't know it yet. Apparently that box office foyer, where he said he went to smoke, it's a hot spot for illegal currency trading. And because he looks naturally suspicious . . .'

'Nonsense,' Molly protested, but under a dazzling smile.

'Well for some reason connected with his manner or appearance he was actually under observation. That's from the time he left his seat until well after the murder. The investigating officers watching him weren't in any way connected with Grinyev's lot. Different directorate. It was only because of the murder he was sent a copy of their report today.'

'Well I'm very glad for Nigel. He's here, by the way. With Edwina and Candy. In seats next to us over there. Can you see? I've pretended to him I know nothing. I thought it best. He's quite chirpy, really.'

'So I note. Putting on a brave face is obviously preferable to looking guilty and ashamed,' he answered without allowing the bitterness to show in his face.

'I'm still not clear who had the genuine birthmark. The real Frenk or the murdered one.'

'Neither of them. The imposter acquired one to assist identification. He wore it in the photo used for his passport and visa.'

'And Nigel had a sort of portable mark he put on when required? For the same reason? To fox some people into accepting him as Frenk?'

'At the airports. Worn under his hat which he took off when confronting any official in his Frenk role. If it hadn't been for Peregrine we'd never have got onto it.'

'You'd told him Frenk had a prominent birthmark. Why?'

Treasure said slowly: 'Don't know really. Some sort of premonition perhaps. Anyway, as soon as he saw pictures of the real Frenk he figured we'd had a different one here.'

'Peregrine had a rough time?'

'Fairly. But he'll survive.'

'And do we know yet how the dead man got the use of Frenk's passport with his own picture in it?'

'Plus his personal details generally. Obviously with the real Frenk's co-operation, which would have removed all difficulties. It was a new passport. He'd never applied for one before. Same goes for the visa. I'd like to know who brought those prints to England. Or the negative for them.'

As he finished the sentence Treasure's gaze fell on Mrs Vauxley who was limping up the central aisle. Miss Harwick was behind her, carrying her employer's impedimenta.

Molly's eyes followed her husband's. 'And you don't think Daphne Vauxley is really involved?'

'I can't believe it. Not knowingly involved.'

'But Nigel was told to introduce her to the phony Frenk?'

'To identify her, perhaps. For a reason she may or may not have been aware of.' He continued to study the subject of his comment. 'I may be wrong, but I don't accept . . .'

'We'd better go to our seats,' Molly interrupted. The players were moving onto the stage from a door immediately behind the couple. Most of the audience was now seated. The Treasures took their places on the left-hand side of the aisle in the seats behind Mrs Vauxley and Miss Harwick. All the other members of the Baroque Circle— except for Canon Emdon—were present and placed close-by. Unlike the seats allocated at the opera, this time the group had been put more-or-less together. The Blintons, looking subdued, were beside Mrs Tate and Reggie in the same row as Mrs Vauxley. Jeremy and Felicity Wander were a row ahead of them.

'Dying to hear more about the 'phone call,' Candy leaned across Molly next to her and whispered loudly to Treasure just as the leading violinist, an attractive female, appeared and was greeted with enthusiastic applause from the packed audience. Soon afterwards the conductor came on. He was a large, broad, pink man, fleshy faced with small eyes, a square shaven head, and a bulging neck which, when he turned to conduct, seemed to be threatening to burst his stiff collar. In the same way his back was soon to appear to be testing the seams of his tailcoat.

The whole orchestra was even so impeccably turned out, the men in full evening dress, the women in becoming black dresses. They were a credit to East German elegance if not to its musicality: the playing was to prove unremarkable.

'That conductor looks as if he belongs in a braided uniform and a park bandstand,' Molly observed during the applause after the Mozart overture.

'And the band should be there with him,' her husband responded. 'Those flutes were anything but magical.' Idly he watched the percussionist adjusting a drum, and a trombonist take his instrument apart and blow it through.

During the violin concerto that followed the banker found it difficult to give his attention to the orchestra, though this was not entirely due to the shortcomings of the performance. He didn't much care for the violin as a solo instrument, and his ruminating thoughts were tending to follow his wandering gaze.

Was Dirving—restless legs protruding along the row— telling the truth about Miss Harwick? At the end of that painful interview the actor had sworn her visits to his room had been made when he hadn't been in it—that he'd given her Frenk's key so that she could use the bathroom there at particular times. It was because he had protested the lady's pure reputation too stoutly and for too long, while going on to impugn someone else's, that Treasure had come to doubt his word.

Could Miss Harwick—sitting quite still in front of Molly—conceivably have been the person Dirving was really intended to introduce to Frenk and not Mrs Vauxley? You could hardly become acquainted with the employer without being aware of her companion. But why should Frenk have needed instant introduction to either?

Treasure considered Mrs Vauxley's back: hers was a figure which even in that presentation, or perhaps especially in that presentation, epitomised the essence of British rectitude. It was almost untenable that she could be mixed up in a murder. His eyes dropped to take in the neatly arranged accessories under her seat—the capacious handbag, the stick, the woollen cardigan brought probably for fear that the building, predictably over-heated like all the others they had visited, should freeze over without reason. No doubt Miss Harwick had been obliged to do the bringing.

Edwina Apse interrupted the last train of thought by leaning forward, re-crossing her legs and arranging her skirt over them. This was a ritual that would hardly have gone unremarked by any man in sight of it: they were very shapely legs and the movements were very graceful. Because he found Edwina so agreeable—and that was putting his feelings towards her at their mildest—the banker deplored her involvement with Dirving. He had always considered the actor unworthy of the women who appeared ready to indulge him in one way or another—a group which included not only the man's ex-wife who the Treasures had known, but also Candy, Mrs Vauxley and, it seemed, most of the other women in the Baroque Circle, Molly not excepted.

Dirving had freely admitted to Treasure that his room was empty at night because he had been, as he put it, shacking up with Edwina. Granted the admission had come to strengthen his insistence that he wasn't doing the same with Miss Harwick—but that was exactly why the banker had reservations on both parts of the statement.

When, before dinner on the previous day, Edwina had come out of her room accompanied by Dirving, her attitude had made it clear she was less than enamoured with him—but perhaps this had been calculated. If it had been an act of self-indulgence later for Dirving to boast to Treasure that he had been sharing Edwina's bed, it was one he had quickly regretted when he had come to insist Edwina had not been aware of his two-man impersonation. That had been an assurance which, in the circumstances, the banker had felt uneasy about. And he was certain his doubts over whether Edwina had been privy to the Frenk plan had bothered Dirving a good deal—more than Treasure's earlier implied reservations about Miss Harwick.

Evidently the person who had conceived the Frenk plan had an acuity sharper than those of either Dirving or Mrs Lloyd of Coventry—from what Treasure knew of the first and had learned on the telephone about the second. He believed too that there had been something more at stake than the creation of an identity for the now dead man, who had seemed not to have been a person likely to be valued for his knowledge so much as for something in his possession. And if this was right, and if Grinyev's conviction that the end product involved was a valuable stolen painting, then Edwina's intelligence could make her a front runner as the brain behind the whole enterprise. And her affinity with Coventry compounded that conclusion.

It was because of the geography—Frenk, Mrs Lloyd and Edwina all being connected with the same city—that Treasure was having so much difficulty clearing Edwina from suspicion in his own mind. Even so he was trying.

Clarence Emdon would know how to handle a stolen picture. He was at home in the fine art world and could probably find a source for the kind of funds needed—assuming he wasn't such a source himself. The same probably applied to Reggie Tate, at least in terms of expert knowledge—and they said his mother was wealthy. Could Sol Blinton have been putting a smoke screen over his most serious intentions by too lightly covering his lesser clandestine activities with the refuseniks—a similar ploy to the one Emdon might have been using over the painting of the village saint? And what about the under-

paid Candy? She had the expertise and energy at least to
bring off a dishonest coup and to get her own back on
the art establishment which rewarded her learning so
meanly. And was Amelia Harwick really as downtrodden
as she appeared? Earlier the banker had been convinced
she had quietly captivated Dirving—and he wasn't at all
sure yet he'd been wrong, nor about the other consequences that such an involvement might entail.

But in these postulations was he simply demonstrating
a concern for Edwina he didn't feel for the others—
especially those others who were not female or, even if
they were, then not so beguilingly so to maturing bankers!
And on second thoughts were any of them really capable
of raising the cash that had to be involved? Come to that,
was Edwina? He frowned to himself as his glance again
moved along the row. In his experience an attractive
intelligent woman could usually borrow money *in extremis*
if she couldn't find it any other way. Which brought him
back in a circle to the inescapable Coventry ingredient.
Was there anybody else . . . ?

'Very insensitive playing, I thought,' Molly commented
over the noise of the clapping at the end of the concerto.
As she added her own token applause she continued quite
loudly: 'That pace was positively martial. You could
almost believe it *is* a military band. Now I'm certain the
conductor belongs in uniform.'

'Failed army officer attempts classical music con as last
resort,' offered Candy from Molly's other side. 'Pleads
he did it for the money,' she added with a giggle.

'You know, that could be absolutely right,' uttered
Treasure, but almost to himself, his gaze fixed on the
piglet-eyed, bowing conductor. What he'd said had not
been so much a comment on the girl's remark—more a
spontaneous reaction to the notion she'd just sparked.
Suddenly a lot of apparently unrelated things began fitting
together in his mind.

Mrs Vauxley turned around. 'Heaven knows what

they'll do to the Beethoven after the interval,' she observed savagely, then made to get up.

'D'you want your stick? Allow me,' said Treasure delving under the chair in front.

'Only because I need to go to the ladies, and there'll be a queue. Like last night. How kind of you.' Mrs Vauxley took the proffered aid from Treasure. 'My bag too, Mark. If it's not too much trouble. No need for you to come, Amelia. Not if you don't need. I didn't see a bar,' the older woman added pointedly as though her companion were an alcoholic in need of restraint or discouragement. Then she straightened and joined the people moving up the aisle. Treasure fell in at her side, following a new determination not to leave her. Molly stayed, talking to Candy and the others. The Wanders too were still in their seats, although Jeremy was glancing back with an uncertain expression.

Unexpectedly there was no queue outside the ladies' room half way down the long staircase. 'Ah,' exclaimed Mrs Vauxley looking vexed at her accoutrements, and clearly now wishing she had brought Miss Harwick along.

'You won't need the stick after all. Let me take it,' said Treasure smiling.

'If you wouldn't mind? It'll just be an encumbrance in there.' She altered her voice to a piercing stage whisper and narrowed her eyes. 'The arrangements are always very cramped in this country, as well as unhygienic.'

When Mrs Vauxley had taken herself off, Treasure moved across to the men's room. The cubicles were small as the lady had pointed out, but he found a vacant one and firmly locked himself in.

# CHAPTER 20

'I still think Beethoven's Seventh in twenty-nine minutes eighteen seconds has to be a world record,' growled Jeremy Wander while helping Mrs Vauxley off the coach. They had sat together on the short journey. He handed back her stick.

'With the strings a critical second slower than that. And never quite catching up with the conductor who beat them by a short head. On a thick neck. What a riot,' expounded Candy Royce, chuckling as she stepped down to join the others.

'It was a spirited performance. You could say eighty per cent proof,' offered Miss Harwick who seldom attempted drollery but wanted to say something bright because Treasure had just taken her arm.

'I've never laughed so much at a concert,' said Sol Blinton, lifting the back of his collar against the stiff breeze. 'Maybe they were worried about catching the plane back to Leipzig.' He was walking between his wife and Molly.

'I don't really think you missed anything by not coming back after the interval.' This was Miss Harwick to Treasure again.

'Except the hilarity. By the way, there really wasn't a bar.' He gave her a conspiratorial smile to which she responded eagerly.

'Didn't think classical music was supposed to be

funny,' said Gloria Blinton uncertainly. 'Oh, isn't the reflection on the water lovely?'

'And will you just look at those buildings? Aren't they great?' The slight Mrs Tate was enthusing close behind but wobbling a bit with the buffeting wind fairly driving her along.

'It was worth coming for that view all by itself,' Edwina agreed, putting a supporting arm through the older woman's.

Despite the problems attending their trip, the members of the Baroque Circle were determinedly enjoying their last minor excursion. Instead of returning directly to the hotel after the concert, as originally arranged, the coach had taken them over the bridge between the Hermitage and the Admiralty to Strelka Point—a granite-walled, half-circular promontory jutting into the water just upstream of the bridge. The panorama being exclaimed upon is the most celebrated in Leningrad, especially at night when the impressive string of buildings back across the Neva are sensitively illuminated.

'Bit cooler, wouldn't you think? Yah,' said Felicity Wander who had been last off the coach with Dirving. She wrinkled her nose and bared her teeth at the wind like a scenting hare.

'It'll be in our backs over here. Water's high too. I'd say less than eight feet below the top of the wall,' said Dirving who hadn't been saying much all evening.

'Yah, and choppy. But you can't see the chunks of ice floating in it like you can in the day.' For once Felicity was wearing her glasses.

'You will when the moon comes out in a minute,' said Mrs Tate who Felicity had joined, standing above the water. 'Strong current running too.'

Now the whole group was lined along the river wall. Miss Harwick was next to her employer with Treasure on her other side. Wander was on the far side of Mrs Vauxley.

'Shall I take your stick?' Miss Harwick enquired.

'Yes,' Mrs Vauxley replied tersely, thrusting the object on her companion, then continuing her interrupted conversation with Wander. It was customary for her to dispose of any encumbrance not actively in use in this way—and usually without thanks. The foot-wide wall was low enough for her to lean on, so she didn't need her auxiliary seat.

Miss Harwick laid the stick on top of the wall just as Treasure, leaning forward sharply to say something to Wander, jogged her arm. Her hand hit the stick which shot off the wall into the water.

'Oh no!'' Miss Harwick cried in horror.

'I'm dreadfully sorry.' Treasure reacted loudly.

'Look it's going to float. It's drifting away,' called Mrs Tate.

It was at the same moment that the shirt-sleeved Wander hit the water with a mighty splash.

There were gasps all around the group. The man had jumped into the icy river without hesitation. He had simply shed his jacket and sheepskin coat together, pulled off his shoes, and launched himself over the parapet.

'He must be crazy,' said the astonished Reggie Tate.

'Lifebelt. Everybody look for a lifebelt,' shouted Sol Blinton.

'I'll fetch a policeman,' called Candy, turning about and starting to run back towards the road.

'I don't understand,' said Mrs Vauxley and meaning it.

'Yah, he's a super swimmer,' Felicity offered with incredible coolness.

'He'll need to be. Is he drunk?' This came bluntly from Dirving who was now behind Treasure. With the others they watched Wander recover from his drop, wipe the water from his face and strike out for the aluminium stick which was certainly floating—but some four or five yards away from him towards the main stream where the ripples from his initial contact with the water had helped to push it.

'He's going to freeze. Darling, what can we do?' Molly

spoke at Treasure's side. 'Is he quite mad?' she added in a whisper.

'He's proving a point,' the banker answered without taking his eyes off the swimmer.

'But not winning one,' Molly answered.

'No. I'm afraid it's my point.'

Wander still hadn't reached the stick. It had seemed to be only just beyond his reach but his arms which had thrashed out vigorously seconds before were visibly weakening. It was difficult for those watching to discern whether the stick was moving faster than the swimmer. Then suddenly the moon cleared of cloud and shed a detailing light on what was happening. The wind off the near shore plus the current were carrying object and pursuer on a diagonal course towards the main stream. The further both got from the lee of the low river wall the faster they moved—except the distance between them had definitely increased. The glinting stick was just visible still.

'You know he's going to be carried away,' uttered Dirving almost under his breath.

'Look at what's behind him.' The horrified Mrs Tate elbowed those on either side and pointed at a huge cluster of fused ice-floes moving very fast on what appeared to be a collision course with Wander.

'Can he get up on it?' asked the ingenuous Gloria whose words the others ignored.

They could all see Wander was hesitating, but from the shore it wasn't clear whether this was because the stick had sunk, or because the swimmer had calculated the increased danger he was in.

'Jeremy, come back now!' roared Reggie Tate cupping his hands. Some of the others took up the cry.

'But how will you get him out?' This was Edwina.

Nigel Dirving began taking off his topcoat. 'If he can make it back, we'll pull him up. Two of you can lower me down head first . . .'

'I don't think that'll be necessary.' Treasure was

looking to their right. The wind had masked the noise of the engine but a big black motor-launch with a cabin midships had emerged from under the inshore span of the bridge. It was doggedly riding the choppy water, its high prow throwing a lot of spray. The searchlight above the cabin came on now, its beam flickering across the water until it picked up the swimmer and held him. Then there was a sharp engine spurt, with water cauldroning behind the low, rear section of the vessel where two life-jacketed men were crouched at the gunwale.

The intention had evidently been to swing the bow of the fast-moving boat hard to the left into the wind just after it came up to Wander, to let him drift down to the after part of the vessel where he could be hauled in over the shallow gunwale there. But whoever was steering hadn't seen the ice-floe. What happened took only an instant, but the result was devastating.

Those watching horrified from the shore saw the boat's bow come around to slap into the packed ice—with Wander's head squeezed between the two like a nut in a cracker.

The jagged ice reared back and for a second Wander's head and raised arms were exposed, illuminated by the searchlight—the head bloody, the arms and empty hands held up but strangely lifeless; there was no stick. The gap closed again before either of the men could reach the swimmer although they had both scrambled forward as the boat's engine was thrust into reverse with the bow still swinging to port. One of the men signalled to the helmsman, crossed the boat, then jumped into the water on what was now the windward side. It was several seconds before he bobbed up again—and in full sight of the onlookers. He had Wander's body in his arms.

'Oh no. No,' breathed Felicity. Molly took her shoulders and tried to turn her away from the sight, but she wasn't to be moved.

'I know the man who jumped. He works for Colonel Grinyev,' said Sol, suddenly proud of the acquaintance.

'They both work for me, Mr Blinton,' came Grinyev's voice from behind. He was standing beside Candy Royce.

'I found a policeman,' said Candy dully.

Sir Jeremy Wander was dead when they brought him ashore.

'I think I'd rather walk. It's such a gorgeous still morning after that awful wind last night,' said Molly taking Mark Treasure's arm and blinking in the sunshine. It had been dark still when they had arrived at St Nicholas cathedral by taxi an hour before.

'Bit under a mile. Do us good,' Treasure smiled approvingly. He had snatched three hours' sleep only— not counting short naps while awaiting telephone calls in Colonel Grinyev's office in the early hours.

He had kept his promise of the day before to take Molly to the seven o'clock mass. The congregation had been quite small and made up mostly of elderly women who had treated the tourists with more surprise than suspicion—as well as with tentative half-smiles. The two had found it difficult to follow the service but enjoyed the atmosphere of worship in a thoroughly baroque building set in a garden. St Nicholas had been the choice of the unfortunately still restricted Canon Emdon. Mrs Tate had intended to come with them but, like all the others, she had missed a good deal of sleep and hadn't appeared by the appointed time.

'How d'you feel, darling?' Molly enquired as they followed a shrub-lined pathway out of the cathedral grounds, with what was left of the winter's snow glinting on evergreen leaves on either side.

'I feel less fraught.' He shook his head. 'Still responsible for what happened of course. I'd really no idea anyone'd be fool enough actually to chuck himself in. Grinyev thought it possible. He was right. I was simply expecting a less dramatic reaction.'

'You weren't responsible. Jeremy was crazy. Felicity

said so herself. Several times to Edwina and me.' She looked up into his face. 'You want to talk about it yet?'

'Sure.' He had been past discussing anything when he had got back to their room at three-thirty in the morning. Since they had got up neither the time nor his feelings had been right for conversation. 'You know it was the German conductor, your military bandmaster, who put me on to Wander?'

'Because he was an over-sized Jeremy? Those eyes. The generally over-fed look?' She grimaced. 'They were a bit alike.'

'Mm. And Candy's remark about his being an ex-soldier gone crooked.'

'Jeremy being an ex regular.'

'Much more than that. You told me ages ago he'd been in one of the old provincial regiments. As local gentry it almost had to have been the Eastwick Yeomanry, recruited from Easthamptonshire and Warwickshire. And he *was* in the Eastwicks. Retired as a captain. I asked him when we were coming out of the Philharmonia.'

'And it meant something?'

'I thought so.' They turned into Mayorova Prospect that led directly to their hotel in St Isaac's Square. What traffic there was consisted mostly of buses—empty buses which made one wonder why there were so many of them. The gilded spire of the Admiralty sparkled in the sunshine and was clearly visible at the very bottom of the avenue. As Valya had said, it was difficult to get lost in Leningrad.

'The husband of Mrs Lloyd was a corporal in the Eastwicks,' Treasure went on. 'Earlier I'd been hung up on the idea whoever was involved with Frenk was probably connected with Coventry.'

'Except Nigel Dirving wasn't.'

'Only indirectly when Mrs Lloyd acquired some of his debts, and eventually all of them. That was obviously by intention.'

'So he was connected through a not so obvious thread.

Not like Edwina who actually lived there but had really never met Frenk.'

'Nor any of the others involved,' he replied firmly. 'No, the thread was Albert Lloyd, deceased, from Coventry in Warwickshire. He must have served in the Eastwicks under Captain Sir Jeremy Wander, owner of Wander Hall in the next county. Possibly his company commander.'

'But he was long since dead.'

'Which moves us along to his widow, a raver past her peak, who is doing surprisingly well on an army pension. Has her own house, her own sauna clinic, her own money lending business, and a tenant upstairs called Rudy Frenk. That was another thread. And quite a thick one.'

'So Mrs Lloyd had a backer, you thought?'

'Well, I couldn't believe the woman described by Peregrine Gore possessed the material and mental resources to fund this caper. Not involving the lifting of a priceless Raphael from the State Hermitage.'

'Nor the conjuring up here of a non-existent member of the Baroque Circle?'

'And I didn't believe she'd organised his cold-blooded murder either. There had to be a puppet-master. Someone who was pulling all the strings. A machiavellian operator with a first-rate twisted mind.'

'Who kept the puppets separate.'

'So each did a job without knowing what the whole operation entailed.' He stopped speaking as they hurried across an intersection just ahead of a changing light and a bus revving up for the off. 'I was certain the big boss couldn't have been Dirving,' said Treasure as they reached the other side of the road.

'And you didn't want it to be Edwina, because you're really rather fond of Edwina.' She squeezed his arm affectionately.

'She might have managed everything else, but not the murder. Too brutal and too expert. And none of the others seemed to have the totally right connections. Although I couldn't be sure. Circumstantially Wander was beginning to look right. And then I recalled something more factual about him.'

'Let me guess. He gave Daphne Vauxley the sitting stick.'

'Not only gave it her, but kept it in sight virtually the whole time when she was out with it. And it was the perfect repository for the painting. In an emergency it even floated,' he added bitterly. 'It came to me when I was watching one of the players take his trombone apart last night. When I was still trying to figure why Nigel Dirving had been instructed to introduce Frenk to Mrs Vauxley.'

'It wasn't Daphne he had to know so much as her stick?'

'Exactly. And do you remember where it was on the coach? When we left the airport?'

'Mm . . . on the row of seats behind us probably. With the other things. Immediately behind Daphne.'

'And immediately in front of the bogus Frenk. A ready-made opportunity. It took me five seconds to unscrew the base and take out the rolled up canvas in the gents last night. It wouldn't have taken our Frenk much longer to put it in. Pretending to fiddle with his belongings on the seat. It was pretty dark in the coach.'

'And that was his job done?'

'Unfortunately for him.'

'Because Jeremy killed him. Why?'

'Either because he'd have been much more of a liability alive than dead—here and in England. Or because he'd been promised too much for doing the job. I think the second reason. Or it could have been a combination of both. But Jeremy was pretty generous with his advance promises. Dirving was to get a hundred thousand for his part. Our Frenk may have been in for half the take. Easy to offer but maybe hard for Jeremy to stomach, once he actually had the picture.'

'And who was our Frenk?'

'Someone called Vasilefski. Sergey Vasilefski. A disappointed aspirant to Intourist, doing time as an international telephone operator here in Leningrad, and carrying a chip on his shoulder. Spoke good English.'

'We know.'

'And German. Also something of an athlete.'

'And the colonel knows Jeremy killed him?'

'He'd have deduced it anyway. Once we both knew Jeremy was behind the theft of the picture.'

'His alibi for the interval at the opera . . .'

'So called alibi. Even if it happened as he said, it gave him time to buy champagne and get from the bar to Vasilefski on the balcony. He was expert at barging his way through crowds. Remember his performance at Heathrow?'

'So you think Jeremy arranged to meet Vasilefski on the balcony?'

'I'm certain of it. For a glass of champagne, probably, which Jeremy was to bring.'

'With poor Vasilefski in time to be at the front. With his back to Jeremy ready for . . . Oh dear.' Molly shuddered. 'But if Colonel Grinyev knows all this too, surely Jeremy wouldn't have got out of the country this morning? He'd have had to stand trial here? Go to prison?'

'No he wouldn't. Ironically he was quite safe.'

'But they'd never have let him . . .'

'Yes, they would. He'd have got away with the murder. In this country at least. I'm sure of it.' Treasure's tone was deadly serious. 'Not the picture, of course. You see I did a deal with Grinyev. In the Square of the Arts, outside the Philharmonia. A deal it suited him to keep. It was while you were listening to the Beethoven last night.'

# CHAPTER 21

'Can we look at the canal for a minute? That's such a pretty street.' On Molly's whim they stopped to lean over a wrought-iron balustrade, contemplating the nearly still water that ran under the main avenue at an intersection and down the centre of the crossing street to the left. Then, puzzled, she asked: 'But you didn't know anything for certain at the concert?'

'That Wander was the villain? No. And I didn't tell Grinyev I thought so either. I simply rang him at his office and told him I could get the painting back. Actually it was in my pocket at the time and I couldn't get rid of it fast enough. I said Frenk had been the thief, that Frenk was an imposter and almost certainly a Russian, that I thought I could sniff out the murderer, and that I'd trade the painting and the information for safe passage home this morning for the whole of our group. No matter what.'

'Meaning you knew one of us was guilty.'

'He had to assume something of the sort. And so did I. Anyway, he drove over straight away. Met me in the foyer. Insisted we did all the talking outside, in the middle of the square, where we couldn't be overheard. I suppose I was almost as anxious as he was to find out who the murderer was, but not necessarily to have him locked up for ever in Russia.'

'Him, or it might have been a her? Who had to be locked up,' Molly added earnestly.

'That's right.' He cleared his throat. 'Anyway, Grinyev was happy to trade. On my terms.'

'Because he'd get the painting back.'

'And because I could prove it was stolen by a Russian,' Treasure replied slowly. 'That didn't suit at all, of course. Though it was convenient the fellow was dead. Made it possible to return the painting and say nothing. If a foreigner was accused of the murder, one of our party, the whole story would have to come out—even with a show trial.'

'With Jeremy, Nigel, Edwina or somebody pleading guilty to everything, and telling all so as to get a light sentence?'

'I don't believe Grinyev was thinking that far ahead. Only that if one of us did do the murder the same person simply couldn't have stolen the Raphael, because we weren't here when it was pinched.'

'Except Mr. Vaseline . . .'

'Mr Vasilefski was here. Yes, because he lived here and succeeded in nicking an old master and hoodwinking the authorities by becoming an instant British tourist, complete with visa. Not a compliment to any part of the security system. I doubt they'll ever reveal here that the real Frenk is alive and well and living in Coventry. They will at home, I suppose. If it's been announced he's been murdered in Leningrad.'

'To say it was a mistake?'

'Mm. But hardly a front page item. Here I imagine the murder hasn't been announced. And like the stealing of the painting it never will be. Keeps Nigel Dirving out of trouble for his part in the whole business.'

'But the colonel has to know now we brought in a nonexistent member.'

'And how it was done. But he's . . . overlooking it. Part of the general amnesty. Part of the deal.'

'And you're satisfied Nigel didn't know about the painting?'

'Pretty certainly. Nor that Wander was his paymaster.

Nigel thought he'd been hired to fix safe passage for a dissident Russian. That's all. His only contact was Mrs Lloyd. Wander was very circumspect.'

'And you were sure whoever knew the painting was in Daphne's stick would go berserk when it fell in the river?'

'Wouldn't you have? If you'd managed the whole exercise? Think of the expense already involved. The risk.'

'I still wouldn't have dived in after it.'

His face clouded. 'I might have known Wander was capable of it. With everything at stake. He was pretty fit and, I suppose, decisive, in a mad kind of way. He calculated the risk, thought he'd survive, and jumped. Hoped we'd all put it down to an impetuous nature. Anyway, yes. I told Grinyev we'd almost certainly get a leading reaction from the guilty party. He agreed.'

'And he let you set the trap using poor Amelia Harwick as accomplice. Who you briefed on the way from the concert. On the back seat of the coach.'

'She was surprisingly compliant, particularly since I couldn't explain why I wanted the thing dropped in the river. With sound effects.'

Molly's eyebrows arched. 'I'd guess Amelia would do most things you asked of her on the back seat of anything. Still, full marks. She had to cope with the stage management—and weather Daphne's disapproval, after all.'

'Strangely, that didn't seem to bother her. But I had to promise I'd replace the stick if it wasn't recovered.'

'And the colonel set up the motorboat?'

'Which was supposed to be in evidence when we arrived. I assumed something had gone wrong with the arrangements. That it wasn't coming.'

'And police reinforcements were laid on around Strelka Point? I didn't see them. Because they weren't needed?'

'Because there weren't any. Grinyev used a handful of his own picked people, that's all. And he was there himself the whole time. In the background.'

'You counted on his having the authority to do a deal of that size. And not to trick you. After you'd handed over the painting. Wasn't that the biggest risk?'

Treasure leaned further out over the water. 'One understands that high-ups in the KGB are a law to themselves.' He paused, pouting at their reflection below. 'In addition, of course, I trusted him. He was genuinely determined to get the Raphael back because he was genuinely, morally disgusted about its being pinched. And so was I. Does that sound pompous?'

'A bit, but then you are a tiny bit pompous. It suits you, darling.' She kissed him lightly on the ear. 'So how did they eventually identify Vasilefski?'

'Through a baggage claim ticket I found in the stick with the picture. From the Moscow station here. He'd checked in a suitcase. His Russian identity card was in it, with his Russian clothes, a false beard and the bottle of dye he used to make the phony birthmark. I suppose if anything had gone wrong the suitcase was his way back. So he kept the ticket.'

Molly slipped her arm through his again as once more they moved off down the avenue. 'How d'you suppose Vasilefski got recruited by Jeremy? Then got all the dates and timings arranged?'

'It wasn't that complicated a plan. Anyway, thanks to Peregrine Gore we know. Pretty certainly. The real Frenk has a friend, a close friend apparently, who works in a main telephone exchange. Like Vasilefski. I imagine the two could have been conversing for days on end if they'd wanted. Or nights, more likely. It's the way night operators kill time. Talking to each other.'

'Like radio hams?'

'Exactly. From what Grinyev's learned already about Vasilefski, he was a pretty disaffected comrade. It wouldn't have taken him long to impress his disaffection on the other chap—and his plan to steal a painting.'

'He'd have risked being overheard?'

'If he was really fed-up. And desperate. In any case

I've never heard of telephone operators being tapped. A calculated risk I'd say. Vasilefski took it. Anyway, the other chap tells Frenk, who tells Mrs Lloyd, who tells Wander. Or that's the most likely synopsis.'

'Except the two men would know nothing about Wander?'

'Or his probably intimate relationship with the widow of a corporal who died while under his command. Incidentally, Frenk's friend was here recently. Peregrine saw a photograph. Probably that's when the plan was completed, the orders passed, and when Vasilefski's passport photo was brought out. It all fits.'

'Well, bully for Peregrine.'

'And his incredible bent for observation and retaining detail. Did I tell you, when he left the Lloyd house he thought he was going to be arrested by a police driver? In fact the man was a keen rally driver trying to decide whether to invest his all in a Scimitar. That's the car Peregrine drives.'

'Sports car? Not wildly expensive?'

He nodded. 'The copper was just coming off duty. The wily Peregrine picked him up shortly after at the police station and let him try out the car on a trip to Evesham and back. It's not far.'

'That's where Frenk shared the cottage with his friend.'

'Mm. After his experience with Mrs Lloyd, Peregrine felt he might need support when he called on the other two. The policeman provided that without knowing it. He was still wearing his uniform jacket. Put the fear of God into the friends even though he stayed outside, looking over the car engine, while Peregrine was in the cottage.'

'But they didn't tell all? I mean, they didn't give Jeremy away, or anything like that?'

'They might have done if Peregrine had known what he was looking for. As it was he was boxing in the dark, but he got enough to confirm the Frenk we had here was an imposter.'

'And enough leads for my deductive husband to work

on. But why d'you suppose Mrs Lloyd gave Peregrine the Evesham address in the first place?'

'Because she really didn't suspect him of anything sinister and seems to have fancied him. She might have wanted Frenk to check him out properly. In the country, where it'd be easier to hold him prisoner. If necessary till we got home today. Easier than it was in Coventry. And where there were two men to do it. I'd guess they had orders to restrain anyone who threatened the plan. It didn't need to be for long. I also got the impression Mrs Lloyd was really trying to set up a jolly rural excursion for herself with Peregrine and his flash car. He'd quite put her off her guard for a bit.'

'Then he scared her?'

'Yes. By lifting a photo of Frenk and thereby wiping out his credibility. She panicked. But it demonstrated how much was at stake. Locking him in Frenk's bathroom was a pretty bizarre thing to have done.'

Molly shaded her eyes. 'Isn't St Isaac's lovely in the sunlight? What a shame it's a museum.' They were entering the square on the west side. 'It'll be my turn again to look after Felicity. After breakfast. With her packing and things. Unless she's decided to stay on.'

'Grinyev said she could. But he also said if she preferred to leave, they'd fly the body to London very soon. In a day or two. Because it was . . . a simple accident, as he put it, witnessed by a dozen of us. There'd be no complications this end, and none expected at ours. He's already had signed coroner's depositions taken from three of our party.' He gave a dismissive grunt. 'Felicity seemed pretty collected in the circumstances. That's when I last saw her.'

'Sounds callous but I don't believe she's going to miss him. Obviously it's been a shock, but I'm certain she didn't care for him. Not any more. Not for a long time. And never so much as for her horses and children. He had too many girl friends for one thing. And I'm certain she knew. Everybody else did. And about his very earthy tastes in that connection. If your Mrs Lloyd was one of his string she'd have been at the upmarket end of it.'

'Could Felicity have known what he was up to here?'

'Not a possibility,' Molly answered firmly. 'She's totally straight and not very bright.'

'A useless confederate?'

'And a dangerous one. He wouldn't have trusted her. Such a devious man. Once he'd sold the painting of course he could spend what he liked on Wander Hall. There's a fortune needed for the refurbishing.'

Treasure frowned. 'A laudable intention. One should give him that. Rescuing the stately home. Making it fit for sightseers to trample round. Or on.'

'Except it was his fault it was left to fall down in the first place. He'd talked about restoration but totally neglected it for years. Then they got a modest offer from a rich American. Felicity wanted them to accept. She was telling me this yesterday morning. He refused to sell because the offer gave him the idea he could get much more. That's if he did restore the place. But the cost to date has practically bankrupted them, apparently.'

'Is the American offer still on?'

'I gather, yes.'

'So now she'll sell?'

'And go on living in the little dower house. Quite happily too, I imagine. So it'll all come out right. Deep down he must have been a loathsome creature. I'm sure she'll be much better off without him.'

Molly's last words stayed in Treasure's mind as they crossed the road to the hotel. He pondered why anyone doubted the generalisation that a too easy pragmatism governed female character assessment. At that moment the gleaming, phallic Admiralty spire caught his eye again. Catherine the Great would no doubt have been one of the few women man enough to concede the point—but only because if she conceded anything she had done it with total impunity.

* * *

Two hours later the thirteen remaining members of the
Baroque Circle were boarding the coach for the airport.
As he walked out of the Astoria, Canon Emdon gave an
extravagant performance of sniffing the fresh air denied
him since the day before. Mrs Vauxley, just as pointedly,
leaned heavily on the arm of Amelia Harwick in punishment for having been deprived of her normal support.
Candy Royce was standing at the coach door checking
documents with Valya Sinitseva who was looking pert and
efficient in her black leather coat. Candy winked at Miss
Harwick as they both helped the older woman who was
making heavy going of the steps. A stony-faced Felicity
Wander followed, accompanied by Molly and Nigel
Dirving. The actor was clearly aiming to please, carrying
the hand baggage of the other two, dancing attendance at
the steps, addressing pleasantries to Candy and Valya.

'Nothing more from the British Embassy?' Treasure
enquired of Grinyev who had just joined him where he
had been waiting on the pavement outside the hotel. The
banker had himself spoken by telephone to the Counsellor
in charge at the Embassy an hour earlier.

The colonel gave his nervous smile. 'It seems they're
a lot more concerned about the accidental death of a
British aristocrat than the murder of an ordinary British
subject.'

'Only because they're relieved it wasn't a British
subject who was murdered.'

Grinyev looked doubtful. 'The doctor is still coming
from Moscow. To see Wander's body. Now he's to be
accompanied by an attaché. A lot of trouble over a thief
and a murderer,' he added, but the tone was nearly
apologetic. 'I'm glad Lady Wander is leaving. It's best
for her.'

They watched the Blintons emerge and cross the road
to the coach. Sol stole a glance at the colonel, and lifted
a hand tentatively in greeting. The gesture was returned,
but just as tentatively.

'You've got a nerve,' whispered Gloria to her husband when they were well out of earshot.

'And I've also got the letter,' replied Sol, inwardly delighted at winning the last round, but outwardly solemn to show his contrition.

'Why did Wander use Blinton's knife to do the murder?' Grinyev asked Treasure suddenly.

'Quite simply I think he was ready to sacrifice the old boy.'

'But there are four million Russians in Leningrad, and quite a lot of them were at the opera that night.' The colonel had been carefully studying his shoes again. Now he looked at Treasure with lips pursed.

'And not one of them with the remotest interest in doing away with Frenk the imposter who'd never been here before. Who had a brand-new British passport which the real Frenk has conveniently denied all knowledge of. If Vasilefski had evidently been killed by a Russian it would surely have involved much more strenuous searchings into his antecedents. Or so it would have appeared to Wander.'

'And he'd have been right. I believed it must be one of your party. Not Blinton necessarily, but one of you.'

'And it was much less of a problem to the USSR if it was.'

'Correct.' The KGB man nodded. 'So, Wander got it right in theory but wrong in practice. Once he'd got the painting he aimed to rid himself here of an expensive liability. Also an enduring risk.'

'Now shall you tell me, Colonel, why Mrs Vauxley's stick wasn't taken apart when you searched her along with everyone else?'

A heavy, dejected expression suffused the other man's countenance, the weight of it reflected in the sudden droop of the shoulders. 'Because she was sitting on it. While she was waiting to be searched. While they went through her handbag. It didn't occur to anyone.'

'We're all human, Colonel.'

Grinyev seemed to consider the point, then his whole frame began to shake with the laughter that sounded from the back of his throat but hardly showed on his face. 'You think the woman officer responsible should be court marshalled for incompetence?' he asked, still grunting with amusement.

Treasure hesitated.

'Of course you do,' Grinyev answered for him. 'And so do I. I'm throwing the book at her. Because I'm human too.' He began to laugh again.

Edwina came hurrying out of the hotel—the last of the group and looking very glamorous. She waved to Treasure before boarding the coach. He wondered what diversionary part she might have agreed to play for Dirving, at the airport coming in, if Sol Blinton hadn't proved more suitable and been substituted at short notice. The actor had needed someone for that vital role: Treasure had reluctantly deduced it must originally have been Edwina. And did that signify her larger involvement in the whole scheme—or just a romantic one with Dirving? Treasure hadn't pressed for confirmation or enlightenment on this—only he disliked Dirving the more for endangering the girl's safety.

None of this was strictly fair, but it fitted the banker's feelings both towards Edwina and the man who claimed to be her lover. It also coloured Treasure's final question to Colonel Grinyev.

'If Wander hadn't killed himself, you'd have allowed him to leave?'

'Naturally. That was our deal. Like you, I wanted the satisfaction of knowing the name of the murderer.' The Russian shrugged. 'But the victim was someone of so little account. Compared to the gravity of the crime.'

'The murder, you mean?'

'Certainly not. I mean the theft of the Raphael. You don't believe I'd have let your aristocrat go?'

'On the contrary, Colonel, I find it much easier to believe you than not.'

The other man smiled softly. 'Ah, so like many in the West you are finding that to trust us is the same as not to mistrust us? But much friendlier?'

'I didn't say quite that.'

'You have reservations?'

'The attitude has to be mutual.'

'As it was between you and me.' Grinyev gave a contented grunt. 'Please visit the USSR again, Mr Treasure. You and your charming and talented wife.'

Treasure shook hands, then turned on his heels and crossed the road to the coach.

# CHARLOTTE MACLEOD

*America's Reigning Whodunit Queen*

## PRESENTS

"Murder among the Eccentrics of Boston's Upper Crust"* with

**Art Investigator Max Bittersohn and Sarah Kelling**

| | |
|---|---|
| THE FAMILY VAULT | 49080-3/$3.50 US/$4.50 Can |
| THE PALACE GUARD | 59857-4/$3.50 US/$4.50 Can |
| THE WITHDRAWING ROOM | 56473-4/$3.50 US/$4.50 Can |
| THE BILBAO LOOKING GLASS | 67454-8/$3.50 US/$4.50 Can |
| THE CONVIVIAL CODFISH | 69865-X/$2.95 US/$3.75 Can |
| THE PLAIN OLD MAN | 70148-0/$2.95 US/$3.95 Can |

---

"Mystery with Wit and Style and a Thoroughly Engaging Amateur Sleuth"**

**Professor Peter Shandy**

---

| | |
|---|---|
| REST YOU MERRY | 47530-8/$2.95 US/$3.95 Can |
| THE LUCK RUNS OUT | 54171-8/$2.95 US/$3.50 Can |
| WRACK AND RUNE | 61911-3/$3.50 US/$4.50 Can |
| SOMETHING THE CAT DRAGGED IN | |
| | 69096-9/$3.50 US/$4.50 Can |
| THE CURSE OF THE GIANT HOGWEED | |
| | 70051-4/$2.95 US/$3.75 Can |

*Mystery* magazine    **The Washington Post